Restless Waters

A Novel

James Heilly

FarRoad Books

ISBN: 978-0615561394

*To all wild marine mammals endangered by human activity,
and to all people who try to give a voice of protection to
threatened, vulnerable creatures everywhere*

PROLOGUE

《》

This story begins during a time in America when the country was changing—maybe for good, maybe not so much. A new state had been admitted to the union just ten years ago, a land in which I have lived for nearly thirty years, and it is from this new state that the story springs.

I must admit that it is strange, but I have no concrete recollection of how one gets in or out of the state by road. I have always flown. Now, I'm a reasonably bright person, but I also can't seem to explain where this territory meets the mainland of the United States. I only know that it does. When I think about such things, the knowledge simply disappears from my mind. It's almost like a tip-of-the-tongue lapse in memory, where the correct details drift swiftly across my mind, but I cannot capture them when I try because other thoughts are blocking them. Strangely, this happens a lot when I think of certain aspects and details of this state in which I live. It matters little to me, since I have no desire to leave, and it is beginning to feel like I have always lived here.

This new state of which I speak is called Newmont, a large, nearly perfectly round chunk of land, bulging out into the warm waters of the Flobian sea, not far from Florida. Some say it is directly under the effects of the Bermuda triangle. Hmmm. And so it is noteworthy that days, months, and years are not trustworthy measures of time here in Newmont—self-consistent perhaps, but not consistent with how the rest of the country measures time.

It is a wealthy state in some ways and dirt poor in others. It remains a popular destination for both tourists and people wanting to live here, but it has its problems.

It was named Newmont because it has a single mountain in its center, relatively new in geological terms, with an elevation of only 1263 feet, which is really only a large hill. A preposterous geological phenomenon, really.

There remains a wildness about Newmont, almost a pre-twentieth century wildness, both politically, and socially, and this developmental immaturity is one of the reasons it took so long to attain statehood. Newmont is still struggling to tame some of that wildness, to bring democracy into full force, and as a result, a lot of dust is being kicked up over nearly every issue imaginable—none more so than over a single, enigmatic, marine mammal who populated many of Newmont's numerous waterways. The creature is called the manaseal and is closely related to the Florida manatee, except, oddly, it has a fine layer of hair, almost seal-like in nature, over nearly its entire body. It is endangered because it exists only in dangerous Newmont. Certainly the animal is not an explorer like some of its brethren manatees are known to be, and it never wanders far from Newmont's shores.

The animals had originally been called "sealcows," from their somewhat seal-like coat of hair. Regardless, the mammal is large like a manatee, slow-moving, as cute as a large button like a manatee, and entirely friendly to humans. "Manaseal" is admittedly a goofy, semi-hammed-together name, and in its goofiness, very Newmontian. But I think it is perhaps better than "sealcow."

Strange things can happen in Newmont. Never forget that. And finally it became murder, and more, that came puffing its way out of the dust of Newmont's new, crude beginnings as a state. That's what brings us to this story. It was murder, and more, that Grady Able, a young newspaperman, living on the eastern bulge of the state, became embroiled in right up to his eyeballs.

So, let the dust fly, I say, and I'll try to follow its breath-choking Newmontian trails for you.

CHAPTER 1

《》

They call me Manaseal, and I'm in to get warm . . .

Grady Able sat at the dining room table in the dark, sipping away at his cup of black coffee. He stared out through the window over the large backyard, which was just becoming visible in the first ghostly gray light of day. One of Steven's toys had just emerged as a recognizable object, and it got Grady thinking about typical fatherly thoughts such as how quickly children grow up and how relentlessly life sweeps by. The refrigerator hummed quietly in the background. Emily, Krissy, and Steven would be up soon.

The phone rang and shattered the calm. *Who could possibly be calling at 5:45 in the morning*, Grady thought. Duty called, though, and after the second ring, he got up and moved as quickly as possible to the phone on the kitchen wall. He had almost refused to answer the call that morning because he had within him a stubborn, grumpy streak that often took him over immediately upon waking. Even with the caffeine beginning to work in him, his disposition remained sullen. And as it would turn out, that call would transform this Monday morning into a beginning of something unlike anything else in Grady's life, and perhaps he should have never answered it. But he did.

"Hello," he said in a gravelly voice he hardly recognized as his own.

"It's Deputy Myers from the sheriff's office," the caller said.

"What's up, Chris?" Grady said.

"We got a call about an hour ago, a possible 187. I thought you might want to know . . ."

"Thanks, Deputy Myers. I do want to know."

And thus it began.

I am Grady's friend, but I will stay out of this story as much as possible, because it has very little to do with me, other than I have been an observer as Grady pursued the truths he felt so necessary to pursue. I am Grady's friend because his father was a close friend of mine for a good part of my early life, going all the way back to our Boston days. In fact, his father and I grew up together. The circumstances that brought me to live in Newmont later in life, not far from the town his son eventually settled in, have mostly to do with great coincidence. I became friends with Grady through that coincidence, and having known his father as well as I did only lent to that friendship a special closeness that could never have existed otherwise.

I will say only this with regard to my role in the events that unfolded from that early morning in January: I am a writer, and it would have been impossible for me to not tell this story. I do caution you, the reader, though. I have a tendency to exaggerate sometimes, and I am a Newmontian. Right now, I am more emotional than I should be for the sake of objectivity, but that's because I have just begun the telling.

I have often reflected upon that phone call and have found myself wondering if Grady would have chosen differently had he known where it would ultimately lead. On the other hand, I am a strong believer in the proposition that we are who we are, and the choices we make come from the substance of our inner stuff. Grady and I have had many philosophical discussions about that sort of thing in recent years. He once told me, "All I'm looking to do is to have the guts to lead a life I can be proud of and call my own when I finally check out." I have known Grady for more than eighteen years now, and as I see it, the essence of that statement is fundamentally what has always driven him. I'm afraid his definition of a life to "be proud of" comes burdened by a far higher standard than my own, and I think that is why it was impossible for Grady to shy away from anything that might prove to be difficult.

It seems he had always actively sought out difficulty, as if he believed each difficult thing comes from some touch-stone of inner truth by which he must measure himself. He was constantly questioning and testing himself, because he was, in fact, tortured by self-doubt. You would never believe it, though, judging from his outward demeanor, from the way he spoke, and from what you might witness from his behavior, unless you knew him as well as I do. In fact, you would think he was one of the most quietly confident people on earth. And once you got to know him, you would most certainly think Grady Able to be a giant of a man when it came to measuring up in the category of "inner stuff."

He answered the phone that morning, here on the east bulge of Newmont, because he couldn't pass up the opportunity that it might prove to be something worthy of a test. Being a good newsman, Grady had learned long ago that if you didn't make acquaintances and friends with local officials, you weren't going to last long in the business. For a reporter, and the owner of a local newspaper, the tricky part was to make good associations while constantly guarding against becoming too cozy with those in authority, so you wouldn't hesitate if you ever had to work on a negative story about them, and so you wouldn't shy away from asking them critical journalistic questions if you had to. It was sometimes a thin line to walk, grown more thin in this modern age, where business, entertainment, and news had become nearly indistinguishable. Because Grady had gained the respect of several of the deputies in the Sheriff's Department, and because they had grown to like him, they often gave him a heads-up whenever there was something afoot that might be newsworthy.

After a brief conversation with Deputy Myers, the call ended, and Grady found himself suddenly awake. He left the house and made his way to his office. He had a couple of quick things to take care of there, and then he was off to Warm Springs County Park.

He parked his car along the street next to the small warehouse and five small offices on Main street that housed The Tomlin Sands bi-weekly newspaper, which he owned and managed. He had started it eight years ago, and not inconsequently, I remember him once telling me over a cold beer that he believed it had saved him from a lifetime of aimless wandering and searching.

Before getting into what happened at Warm Springs County Park that day, I think it's important to understand how Grady got to this point in his life and how he came to be a newspaperman. It's important because he didn't come by it easily, and the difficulty he experienced along the way put a shape to him, and it put a shape to the way he proceeded as a journalist. And thus it put a shape to this story.

When Grady graduated from the University of East Miami in 1992, jobs were difficult to come by, and so he tried his hand as a cub reporter on a small South Miami paper. After two long years there, with little room for advancement on the horizon, he began to fear he was becoming too far removed from the real truths of life, and from journalism. He was young and foolish at the time, by his own admission, and he nearly smothered himself under the weight of his impatient expectations. Some of his problems were due to what he now admits as gross immaturity on his part, and some of them could be blamed on the times. He wasn't good at blindly following the authority of others, for one thing, which was often required of young professionals fresh out of college.

Grady suddenly decided he couldn't do that kind of non-journalism journalism work for another single day. On the spur of the moment, and with very little money to his name, he quit his job, went to the Miami airport, and booked the first flight out to Chiapas, Mexico. He had no idea what he was doing, but he had gotten an itch to take a firsthand look at the story that was developing there surrounding the Zapatista revolution. Subcomandante Insurgente Marcos, who had founded the Zapatista Army of National Liberation, had led an uprising in 1994 to take back his native country from the government. Grady felt he needed a good dose of reality, if nothing else, and he rationalized his reckless behavior to himself by saying that maybe there would be a byline or two in it for him as a freelance journalist.

The Chiapas natives were trying to stave off the ongoing exploitation of their culture and natural resources by the Mexican government. Their struggle had become legendary around the world. When Grady arrived there, a poor Chiapas Indian farming family, through their great generosity, had invited Grady to stay with them in the hills of the Lancandona rain forest not far from San Cristobal de las Casas, the town where two years earlier Marcos had made a daring takeover.

Grady was there when it all began to come to a head. As I remember it from reading about it, and as Grady relayed it to me, in 1996, the Zapatistas had drawn up the San Andres Accord, which represented the structure for returning sovereignty to the Chiapas Indians. Unfortunately, in 1997, forty-five Tzotzil Indian refugees, mostly women and children, were slaughtered by pro-government paramilitary soldiers, in what became known as the Acteal Massacre. This brought swift international condemnation, mass protests in major Mexican cities, and calls for the resignation of then president, Zedillos.

Grady never did manage to receive a byline for the story, but he stayed with the Chiapas Indians for almost three years and wrote a book about the revolution called *Colored by Earth*, this named after an expression the Chiapas people commonly used to show how closely they were attached to the land.

When Grady returned to the U.S. in early 1998, he was demoralized and angry, and he floundered about trying to figure out how to proceed with his life. His book about the Chiapas people and their struggles was a depressing effort for him, because at the time of the writing, it looked as if nothing would ever be resolved in Chiapas from the standpoint of nailing down indigenous people's rights to their land and to their sovereignty, this despite all their courageous battles against the powers that be. To bolster his own spirits, he kept telling himself that the Chiapas people had at least made their cause known to the world, and because of the international pressure that was being applied to the Mexican government, there remained some hope that something could eventually be worked out.

The Chiapas people struggled on, and so did Grady. Most of the fight was with himself, though. It probably would have helped him had he known that a delicate peace was eventually to be forged, after many years of conflict. I have often thought that it would be nice if we could all have foreknowledge of a future positive result for that which we have staked so much hope, energy, and personal pain. That would certainly help us all make our way, wouldn't it? Unfortunately life doesn't work that way. It is mostly a struggle in the dark.

Grady's *Colored by Earth* was published in the spring of 1998, and even though it received good reviews, it was only a marginal financial success. The small royalty checks that dribbled in did help him pay for his basic living needs, but just barely.

The spirit had gone out of him. He drifted from one odd job to another—from construction work, to delivering phone books, to operating the cutting machine in the company that printed those same phone books, to writing obituaries for a small newspaper, to working as a telephone customer service representative for a large telecom company in Miami, and to even delivering pizza. There seemed to be no path that interested him and no future that seemed worthy of pursuit. Grady had become determined to drift, waiting for a sense of worthiness to begin in him in earnest. It wasn't just the demoralization he had experienced from his time in Chiapas. He was beginning to feel that life was so unjust in all ways that all the words written about truth and justice, written in books, magazines, leaflets, and newspapers, even in constitutions of egalitarian nations, now seemed hollow, and that life was more savage than he had ever imagined.

He was young, and his idealism turned quickly into cynicism. The worst of it was the human hypocrisy and stupidity (his word for it) he saw everywhere, and it was more than he could stomach. The kind of stupidity that bothered him the most wasn't that which resulted from a lack of book-learning. No, it was the kind of stupidity that kept a blind eye to everything it didn't like. And this kind of stupidity existed in the educated, as well as the uneducated. It was the kind that refused to examine the complexities of life, refused to look beyond a tiny, safe, narrow corridor which that blind eye wanted so desperately to keep directly in front of it. "Tunnel-vision-stupidity" is what Grady came to call it. He began to believe way too many people preferred to keep things simple to the point where the simplicity, itself, turned into an enormous rationale for believing any supporting lie. He saw himself as guilty of it at times, too.

The phoniness in the attitudes and human behavior he saw upon his return to the U.S., by comparison to the reality he had witnessed for three years in Chiapas, became more and more stark to him. Everywhere he looked, especially in the world of so-called journalism, he saw too often a horrible falsity and people who had filled themselves up with a kind of lifeless plastic, molded by the urge to gather in a few more pieces of silver, an urge that eventually stripped them of all humanity. They had became whores. Too much had become colored by the green of money, and completely NOT "colored by earth."

Grady's father had been a pursuer of the truth, and Grady had always hoped he could be that, too, in some concrete way. He was beginning to believe that in his own beloved country, much of the truth had been buried forever. People just didn't want to see it, or hear it, anymore. More and more, he saw that they ran away from it as fast as they could. And when a journalist can no longer pursue the one thing he is supposed to pursue, the truth of what is, and what is not, then it was no longer an occupation that Grady could value. He was a young cynic in the making, and so he tended to exaggerate the dire nature of things, and this caused him to drift some more.

He felt he had failed terribly with *Colored by Earth* to get at what he thought he should be getting at in his writing. Sometimes he just wished he hadn't written the book at all. In his view, it didn't nearly do justice to the high standards the subject demanded. And justice was the point of human society, wasn't it—or was it? Grady asked himself this often. His own silence of thought as an answer left him even more demoralized.

To make things worse, at the time, Grady also felt himself to be a great disappointment to his father, despite the fact his father had always been quietly supportive of everything Grady had tried to do. I know for a fact that his father loved him very much and was extremely proud of his son, but he was not good at communicating this to him. "No one else can tell you how you should live," Grady's father had told me, but unfortunately, he never said such things to Grady.

In January of 1999, his father died, and Henry Able's death changed Grady's life forever, but oddly, in a positive way. It broke a lot of false chains that had been gathering around him. Events moved swiftly after that. His father's passing had shocked Grady into taking some action, into selecting a direction. It had made him decide he should at least try in some fashion to do what he thought he should be doing.

His father had left him some money, and Grady had used it to cross over into Newmont, into a different time where the calendar years had no meaning, and to start up the Tomlin Sands newspaper in the town of Tomlin Dunes located just north of Creighton Beach. From my observations of Grady, it was at that point when his life began to right itself. When he had gone to Chiapas, I had known then that he would be a tall ship on rough waters, but that it would take a powerful storm to toss that stolid ship on its side and flounder it to the bottom of the sea. He was made of much more inner stuff than he knew.

And helping to further stabilize his ship that same year, he met and fell in love with Emily Linley. After a steamy four month romance, Grady and Emily were married. During the next three Newmontian years, they had two children, a boy and a girl, Krissy and Steven. This forced upon Grady another level of maturity because of the load of responsibility that came with his new life, a responsibility he had never thought himself capable of handling.

In all of this, I'm sure it hasn't gone unnoticed that Grady's last name is Able. This had been the source of jokes and ridicule his entire life, and he had grown to hate his name and what it demanded, but by the turn of the new Newmontian century, he was just beginning to develop a sense of humor about it all.

And that's how Grady Able came to be in the newspaper business, and that's the context in which he took that call from Deputy Sheriff Chris Myers that cold January morning and went down a particular path.

CHAPTER 2

《 》

Curious eyes see curious things . . .

Grady hurried across the street with his travel mug of coffee in hand and called out a warm "Hi" to Ned Lower. The feisty businessman and friend was walking along the sidewalk toward his store, Old Treasures Antiques. They often met each other as they arrived at their respective businesses early in the morning. Sometimes, they found time to chat for a few minutes.

"I suppose that editorial of yours last week didn't help your circulation any," Ned called back after giving a quick glance back toward Grady and offering a brief wave of his hand. Grady could see the familiar sardonic smile on the man's face, and he smiled back broadly and shook his head in acknowledgment. Grady had taken strong issue with the City Council's popular proposed tax incentives to go to the Hirzman Corporation to entice them to move into town. Hirzman had widely advertised they would bring about seventy-five new jobs into the area. Grady, however, had argued in an editorial that the Council had been bamboozled and that it was being completely irresponsible in its actions.

"They are giving away the farm," he had written. "At a cost that will be far too great for this community. The jobs will be mostly minimum wage jobs, with no benefits. And let us not forget that the Hirzman Corporation has a reputation for not being a good corporate citizen." Grady pointed out that the company's track record spelled out their deficiencies quite clearly in the four other towns where they had previously located branch offices. They had been guilty in the past of violating EPA standards, had basically blackmailed other communities into letting them in and then had caused nothing but expense and problems for those communities. "The gain in cheap jobs can never measure up to the costs they are asking this community to bear," he concluded. Grady's editorial, as Mr. Lower had pointed out, would not likely sit well with many in town, including many on the City Council.

Grady loved his community, but he knew that most of the residents of Tomlin Dunes weren't much prone to boat-rocking. During the past several years, he had gotten to know them, and they were good people, a respectful, hard-working bunch, but in general they weren't always very well-informed about complex issues and were apt to see one political ad on TV and believe everything it said. And he knew they were easily frightened into believing their jobs might be in jeopardy when politicians or corporate shills decided to use that ploy to run their will upon them.

He wrote his editorial anyway. And the people of the town had a certain grudging respect for the backbone he showed, even when they disagreed with him. And so his circulation numbers had not suffered.

Once inside the small Tomlin Sands building, and inside his small office at the back of the building, Grady took a quick look at Jesse Merlin's "Sports" column. Jesse had proven to be a reliable writer for him, if not extremely stirring with his words about fishing in the area. After reading the first paragraphs about John Clayton winning the weekend lure casting tournament, yet again, Grady said to himself that it was the same-old, same-old, but nonetheless acceptable for what it was.

He was in a hurry, so he quickly closed the file on his computer. He grabbed his dark brown leather notebook, the one his father had given him many years ago, and then took his well-used miniature tape-recorder from the top drawer of his desk, also a gift from his father. Not that Grady thought he would need it, but it had become his habit to carry it along whenever he went out into the field to do a story. It made him believe there was a chance something important might warrant its use. More importantly, it made him think of his father.

Before putting on his jacket and leaving the office, he gave Nuck Landers a call. Grady knew this was a story that was likely to need a photographer, not that Nuck was really a professional photographer, and not that that was the real reason Grady took him along with him on story calls.

"Can you meet me at The Donut & Coffee Shoppe in fifteen minutes?" he asked.

"Sure thing," Nuck responded in his usual concise manner.

Nuck was accustomed to being called out on jobs by Grady at a moment's notice, although he wasn't always around when the phone rang. That morning he happened to be. He was sipping on a hot cup of his own special herb tea and coffee mix, which no one else who had tried it could stomach.

Nuck was a strange, quiet, older man, hard to say exactly how old, somewhere between 40 and 70, who had lived in Newmont most of his life. He had grown up in Yellowknife Canada but had then moved to the Newmont territory when he was ten and had lived here ever since. The details of his life remained elusive to Grady, and to everyone else who knew him. He was a tough and grizzled character, not afraid of much, and full of a certain down-home country wisdom that Grady liked. Nuck often told Grady that he had a lot of Canadian-Indian blood in him. Grady found Nuck to be a very interesting, enigmatic man, as if he had come from someplace different from the rest of humanity. Even his name was a mystery, though Grady had some theories. When he asked Nuck how he had come by it, and what it meant, he only responded by saying, "That's just what people call me." He had no family, at least none that were alive that Grady knew about. Grady had taken an instant liking to the man because Nuck seemed to have an abiding respect and love for life and nature and all that is vulnerable within it—and yet he was also tough as nails.

When Grady arrived in the parking lot of The Donut & Coffee Shoppe, Nuck was already there, sitting in his 1956 greenish station wagon, a car he had found somewhere and purchased for $100 and then managed to get running. When he saw Grady pull up, he got out of his car with his camera and camera bag hanging around his thick leathery neck and came over and climbed into Grady's white, well-used SUV. Nuck's camera equipment was old, everything purchased at auctions, pawn shops, and from classified ads in the paper, but Nuck did know how to use it all, and he did so with competence.

"Good morning," Grady said. Nuck made for an imposing figure with his enormous shoulders set on a sprinter's frame. He always reminded Grady of an action figure, Superman-like even, in certain respects, except he had hair that grew down well past his shoulders and a square jaw on a weathered looking face that was round as a cantaloupe. His eyes were brown and set under heavy brows, and they seemed a little too open to keep Nuck as properly hidden from the rest of the world as he would have liked. They were animated eyes, flaring and receding, turning from side to side with strained attention to all that was going on around him. He was a nervous man inside but solid as a rock outside.

"Mornin'," Nuck said in return.

Grady looked at him and smiled inwardly after fastening his seat belt, "Did I wake you with the call? Sorry if I did."

"No."

Nuck Landers was normally a quiet man, sometimes not saying a single word for hours at a time, but then on a rare occasion, when the moment struck him just right, he would become talkative, and he would go on and on, as if he was expressing all those thoughts he had stored up during the many hours of quiet. This was not one of those moments, however, and the two men drove in silence the twenty-seven miles to the county park.

Nuck had turned out to be an especially good investigator for Grady, despite the fact that, for some yet unknown reason to Grady, Nuck refused to be called a "news investigator" or "reporter." Grady thought it must have something to do with some unpleasant event in his past, but he could only speculate, because to ask Nuck about some personal detail of his life brought such a tortured look to the man's face and such silence in response, with those large brown eyes staring back in a frightened, pleading fashion, that people quickly got the message that his private life was off limits. Nonetheless, Grady knew that the man had a photographic memory, which he combined with a keenly observant interest in both physical detail and human behavior, and these traits made him a very useful news investigator, indeed.

How did this improbable team come to be? Nuck had come into the office one day, a year after Grady had opened the paper, asking if there was any work he could do for him. In return, Grady had asked him, "What kind of work do you do?" And Nuck quickly replied, "I don't want to be an investigative reporter, that's all." It was an odd answer, but the look on the man's face was intelligent and filled with such a genuine intent that Grady understood right away that he was dealing with a very special person. He was quickly to learn that he was a person with wishes and sentiments that could not be easily ignored. It was this strange, honest way that had first won Grady over.

"Have you ever used a camera," Grady had then asked during the unusual impromptu job interview.

"Maybe once or twice," Nuck had responded honestly.

"Okay, I'll give you a try."

Grady didn't really care how good a photographer the man was. He could certainly take photos as well as Grady could. So, Nuck became the official, and sole, Tomlin Sands photographer. Grady was frankly very tired of doing most of the photography work himself. It was necessary work he didn't like in the least. More and more, it had been getting in the way of his note-taking and interviewing time, and people didn't take him seriously as a journalist when he showed up looking more like a photographer than a reporter. Not only that, he knew nothing about photography in any real sense. He knew how to focus and press the button. That was the extent of it. The paper was doing reasonably well, and Grady decided it was time to step it up a bit.

So Nuck thereby became the photographer for the Tomlin Sands bi-weekly. He had turned out to be a very good photographer, too. It quickly became obvious to Grady that the man began studying the craft in a serious way after he was hired. He had eventually become so good, in fact, that he had even won a photography award last year in the annual Tomlin Dunes Beach Library and Art Society contest. Grady knew that award had filled Nuck with great pride, but the man never said a single word about it.

The hiring of Nuck had turned out to be one of the best things Grady had ever done for the paper. There was a mystique that attached to the large man, his appearance, and his manner, when he went on assignment, with or without Grady. He carried himself with an honest demeanor of substance that was rare these days in our world of theme parks, theme restaurants, theme this, and theme that. He was a prodigious man, in every way. He was the kind of person, upon first meeting, you felt you could put your trust in and not be disappointed.

Grady always took him along on any unusual story that might require some investigative work, even though the premise for having him along always had to be, "I might need a few photos for the story." The truth was, Nuck loved being involved in investigative work on stories—he just didn't want his job title to reflect that in any way. Beyond that, Grady and Nuck had become good friends.

And so, the two men drove to Warm Springs County Park. They didn't know it yet, but they were embarking on the adventure of a lifetime.

CHAPTER 3

《 》

I heard a dangerous sound, but it was too late . . .

They arrived at the Park in the cold of a mid-January morning. Grady had always believed it was one of the most natural and beautiful parks in all of Newmont, and he had taken his family there on many occasions to picnic, swim, canoe, and to enjoy watching the manaseals swim or rest in the double S-shaped spring run when they were in during winter months. The Spanish moss was hanging from the limbs of the old live oaks that lined both banks of the spring, and a silvery mist smothered any view of the run beyond a hundred yards in either direction. A county ranger was out in one of the park's canoes, a diver was in the water, and two state police officers were in another unmarked aluminum canoe. Grady could see something floating on the surface of the water, half-submerged, near the diver—a human body.

"She's got a large wound on the side of her head," one of the officers called over to the shore.

"Yeah, okay. Bring her over. Carefully," said the state police officer heading up the investigation. "Let's try not to muck up any of the evidence before the medical examiner has a chance to have a look at her . . . You got the flashlight you found floating in the water?"

"Yes," said the officer in the canoe. "I bagged it."

The investigating officer, Lieutenant James, noticed Grady and Nuck, who were now standing on the boardwalk at the top of the bank. He looked straight up at Grady and then turned to the Sheriff's deputy who was standing next to him. "Who're they?" he said. "And what the hell are they doing here?"

"Oh, that's Grady Able and his photographer," said the deputy. "He's a reporter from one of the local papers."

Lieutenant James returned his eyes to the ongoing work of his fellow officers in the water. He had a Newmont Criminal Bureau of Investigations (NCBI) emblem on his shirt sleeve. Grady guessed that due to the suspicious nature of the death, and where it had occurred, the county officials thought they might need the state's expertise and crime lab to give them some cover and to make a proper investigation in such a delicate situation. The county was in the process of selling the park to the state, after which it would become a state park. And maybe there had been a jurisdictional battle that had gone on during the wee hours of the morning between various state and local investigatory agencies. Apparently the state's NCBI had won out, but there was a coordinating effort going on as evidenced by the fact that standing next to Lieutenant James was a Timpkin County Sheriff's deputy, and standing only a few yards down from them was an officer from the Department of Environmental Conservation (DEC). The DEC officer was there because the woman's death had occurred in sensitive manaseal waters. There were also several county park rangers present.

Grady and Nuck watched as the two NCBI officers worked in the spring run. There were a few manaseals swimming quietly about, and a group of about fifteen were lying on the bottom, resting. They had come in from the colder waters of the Hopkins River. Manaseals could stand warmer waters than their relatives, the manatees, but they could not live in water that was colder than 64 degrees for very long. If they failed to find refuge in warmer waters during sustained wintry spells, they were likely to suffer cold stress that would make them more susceptible to infection, disease, and death.

People died all the time in Newmont waters from drowning and boating accidents, so the death in the spring run was not all that unusual in that regard. What did make it unusual, however, were some of the facts surrounding this particular death. The dead woman had been a manaseal lover and a volunteer for the Nature Protection Foundation (NPF), and there were suspicions already surfacing among the investigators that her death might have been the result of foul play. She had been volunteering at Warm Springs Park the day before and had been handing out literature about protecting manaseals.

Manaseal protection had become a contentious issue in Newmont, with certain boater groups, boater marine industry lobbyists, and aggressive developers fighting against every possible regulation of their activities and commerce in the wild state of Newmont. Manaseals were dying in record numbers due to human causes, and some regulation was needed if the species was to avoid eventual extinction, not unlike the situation the manatee faced in the state of Florida. Being a subtropical paradise, Newmont was one of the fastest growing states in the country, and that growth was putting pressure on every aspect of the environment.

Grady was the chief cook and bottle-washer at the Tomlin Sands Bi-Weekly, but that morning he had on his crime-reporters hat, since he didn't actually have anyone on his staff who was a real crime reporter. In fact, besides Nuck, he had only four other full time people working at the paper: his wife who did a little of everything, a young man named John Hands, whom Grady had just hired on to oversee the actual printing of the paper, Jesse Merlin, who was Grady's assistant editor, and Grady's old friend and right hand man, Doug Waxel, who was the official layout person. Grady counted on Doug to do a little of everything, too. Also, there were always several part-time employees on hand to assist in the workload.

As Grady watched the Newmont state police officers gently pull the woman's body to the shore, he happened to notice a small folded piece of paper resting in a dense growth of ferns just off the boardwalk. Who can tell what makes a person take notice of certain things and not of others. There were pieces of paper here, there, and everywhere that had been strewn by the high winds of the previous night. This particular piece of paper caught Grady's eye, probably because he was standing next to it, and probably because he noticed that it was larger than the other pieces of paper nearby. It was also folded, and that suggested something possibly more important inside.

He reached down under the railing and picked it up, being careful to hold it by its very edges. He looked around to see if anyone other than Nuck had taken any notice of his actions, and satisfied that they had not, he gingerly unfolded the paper.

The following was written inside in an artistically sweeping hand: "Please call me. We've got big trouble." Beneath this brief message was a phone number with a Trembly Bay area code. And at the very bottom was a single word, "Rantle." The note had been crumpled and then un-crumpled, probably more than once.

One of the officers called out from the bank, "We've got an ID. Marcy M. Appleton, 763 South Tremont Street in Port Sun Beach. Born May 8th, 1981. Her Newmont license photo seems to match."

"O.K. Let's get her in a bag," said Lieutenant James, the head of the investigation. "Leave it open, though. The ME will be here soon."

"Sir," a junior officer broke in, coming up the boardwalk past Grady to the observation platform just above where the girl's body lay. "I've got a ranger here who might be of help."

"Help is a good thing," the Lieutenant said.

Nuck was looking around with interest and taking a lot of photos. Grady had told him a long time ago, "I don't want you going cheap on the film when you're out on a potentially good story." He knew his friend's equipment was well behind the times and that he still used actual rolls of film. Grady had been wanting to buy him a good digital, but he knew that might not go over well.

Nuck began eyeing the observation platform carefully and looking up into the trees. Grady glanced at him and then looked at the approaching officer, who was accompanied by a park official.

"Ranger Compton here thinks he might know who the woman is," the officer said as he came up to Lieutenant James.

"How's that?" the lieutenant said.

"I got a glimpse of the floating body early this morning when I first got here and saw all the commotion. I thought I recognized the T-shirt she was wearing."

"Take a close look at her, then," the Lieutenant said to the ranger. "She had ID on her, and we think we already know who she is, but take a look, anyway."

"All right," the ranger said.

Lieutenant James called down to his officers on the bank of the spring run and told them to let Ranger Compton have a look at the victim. The body bag was lying in a lush growth of ferns.

After climbing over the guard rail of the boardwalk and carefully making his way down the steep bank, he took a good look at the body. "Yeah, that's Marcy alright," he said. "She was here yesterday, running a volunteer table for the park. It was part of our Manaseal Days celebration. She was staying in the park campground for the weekend. It's so sad."

"You know any reason why she might have ended up dead in the spring run?" Lieutenant James asked pointedly.

"I can't say that I do, but I do know there was some sort of an incident yesterday. I'm not sure it had anything to do with her death, though. There was a small group of men giving Marcy a hard time. They were hanging around her table and harassing her at every turn, calling her a liar and speaking out whenever she gave information to any of the park patrons. A woman came to the ranger's station and complained about the men. That was at about 2:30. I immediately went down there with another ranger to tell them to stop bothering Marcy and to quit raising a ruckus. When we got there, there were three men still shouting at her, calling her a liar and 'enviro-nazi,' you know, that sort of thing. It was pretty ugly, and it began to draw a fair-sized crowd. We don't put up with people causing a disturbance. It's very rare, but we don't put up with it at all.

"They were nothing but trouble from the beginning. The DEC officer patrolling the park had caught them swimming with the manaseals earlier in the day up near the springs area of the run. They had ignored all the signs and warnings to keep their distance from the animals. They were loud and obnoxious and were apparently yelling obscenities at the animals. As I understand it, the DEC officer had to ask them to get out of the water. He questioned them harshly, gave them a talking to about harassing the manaseals, and because they answered him in a polite, responsive way, he reluctantly agreed to let them stay in the park as long as they did not go back in the water. We try to work with people as much as we can. After they started the ruckus later in the day, however, we had to restrict them from the springs area entirely. I told them they could continue camping in the park, but we didn't want to see them anywhere near the manaseals or that part of the park, and if we had even a hint of any more trouble from them, they would be asked to leave the park and would be banned forever."

"Were they members of a boater's group?" Lieutenant James asked. "Know anything about them?"

"I don't know for sure. From what they were yelling, they appeared to be against increased manaseal protections, and they were outspoken about it. Even if they are members of a group or organization, you know that within any group, there are always some loose-cannon types. There's always been that small number of boaters out there who don't like anyone telling them what they can, or cannot, do, manaseals or no manaseals. Don't misunderstand me, though, Lieutenant. We at the park aren't against boaters. Not at all. We all own boats, go fishing, water-skiing, and have fun on the water. We just want boaters to learn to be careful around manaseals and to slow down a little so the creatures will be around for our grandchildren to see."

Grady didn't say anything, but he thought to himself that unfortunately, there are always a few radical people out there who believe the government shouldn't regulate boating at all, or apparently anything else for that matter. Every once in awhile he'd receive a Letter To The Editor from some such in his paper, which he always printed, because he strongly believed they have a right to their opinions, but which in return always brought in a lot of angry responses from manaseal lovers, conservationists, and nature lovers in general."

"It's something to look into," Lieutenant James said, turning to one of his junior officers. "Johnson, let's find out who these individuals are. I want you to interview each of them."

"That should be easy," said the ranger. "They're camping in the park for the week. In fact they're located only five sites down from where Marcy Appleton was camping."

"Lieutenant James," Grady interjected. "I found something I think you might want to take a look at." He held up the folded piece of paper he had picked up a few moments ago, making sure to grasp it delicately by the thinnest of edges between a widespread thumb and middle finger.

"What's that?" the lieutenant asked, looking at Grady as if he were some kind of bothersome bug.

"I found it along the boardwalk over there," Grady said, pointing to the exact spot. "It may be nothing. Don't know if it has anything to do with the girl's death, but I thought I'd bring it to your attention." Grady walked over to the rail and passed the note to the lieutenant who gave him a frown in return.

"You know better than to touch anything here. We're trying to do an investigation."

"I know. You're right, officer. I shouldn't have picked it up, but it caught my eye. I was careful with it, though, as you can see. I didn't touch any of its surfaces." Grady offered the man a smile, hoping it might be winning enough to ease some of the disgust he was sensing coming from the lieutenant. He knew he shouldn't have picked up the piece of paper, but it had spoken to him in that language exclusive to curiosity, and in so doing, it had compelled him. "I was afraid the wind might blow it away," Grady added. Though truthful, he knew it sounded lame. It was one of the reasons he had picked it up. The gusty wind was shuffling it back and forth and was threatening to sweep it away when he first saw it. But he knew that was just a rationalization.

"Yeah, sure, you were afraid of the wind," the lieutenant said, looking at Grady once more and then at the piece of paper. He opened it, also holding it only by its edges. After quickly reading it, he then slipped it into a small plastic evidence bag he withdrew from the rear pocket of his pants. "It might be something. We'll look into it, and we want to thank you for your brilliant detective work, Mr. Able," he said sarcastically.

"You're welcome," Grady said and smiled again in a self-deprecating manner.

"Now don't touch anything else around here. Alright?"

"I promise."

The state police and DEC officers were at the scene for an hour or so longer, looking for evidence, collecting samples, all the usual things. The medical examiner came and retrieved the body, not willing to make a final determination of the cause of death until he could make a thorough examination of the body back at the autopsy room in the morgue.

There didn't appear to be much outward physical evidence in this case, other than the girl's body and her injuries. She did have a severe wound to the back left side of her head. One of the investigators surmised that she might have been struck from behind, but Lieutenant James said, "We'll have to wait and see what the ME finally comes up with."

Grady got the sense from the way the officers were talking among themselves that they were beginning to solidify their belief that foul play was involved in the young woman's death. The three men who had been causing trouble in the park the previous day were definitely at the top of their list of prime suspects, though the investigators probably wouldn't be announcing anything officially until they had more evidence to go on.

Grady asked Lieutenant James if he and Nuck could walk out onto the observation platform to take some photos. Grady promised to not disturb anything. The lieutenant looked at him sullenly, but after a brief pause, he reluctantly gave permission.

"My boys have already taken prints and photos of every square inch of the place, so you shouldn't be able to do too much damage," he said.

The investigating team wrapped things up, put police tape around the entire scene, gave the proper warnings to the park officials to make sure nobody touched anything, and then packed up and left.

Grady and Nuck ducked under the police tape that barred entrance to the observation platform and walked out onto it. Grady went to the railing and peered into the clear water. He sensed that Lieutenant James was watching them, and so he gave a quick glance in his direction, but the officer was already walking away along the boardwalk. There was still a fog lingering on the surface of the water, but when Grady looked straight down, he could easily see gar, bass, mullet, some kind of bottom feeding sucker, tilapia, and other fish he couldn't identify, swimming lazily in the spring.

Nuck was busy examining the platform. A heavy thunderstorm had pounded the area the night before over on the coast in Tomlin Dunes. It was obvious that a strong storm cell must have come through the park, too. Everything was drenched, and there were limbs, air plants, clumps of Spanish moss, and leaves down everywhere. Matted, soaked debris laced almost every square inch of the boardwalk and the deck of the observation platform. As Grady looked about, he kept a curious eye on Nuck, who was now looking up with great interest into the enormous oak tree that overhung the platform. Grady could see something was stirring in his friend's mind.

Nuck looked from the tree back to the platform. He then looked into the tree again and studied it carefully. Following Nuck's eyes, Grady suddenly noticed burned limbs at the top of the tree. He, too, looked down and then over at the railing of the observation platform. He moved quickly over to it and looked into the water beneath the platform. He then looked back at Nuck, who was still examining the tree.

"Lightning, you're thinking?" Grady asked.

"Yes."

If Nuck hadn't been terrified by lightning when he was a child back in Yellowknife, he probably would have never noticed the telltale signs of a lightning strike in the tree, but he had come to be very keen on the subject. When he was only five years old, lightning had struck his family's home and had burned it to the ground.

As Nuck looked into the tree, he probably remembered that experience of long ago, remembered the night sky lighting up like day for an instant and the simultaneous explosive crack the bolt had made when it struck. He probably remembered the burning smell, too, and the crackling sound that had quickly followed, and he probably remembered his terror more than anything, that the sky could single him out so definitively and send such a destroying strike down upon him and his family so quickly and so unexpectedly.

"Take a few shots of the platform and the tree, and I'll meet you at the rangers station as soon as you're done. We've got a lot to do and not a lot of time to do it in, I'm afraid."

"You thinking what I'm thinking?" Nuck asked. There was excitement in his eyes, and his leathery face was tight with intensity.

"Maybe," Grady said. "We'll talk about it in the car on our way back to the paper. First, though, we've got a lot of groundwork to do, and we absolutely need to keep our theories to ourselves for now. Otherwise, something might fall through the cracks and come back and bite us right in the ass. I'll need you ready with that camera of yours, though," Grady added, making sure to mention that photography would be essential to their tasks. It was what Nuck wanted to hear. He took hold of the camera that was hanging around his neck and gave it a wiggle to show he was at the ready.

Grady hurried off with long strides, his longish sunbleached brown hair bouncing over his ears beneath his well-worn baseball cap. He wanted to talk with the four county rangers who were present in the park the previous day. He found them all gathered in an office at the end of the park's information building. The door was open, and one ranger was leaning against the door frame, half in the room and half out, listening to the conversation inside. Grady leaned in next to him and looked into the room.

"Excuse me," he said. "Would it be all right if I ask you men a few questions?"

"Fire away," the park manager said. "Come on in and make yourself comfortable. We've got some hot coffee if you want a cup."

"That'd be great," Grady said as he moved into the room. "I'm sorry for interrupting your conversation, but I just need to know if any of you saw anything or know anything that might help in understanding what exactly happened to the girl. I know the investigators have already questioned you about all this, but if you don't mind, I'd like to go over a few points again."

One of the rangers poured Grady a cup of coffee and asked him if he wanted cream or sugar. Grady said no, and the steaming cup was handed to him. He took a couple of sips, and it was good. He got on with his questions, the usual who, what, where, when, and why.

The rangers didn't have much to add to what they had already told the investigators, except that one ranger said, "The only thing I noticed was, Marcy seemed quite down yesterday. She hadn't been here in awhile, not since late November, but whenever I had seen her in the past, she had always been very cheerful and friendly, and very talkative. When I said 'hi' to her yesterday on my rounds, she gave me the weakest of tiny smiles and the tiniest wave of her hand, and then she looked immediately down at the ground. It's probably nothing, but it was just something I noticed."

When Grady finished asking the few questions he had to ask, he thanked the park personnel and went outside and found Nuck sitting at one of the picnic tables waiting for him. Grady gathered him up, and they drove to the campground, which was about a mile down the road.

Grady first interviewed the campers around Marcy's site to see if they had heard anything. Nuck took more photos. There was a middle-aged couple staying in the site to the right and a group of six seniors were camping from a large RV to Marcy's left. Upon interviewing them all, they said they hadn't heard anything of consequence. Marcy's light-green, high-mileage economy car was still parked in front of her small tent. She must have walked to the park in the middle of the night, Grady thought. The picnic table was bare except for a single brown paper bag weighed down by a stone and a lot of small sticks and twigs with an air plant or two and strings of Spanish moss that had blown down from the trees surrounding the campsite. Grady opened the bag with a stick and took a quick peek inside, but it was empty.

The state investigators had finished at the campsite earlier, with their finger-printing and evidence gathering, and they had marked everything off with police tape. Nuck took several shots of the campground, including the paper bag. They then went to talk to the three boaters that had been involved in the commotion the day before.

Just as the ranger had said, they were located in a site five down from Marcy's. They were highly defensive when Grady introduced himself as a reporter, and they immediately began to give him an attitude. At first they refused to tell him much of anything useful, other than they insisted they had nothing to do with the girl's death.

"Just because she's one of those bleeding-heart manaseal lovers that wants to take all our boating rights away, doesn't mean we killed her," said one of the men. He was large and highly overweight. He gave Grady a nasty, "back-off" smile beneath his scraggly white beard. "If that's where you're goin' with your reporter questions," the man continued. "You're not gonna stick us with her death. We don't have to talk to you, anyway."

Grady didn't bother using his tape recorder, but he did scribble down a few notes in the dog-eared notebook his father had given him many years ago.

The other two men said little in connection with Marcy's death, but they did manage to give Grady an earful about their political beliefs and about how there were too many manaseals in Newmont waters, anyway.

"That's why they're dying," one of the men said. "There's just too damned many of them, so of course some of them are going to get run over by boats."

"Too many of 'em?" Nuck asked when he heard this, his voice rising higher than normal. Grady looked at him nervously. It wasn't like Nuck to present any kind of a challenge to anyone. Grady wasn't sure where this was going to lead, since obviously, Nuck did not like what the boater men were saying.

"Yeah, that's right. You got a problem with the truth?"

Much to Grady's relief, Nuck remained completely professional and made no further response. He did, nonetheless, train a hard unyielding eye upon the man, which made him eventually look away.

That was about all Grady could handle in the way of interviewing the men. They were crude and obnoxious, and he knew he wasn't going to get any useful information from them, anyway, so he thanked them for their time and called it a day for the preliminary interviews. He and Nuck then hurried back to Marcy's campsite, climbed in Grady's vehicle, and they drove back to the paper.

CHAPTER 4

«»

A Peaceful home disturbed . . .

As they got out of the car outside the Tomlin Sands Newspaper building, Grady asked Nuck if he could stay around for awhile. "I might need you a little later in the day," he said. Nuck nodded in response.

"Could you also get your photos developed and pick three you like best."

Nuck offered a single nod and gave an acknowledging tap of his old photography bag that he had slung over his shoulder. He then walked off down the street toward Henry's Photo. There would be no digital cameras in his near future, Grady thought as he watched after him, but he knew one day, a year or two from now, he would show up with one, probably used, and not a word would be said about it.

Grady closed the car door and hurried into the Tomlin Sands building. He went immediately to his small office and plopped himself down in his large comfortable swivel chair. Gnawing at him was the feeling that there was more to this Marcy Appleton story than first appearances were letting on. There was an urgency to it, too. He knew he had to hurry if he was to pull together the loose ends of this story in a sufficient way to be able to write a cursory story for tomorrow's paper. He thought he and Nuck were onto something the investigators had overlooked, but he needed to find out more about what was written on that note, and he needed first to find out if the note was even written to, or by, Marcy Appleton. The investigating authorities would certainly be doing that.

He took out his notepad and looked at what he had written under Marcy Appleton. Her date of birth and her address were scrawled there, as well as the brief message that had been written in the note he had found, including the phone number. He was a big believer in taking the most direct route when doing investigative journalism. If you had a number, you called it, but he also was a big believer in using all the information at hand to provide that direct route some chance of success. First, he was hoping to get a name for the number, so he typed it into one of three public reverse lookup search engines he used on the internet to track down people from their phone numbers. If the number was unlisted, though, he'd be out of luck with that method. There were others, though, he could resort to.

Luckily, his first search did find a hit, listing the number under a Linda Herrero, 1208 West Weatherly, Warm Sea Breeze Apartments, #701c, Trembly Bay. Thus armed, he dialed the number.

"Hello," a young woman answered.

"Hi, my name is Grady. I'm a reporter with the Tomlin Sands, a small newspaper over here on the eastern coast of Newmont. May I speak with Linda Herrero, please?" In Grady's experience, he had found it better to be up front with most people under most circumstances when trying to dig for information, especially when talking to a complete stranger over the phone. He could have claimed he was from the Division of the Newmont Lottery or some such nonsense, which might have gotten some initial attention, but such a tact could also backfire and alienate a person who otherwise might have some useful information to offer.

"I'm sorry, Mister. Linda is no longer here. She moved a long time ago."

"Do you know where she is living now, Ma'am?"

"No, I'm sorry. I don't know that."

"Did you know Linda very well?"

"No, I didn't know her at all. I only met her once when she came to pick up the rest of her things. I moved into the apartment she was vacating."

"I apologize for bothering you, and thank you for your time."

Grady hung up before the young woman had a chance to begin asking questions of her own about why he wanted to see Linda. There was no time for that. He then performed another search to see if he could find any Linda Herreros in the greater Trembly Bay area. He believed the investigators were on the wrong track in thinking the three boater men at the park were possibly responsible for the young woman's death. Before he could run his theory by the authorities, though, and more importantly, in a news story, he had to talk to Linda Herrero, and make certain it didn't lead to further evidence suggesting that his theory might be flawed, possibly even providing further evidence that implicated the ruffians at the park. At this point, he wasn't even certain that the piece of paper was Marcy's at all. But if it was, then the words, "We've got big trouble" had to be investigated to see where they led.

A story like this could be dicey, especially when it was one that might turn out to question the thinking of the investigators of two prominent Newmont law enforcement agencies. He had to first make certain he was on solid footing, and right now the ground seemed too easily capable of shifting beneath his feet. His theory, after all, was a bit of a reach, and if it turned out to be true, he didn't want to embarrass the state investigators in any way. He knew it was easy to overlook what Nuck had noticed at the observation platform. Regardless, he didn't believe for a second that the three men were responsible for Marcy's death, even as nasty and as rude as they had been.

It would be a great story to break, but he wanted to get it right. If it was a murder, then the state police and the Timpkin County Sheriff's department would soon be pursuing every lead they had, and that folded piece of paper with Marcy's name on it might turn out to be a lead that goes somewhere. He was hoping he might beat them to the punch, as did any good newsman. If there was a story, he wanted it first.

He did not find a single Linda Herrero in his search, but he did find three "L. Herreros," and he began calling each one. The first call reached only an answering machine. It was a man, and his name was Lawrence. The second call reached a woman named Lisa Herrero, and she knew nothing of a Linda Herrero when asked. The third, and last, try was to a Waterside address, and it was answered by an older woman. And as luck would have it, she turned out to be the mother of Linda.

She answered sternly when Grady asked her if she knew where he could reach Linda. He immediately recognized a distinct Cuban accent. The years Grady had spent in South Florida, before moving to Newmont had given him a good ear for that particular dialect. Grady asked her if he could speak with Linda. The woman began crying immediately in response to this.

"My lovely, precious daughter is gone," the woman said through her tears. "The police say it was suicide, but I know it was not. They are wrong. They are so, so wrong." Then, more tears. Grady tried to calm her, but she was inconsolable—the death of a dearest loved one tends to make us that way. Finally, after several moments of simply listening to Linda's mother talk through her tears about how wonderful her daughter was, he got up the nerve to ask her what she thought was the cause of her daughter's death.

"She was murdered," the woman said sharply. "Those policemen don't know anything. She was ruthlessly murdered."

"I'm so sorry to hear that," Grady said and was silent for a moment. "I know this is a terrible time for you, but Mrs. Herrero, may I ask you if you know a young woman named Marcy Appleton," Grady asked with all due politeness.

"Oh my, yes," Mrs. Herrero said. "I know her. She and Linda were best of friends. They spent a lot of time together, even though they lived across the state from each other. They had gotten involved in something political. I told Linda to keep her nose clean, but she never listened to me. They went right ahead, she and Marcy, and somebody murdered my beautiful Linda because of it." Mrs. Herrero began crying again.

Grady hated having to dig into the heart of this poor woman's misery. He hated this sort of investigative work altogether, but it was sometimes a necessary part of the job. When he had been working in the obituary department of the small South Miami paper, his job required him to call many a grieving family member to try to get a few words to print about the deceased.

"I'm afraid I have some very bad news to give you, as if you needed any more," Grady said. There was silence on the other end of the line. "Marcy Appleton died last night at Warm Springs County Park, over here in Timpkin County. The police aren't yet sure of the cause of death, but I think it might have been an accident."

"It was no accident," Mrs. Herrero said with surprising force through her continuing sobs. "She was murdered too. I just know it. I told them to keep their noses clean, but they wouldn't ever listen to me," she repeated.

"I'd like to come over there right away to see you, if I could," Grady said. "I run a newspaper in Tomlin Dunes over here on the east coast of Newmont, and I'm doing a story on Marcy's death. Would that be alright, Mrs. Herrero, if I came to visit you and talk to you some more about what happened?"

"I don't mind you coming over, not if you plan on telling everyone the truth about my poor daughter and her friend. You tell everyone that they were murdered."

Grady was silent for a moment, but then he said, "I'll be there in about five hours with my assistant Nuck Landers. Thank you for talking to me. I am so sorry for your loss. By the way, my name is Grady Able."

Mrs. Herrero gave Grady her address, even though he already had it on his computer screen from his earlier search. Now, suddenly, there were two deaths he was dealing with, and there seemed to be more and more uncertainty about each. He immediately began to realize that the Marcy Appleton death might actually turn out to be a real story, but it was a story that was likely to draw a whole lot of heat, especially in a place like Newmont. Under normal circumstances, that heat would be good, because it would sell papers, but unless he could be certain that Marcy's death was an accident, there would be a lot of nasty implications surrounding this story. Was it really somehow wrapped all up in the manaseal issues that had been so contentious in Newmont for so many years? He hoped not. When he lived back in Florida, the issue over the related manatees had been contentious enough, but here in Newmont, it was even more so. He was seriously hoping that Linda Herrero's death was, indeed, a suicide and Marcy Appleton's death was, indeed, an accident. No one needed a death related to the manaseals.

In Newmont, the marine mammal was at the center of a great tumultuous political fight in certain districts, especially those with a lot of boaters and a lot of manaseals in the waters. A few boater groups had formed in an attempt to stop further manaseal protections and to even roll back the meager protections that had already been put into place. Several conservation and environmental protection organizations had been fighting persistent battles for many Newmont years to get stronger manaseal protections put into place for Newmont waterways, hoping to secure the marine mammal's existence well into the future, just as they were doing in Florida for the manatee. And they had succeeded in part. The more successful they were, however, the more angry and boisterous became the opposing special interest groups, including some members of the Newmont marine manufacturers industry.

The heated battle had been going on for many years over the issue and was all wrapped up in local, county, state and even national politics. Yielding to major pressure from some of the more powerful boater groups, segments of the marine industry, and neo-conservative, no-government-regulation groups in Newmont, the state had decided to take the pressure off by dismantling some of the protections that had been put in place for the manaseals. At least that was their short-sighted thinking at the time. They hadn't considered the backlash that would occur in the state, however, when manaseal deaths began increasing each year, which they surely would with fewer protections and a growing boating and human population in Newmont, and with increased encroachment by developers into critical manaseal habitat. When that happened, the pressure would be coming from the citizens of Newmont to reinstate the protections and to add even more. They might be a little rough around the edges, but on the whole Grady knew they were a good citizenry. They would begin to blame the state for every new manaseal death.

Not only that, but the intended action bumped up against the state's own species protections laws and federal laws, and the real science was not on their side. To ease protections for an endangered species for purely political reasons, to appease certain conservative special interest groups, also went against even the most basic common sense in a state where the vast majority of Newmont citizens adored the gentle creatures. In a word, as I said, it was shortsighted politically, with no chance of holding up in the long run. Manaseals were as much a part of the character of Newmont as the five-fingered palm trees or the beautiful purplish-green sunsets. It was for these reasons that groups engaged in trying to protect the manaseal had been able to stave off most of these expedient political efforts. But things had gotten ugly in the state over the issue, and shortsighted thinking was working its way into the body politic.

Grady hadn't paid a lot of detailed attention to the issue before that day they found Marcy Appleton's body in Warm Springs County Park. He liked manaseals. He did have a lot of friends who were regular boaters, and they were all good people. As a matter of fact, most of them had no problem with slowing down a bit in manaseal areas to help protect the gentle, friendly mammals. There were a few who thought that the environmentalists were exaggerating the plight of the manaseal and, as a result, expressed the opinion that they didn't see how the animal could be considered endangered. But Grady then would ask them straight out, "You don't think it's okay to run over them, though, do you, whether they're endangered or not?" And the answer always came back as a swift and certain "No." They all agreed that it was essential to work something out so the gentle mammal could be protected well into the future and so that boaters would have as much access to Newmont waters as possible within the context of sharing those waters safely, not only with the manaseals, but with other people and other boaters. But then again, these boater friends of Grady had always been reasonable people. That's why Grady liked them, so he cautioned himself about looking through the filter of his own eyes. He tried not to associate too closely with unreasonable people with extreme beliefs.

From what little he knew, he also had a healthy respect for the groups trying to protect manaseals, because he knew people who worked for some of the non-profit organizations involved, and he knew they were actually working very hard, with very few resources to try to help the manaseals survive, and against some very powerful forces. It was a fervent mission, even though some of the nastier boaters tried to claim that these organizations only existed to provide jobs for those who worked for them. Grady knew that it was a ridiculous accusation, since the biologists and other professional people working for such groups could have garnered much larger salaries with their professional educations and experience had they chosen to work for private industry. He knew they did the work they did out of love and dedication. Grady also knew there is always a big difference between those working for their own selfish interests and those working out of conscience and love for an animal that cannot protect itself or speak for itself. Some of the groups, including the Nature Protection Foundation, were small non-profits, as poor as church mice, but they had nonetheless managed to fight some very tough and effective battles on behalf of the manaseals.

So, Grady had a sense of what was going on with the manaseal issue, but he hadn't become personally involved in any substantial way. And after that morning of finding the dead woman, a responsibility began lurking within him that felt entirely dangerous and rendered all convictions precarious.

Grady did a search of the archives of several of the papers in the Trembly area to see what he could find out about Linda Herrero's death. There wasn't much written about it, but he did discover that she had been found in her apartment, overdosed on sleeping pills, and the police had found a suicide note. After reading everything he could find about the case, Grady then went to his assistant, Doug Waxell, and told him he was making a trip over to Waterside. Doug would have to take over the details of prepping the Wednesday edition of the paper until Grady returned. He gave him a brief blurb of a story about the death at Warm Springs, sticking strictly to the facts, and avoiding all mention of any theories he had. In the following edition, which came out on Saturday, he could present more of the entire story. First, he had to find out what that story was.

Before he and Nuck left, Grady placed a call to the local State Police headquarters.

"Lieutenant James? This is Grady Able from the Tomlin Sands paper. Remember—I was at Warm Springs this morning when you pulled the girl out of the water."

"I remember. You were the Sherlock Holmes guy. What do you need, Mr. Able?"

"I don't need anything, but I wanted to tell you that I think the girl's death might have been an accident. My photographer noticed something on the observation platform that got us both thinking about it."

"Look, we're still examining all the evidence. I guess you know we are leaning toward some sort of foul play being involved. So, tell me how you think she died by accident."

"The limbs near the top the large oak hanging over the observation platform were freshly burned—as if they were struck by lightning. I think it's possible a bolt may have hit the top of that tree and then jumped down onto the woman on the observation platform. Maybe she was sitting on the railing at the time, looking out into the water. When she was struck, perhaps she fell into the spring and hit her head on a stump. I noticed one there in the water just beneath the surface. What do you think?" Grady asked smiling impishly on his end of the phone.

"It sounds very farfetched. Is that what you news guys do these days to sell papers, sit around and dream up cockamamie crime theories of your own that differ from what we come up with, just to be different?"

"No, Lieutenant, I don't think that's what we do. It's certainly not what I do. I appreciate the difficult job you have when it comes to investigating an incident of this nature. And you could be right. I know our lightning-accident theory sounds a bit farfetched, and it could be merely a coincidence that lightning hit the tree above the platform, but I thought I'd tell you what we saw. You can do what you want with it. I'd hate to see some innocent men get prosecuted for something they didn't do, that's all.

"We'll look into it," Lieutenant James said gruffly. Grady knew they could ill afford to do otherwise, now that he had made them aware of some further possible evidence which they hadn't yet considered. That was pretty much the extent of the conversation. He had tried not to ruffle the lieutenant's feathers too much, since he knew they truly did have a difficult job, and since Grady also knew he might need their cooperation in the future.

CHAPTER 5
《 》

We love life, but I am saddened when I sometimes find my friends are coming up missing—or worse, floating dead in the water...

It only took them four and a half hours to drive to Waterside. Grady didn't allow small things such as the speed limit to inhibit him much when he drove. His insurance rates reflected that fact, too, as he had been issued five speeding tickets during the past three years, and he was forced to pay an enormous amount for his auto insurance. He noticed that Nuck was less than overjoyed by his driving, too. Grady found it amusing in a way. Nuck was one of the strongest and toughest-minded men he had ever seen, and yet Grady's driving, which he himself didn't think was all that unsafe and frightening, had Nuck gripping the door handle in a constant state of subdued terror. This was never more true than when he drove the Plain Mountain Highway, which rose up from the flats of Newmont and passed not far from Mount Newmont's summit of 1263 feet. You could see for great distances up there, and Newmontians were very proud of their mountain, or hill, such as it was, but the highway did have a couple of hairy turns near the top that kept the mind focused.

When they reached Waterside, a town just south of Portland Beach on the west coast of Newmont, Grady had Nuck read him the specific instructions he had written down in his notebook. He had retrieved the directions to Mrs. Herrero's home from a map search he had done on the Internet. After making one wrong turn, Grady finally pulled into the parking lot of the Ogden Apartments at 123 West Caloosamonty Street. He parked the vehicle in a small area marked "Visitors," and Grady and Nuck set out to find Building #7, Apartment B.

They wound their way down a walkway that led them between the well-manicured and well-landscaped apartment buildings. There were many beautiful maples and live oaks and a few magnolias providing a lot of shade along the way. There were also many crape myrtles reaching up to the sky with their rich green leaves, but without blossoms this time of year. And there were plenty of azaleas, crocuses, Aztec grasses and evergreen giants landscaped into the grounds. It was a warm, windy day for mid-January, and Grady could feel the sweat growing under his collar.

They found Mrs. Herrero's apartment at the very back of the complex and knocked on her door. She greeted them with a warm smile. She was a smallish woman with medium length black and gray hair combed straight back in a simple fashion, and she had a pronounced stoop to her posture. Grady noticed immediately that her eyes were red from crying. He felt a surge of compassion for the woman and knew she must have suffered incredibly. She must be filled with horrible grief at the loss of her only daughter. He choked back his own emotions and entered.

"It is nice of you to allow us to talk with you, especially under these difficult and tragic circumstances" Grady said. "This is my photographer, Nuck Landers, but don't worry, we won't be taking any pictures unless you want us to, and we certainly won't be using any pictures in the paper unless you give us permission."

Mrs. Herrero nodded hospitably and escorted the two men into her living room and pointed to the couch where they were to have a seat. Grady looked at her with compassion and wished there was something he could do to take the pain away, but he knew that was impossible. Only time and human kindness and understanding could be of any help to the poor woman at this stage of her grief.

"Would you like some coffee or tea, Mr. Able and Mr. Landers?"

"Yes, a cup of coffee would be nice." Grady would have said black with no sugar, but there was a good chance Mrs. Herrero would serve Cuban espresso made with demerara sugar, and he didn't want to insult her with any stupidity on his part. He decided to go with the flow and drink whatever the woman served.

Nuck shook his head no with a motion that was barely perceptible. Grady could tell he was nervous. He had seen him in similar situations in the past, where Grady had taken him along on interviews with grief-stricken people, and Nuck always seemed to absorb the pain of those sufferings right down to the bone. If there was such a thing as an empath, Nuck was certainly one.

"Would you like some lemon cookies?" Mrs. Herrero asked. Her eyes moved questioningly and hopefully back and forth between Grady and Nuck.

"That sounds very nice," Grady said. Nuck didn't respond, but Grady was certain his friend wouldn't be able to resist a cookie or two once the treats were actually sitting in front of him.

Mrs. Herrero went to the kitchen and brought back two cups of Cuban coffee, dark, rich, and foamy, and a small platter of cookies on a tray which she placed on the coffee table between them. They took a couple of initial sips, and then Mrs. Herrero said, "Now, what is it that you would like to ask me about my precious daughter?"

"Well, I know how difficult this must be for you—talking about your daughter—but can you tell me something about the friendship that existed between Linda and Marcy Appleton. Had they been friends for long?"

"Yes, for more than five years. Ever since undergraduate college, they were friends. Real good friends, too."

"You told me on the phone that you believe Linda was murdered. What makes you think that?" Grady took another sip of his coffee and nibbled nervously at one of the cookies, which he found to be quite delicious. Nuck was also eating one. Grady looked over his cup at Mrs. Herrero.

"I'll tell you everything. Someone needs to know. The police didn't want to know anything about it. I told them she was murdered, but they thought I was just an old woman who doesn't know anything. I tried to explain to them that my daughter had gotten involved in something that brought danger to her. And now Marcy's dead too—both murdered."

"Well now, Mrs. Herrero, I'm not so sure that Marcy was murdered, as I told you on the phone. I'm beginning to think her death was possibly an accident. It's one of the things we're looking into. You mentioned that your daughter and Marcy had gotten into some kind of trouble. Could you tell me about that?"

Mrs. Herrero was now staring at Grady. There was no anger, no questioning in her eyes, just an intensity and determination that she was going to get someone to listen to her story and to believe her, and that someone was going to be Grady. Her eyes then softened, as she realized it might be perceived as discourteous. "I have her things. I put her old room back together as best I could with all her possessions from her apartment," she said. "I know it's silly, but I wanted to have the feel of her here again, just like before she went off to college and learned too much. Sometimes you can know so much about things that it brings nothing but danger to you." Tears welled up in Mrs. Herrero's eyes, but she fought them back.

"I know my daughter, and I know Marcy, and I know they had gotten themselves into trouble. I showed the police poor Linda's box of papers. She kept many of her important things in a box under her bed. The officers looked at it all and said they would be in touch, but they never got back to me. Three days later they declared her death a suicide. I read it in the paper. I went down to the police station and asked them why they were saying Linda committed suicide, but they only told me they were sorry, and that the case was officially closed."

"Would you mind showing me the contents of Linda's box of things?" Grady asked. "I know it's very personal, but if there is any evidence in there that might give rise to questions about how Linda died, then it would be important to see it."

"Sure you can see it. It's all I have of her now, and she did not kill herself. Maybe her box of papers can clear her of this awful blight the police have chosen to put upon her name."

"Maybe," Grady said.

Mrs. Herrero left the room and momentarily returned carrying an old, slightly tattered, light tan, hatbox, which was decorated with delicately drawn, light blue flowers. She handed it to Grady who remained seated on the couch.

"I gave that box to her when she was three years old. She loved the old thing. Don't see many hatboxes like that anymore. Women don't wear hats as much these days."

Grady removed the cover of the box and placed it gently on the end of the coffee table. He treated the box with the kind of reverence he knew Mrs. Herrero had for all of Linda's possessions. Inside the hatbox, he found dozens of loose envelopes and letters at the top. Grady began looking through them, and after carefully and reverently setting several aside on the couch next to him, he found one from Marcy Appleton, postmarked January of last year. "Do you mind if I read some of these?" he asked, looking over at Mrs. Herrero. She was seated across from Grady and Nuck in a large chair upholstered in a bright floral pattern.

"You go ahead and read whatever you want to in that box, Mr. Able. I've looked into your eyes, and I believe I can trust you. I'm a pretty good judge of character. And though your Mr. Landers is a quiet sort, and holds himself in reserve, I know he has a good soul. Please help me, if you can," she then pleaded. "Clear my precious Linda's name. You'll see, if you read what's in that box that she and Marcy had gotten themselves into some serious and dangerous business, just as I told the police. They were both very head-strong, especially when it came to doing what they thought was right. They were young and foolish."

Grady looked at the woman sadly and then turned his eyes down to a letter he held in his hand. He read through it quickly, feeling very uncomfortable, sitting there in Mrs. Herrero's home, reading her dead daughter's private communications. The letter said very little, other than it made mention of a "plan" for a lobbying effort that Linda and Marcy were involved in on behalf of protecting manaseals. They hoped to get a state representative or senator to sponsor legislation that would provide better protections for the creatures in the most critical areas of their habitat.

"Did Linda give you any indication before she died that she might be in some physical danger?"

"Yes. About a month earlier. And in the two weeks before she was murdered, she told me often how afraid she was. She never told me exactly why, but I knew it had something to do with what she and Marcy were doing up in Hasselford in the legislature that Spring, something to do with manaseal protection, or some such thing. She just loved those animals. She took me to see them up north, at Darling Springs, two or three times a year, and out to the observation area on the south side of Trembly Bay. In the winter months, they like the warm water from the discharge of an electric power plant there. I must admit, I started to fall in love with them too. They are so friendly. But those damned creatures got her killed. I hate them now."

"You don't mean that," Grady said. "You're just upset, and rightfully so." Grady looked on sadly, without saying what he wanted to say—that no matter what happened to Linda, the manaseals hadn't gotten her killed. He bit his tongue, because he knew Mrs. Herrero's anger was all she had to cling to now.

"Linda had lost her part time job at the Anders, Grebes, and Williams Law Firm," Mrs. Herrero said. "Or someone saw to it that she lost it. She was in her second year of law school at Pellsburg University in North Trembly Bay. After she was fired, she had no income, and she had no money, so she asked if she could move in with me for a few months until she could get back on her feet. I told her of course it was okay. This was about a week before she died, and she never did have the chance to come stay with me here. All she said on the matter was, 'They won't stop me. They deserve nothing but the worst kind of hell.' Such talk from my gentle little daughter. They did stop her, though. I don't know exactly how, but they stopped her by murdering her."

Grady doubted that Mrs. Herrero had made her conclusions based on any sound evidence. She was very emotional right now, and who wouldn't be, but he feared she wasn't necessarily thinking clearly about her daughter's death, and he cautioned himself to not be influenced by her emotions. He looked at her for a moment and then read another letter in the box. This one was from an old boyfriend from the University of Newmont. Apparently they had broken up just before the end of her senior year of undergraduate schooling there. In his letter, the young man had written, "I'm sorry we couldn't work things out, but I hope we can still be friends." Grady had a pretty good idea where that suggestion had gone, but then he stopped himself, because he realized he was making judgments based on absolutely nothing. This wasn't helping, and it probably had nothing to do with what he had come here to find.

"One of the news articles I read during my preliminary research before coming over here mentioned that Linda had died on December 22nd," Grady said out loud, looking up from the box.

"Yes, just before Christmas." Tears were welling up in Mrs. Herrero's eyes again.

"I understand the police found what they called a suicide note in the bedroom of her apartment?"

"They found a message. Only two short sentences. It was no suicide note. I know my Linda. It was scribbled at the top of a piece of paper, and it said, "I can't go on this way anymore. It's time I put an end to it.""

"Do you still have it?"

"Yes. I'll get it for you." Mrs. Herrero got up slowly, showing some arthritic pain in the effort, and then she left the room. Grady read another of the letters while he waited. This one was from Marcy, and she spoke with some apparent excitement about their first meeting with a Newmont State legislator, Senator Hinsdale, about the manaseal protection bill that Ms. Hinsdale had agreed to sponsor. Senator Hinsdale had been a staunch supporter of protecting Newmont's environment and wildlife for many years, including manaseals. Mrs. Herrero returned with the note Linda had written just before she died. She gave it to Grady and sat back down. He looked at her and could see she was about to cry in earnest. It was all beginning to be too much for her, the note, the hatbox of Linda's things, and all of Grady's questions were piling up on her.

"I'm sorry," Grady said. "this is an impossible situation." He then paused for a moment in troubled thought and added, "Actually, in truth, I can't begin to imagine what it's like to lose a daughter or son. I have two children of my own. My daughter's only four, but I don't know what I'd do if I lost either of them. I'm sorry, Mrs. Herrero." He looked at her with eyes that revealed his empathy. "I'm sure you've heard that a hundred times from people, and it probably never does anything to ease the pain, does it?" It was a rhetorical question and was taken that way by Mrs. Herrero. She just sat looking at Grady, tears still growing. She held them back, though, as best she could. Grady wished she would let them flow. It did no good to keep them in.

"I'll be all right," she then said. "Please continue. Read everything. I don't care." Her voice was filled with anger and resentment now. Not at Grady, he knew, but at a world that could be so cruel to take her daughter from her and leave her with only memories, a hatbox full of letters, and strange men pawing through them. "You go ahead and read it all. Read everything in there, until you believe me that my daughter was murdered. You'll see." Her eyes were filled with horrible pain, and the tears were rolling down her red face.

Grady looked at her sadly for a moment and then got back to work digging through the contents of the box. There was nothing else he could do. If he was going to go through the woman's dead daughter's private things, then he was determined to find anything within them that might prove to be important in backing up what the woman wanted to believe so desperately.

He read letter after letter, some from her mother, a few from the brief boyfriend she had, and a lot of letters from her friend, Marcy. In them, they talked mostly about what they were going to do about the manaseal legislation they were working on, but Grady noticed that after about the middle of the legislative session last year, they began talking more and more about a mysterious meeting between a man named Francis Jaimansen and Newmont Senate President Sarcost. Both women chose their words carefully, though, and they avoided speaking in any detail about the meeting, as if they were worried that someone else might read their letters and that there could be consequences to that. There seemed to be a fear, or perhaps paranoia, about that meeting.

Beneath the many letters and other loose papers, some with notes scribbled on them in Linda's handwriting, all of which Grady knew he would have to read and go over at some point before he left for home, and which he now avoided, he saw the end of a tiny brown envelope near the bottom of the large, round, sturdy hatbox. He carefully worked his way down to it with his fingers and retrieved it. He opened the envelope, and inside he found a single key, which he turned over in his hand several times, as he thought about what it might go to. Nuck sat silently at the end of the couch watching Grady with his usual intensity. Whenever Grady looked over at Mrs. Herrero, so too, did Nuck, as he did now.

"Did your daughter have a safe deposit box at her bank?" Grady asked.

"I don't know. She may have." Mrs. Herrero looked at the key in Grady's hand.

"I think this key may open just such a box." He looked at it again. "I assume you have legal authority to open it, if she does have one?"

"Yes, I believe I do. Linda gave all her private possessions to me in her will, and she named me the executor."

"Before I go through these papers any further, would you mind making a trip to the bank she used and see if she had a safe deposit box there. It could hold some important clues about what happened."

"Alright, Mr. Able, let's do that." The woman smiled wanly at Grady. He smiled back. It was the first hint of lightness he had seen on her face. She seemed glad that someone was showing even a passing interest in her bereaved cause to clear her daughter's name from the disgrace of suicide. In her heart, she knew that Linda had, instead, been murdered, but she didn't want anyone thinking that she had died by her own hand. The only way to change their minds was for the authorities to officially declare that they had made a mistake. Until Grady showed up, she could think of no way of changing their minds. Grady was beginning to wonder if the police had even read anything in Linda's hatbox. In just a quick perusal of the contents, he had seen plenty to point towards the "trouble" Mrs. Herrero continually spoke about with regard to Linda and Marcy. Perhaps the police had investigated and found nothing to point toward murder, or perhaps they had decided they just couldn't be bothered with a possible wild goose chase. Local investigators in a not-so-big town such as Temple Hills, in a state like Newmont, were sometimes understaffed and overworked, and if they could dismiss a case easily, with the medical examiner's support, they were more than happy to do so.

It was a half hour trip to the Sunset Coast Bank, where Linda had her account. In the lobby, Grady talked with a receptionist who, after hearing what they wanted, asked them to take a seat in the waiting room portion of the lobby of the bank, which was an area with a couple of comfortable easy chairs and a long couch in front of a coffee table with magazines on it. There were two people ahead of Grady and Mrs. Herrero, but there were three bank associates handling those waiting with bank business.

After about ten minutes, a young man, with wavy golden hair came over to the waiting area and called for them to follow him to his desk. He asked what he could do to help them, giving them a too-large smile. He was one of those newly hired, overly eager bank associates. It made Grady uncomfortable, but he played along with the happy spirit of things, the happy spirit of doing business with the most happy of happiest banks, the great Sunset Coast Bank. Mrs. Herrero remained unaffected, and simply said, "I want to look at my late daughter's safety deposit box, if she had one at your bank." The young man smiled and asked for her name and address, and then after doing a search on his computer, he said, "Yes, she does have a box, and if you can show me some photo ID to prove you are Linda Herrero's mother, we can provide you with immediate access to her safe deposit box. I see here that the legalities of proprietorship have been taken care of."

Mrs. Herrero showed the man her license. He looked at it carefully, had her fill out and sign a brief form attesting to the fact that she was indeed authorized to open the box. "I'm sorry for your loss, Ma'am. Your daughter was a frequent visitor to the bank before she . . . uh . . . passed away. I saw her two or three times, myself. Do you have a key?"

The young bank representative said this in such a fashion, as if it had been included in one of the training films shown to him when he was hired—how to handle a grieving customer—that Grady began to very much dislike his over-enthusiastic youth and naivete under the circumstances.

"Yes, I do," said Mrs. Herrero, holding the key up for the young bank clerk to see. Satisfied that it was indeed a key to one of the bank's safe deposit boxes, he ushered Mrs. Herrero and her entourage of Grady and Nuck to a special vault and opened it. He told them they were free to look as long as they wanted, and he showed them to one of the four partitioned compartments in the vault, each having a small table, where they could look at the contents of the box in privacy.

They waited for the clerk to leave the vault, and then Mrs. Herrero opened the box with the key. Inside, was a manila envelope. She retrieved it and opened it and pulled out a sheaf of papers contained inside, all held together with a large white paperclip. At the top of the first page was written in large handwriting, "For Immediate Release to the Press." Also in the safe deposit box was a single, folded piece of paper and another envelope containing a letter. Mrs. Herrero handed over all that she was holding to Grady. "I can't read very well any more. My eyes are not good."

Grady opened the letter first and read it to himself:

"If I should die before I can turn over the information I have in my possession, it is likely my death was caused by ruthless men who have corrupted our political system for their own selfish gains, and for power, and who are now in pursuit of that information, hoping to take it from me and to keep it from being known to the public at large. From the evidence I have obtained, and which you will find in the envelope marked as such in this safety deposit box, I can tell you that this truth should not be difficult to uncover. It only requires a will to do so. I am placing that evidence here in all faith that someone will put an end to the madness."

Also in the box was a loose letter, not in an envelope. Grady unfolded it and saw that it was obviously written in a hand other than Linda's. It said:

"The enclosed information should fit well with the list of names I know you already have, and it should help you undermine Francis Jaimansen, or at least maybe provide you with some protection, whatever you may decide to do with it. He is an evil man, and I know my brother's boss is not all that clean either. I am sick of it all, and I will be doing my brother a favor if I can somehow separate him from Jaimansen's reach. In any case, here it is. Keep my name out of it, if at all possible. That's all I ask. Stay safe."

The letter was unsigned.

Grady's eyes hardened, and his brow tightened after reading the two letters, because he knew things had just heated up considerably. He looked at Mrs. Herrero with concern. She was leaning over his shoulder, and when she caught the seriousness of his expression, she said, "What did you find?"

Grady didn't respond to her right away, because he was looking with interest at another envelope at the bottom of the steel box. The word "Evidence" was marked in black marker on the outside. It made Grady's heart beat a little faster, because he was a little afraid of what reality he might find within. He brought out the envelope and carefully opened it. When he looked inside, however, he found it to be empty.

Grady looked at Linda's mother now, not quite sure what to say to her, but then finally he said, "It looks like you might have been right about your daughter, Mrs. Herrero. Linda may have gotten herself into some kind of real trouble. Now, I don't know if any of this means she met with foul play, but it certainly has my interest, and I will help you in any way I can to see to it that the truth about what Linda was onto finds its way to the light of day. Unfortunately, this is made difficult by the fact that the evidence she had in her possession, and which was the source of her recent fear and trouble, appears to be missing."

"Oh my gosh," said Mrs. Herrero.

"Do you mind if I keep these two letters for now?"

"No, not at all."

Grady put them in his jacket pocket.

Nuck looked on. His lips were pressed tightly together with frustration now. He exchanged a look with Grady and then looked at Mrs. Herrero. He smiled at her in sympathy, and she smiled back. She was on the verge of fresh tears.

"It'll be all right," Nuck said in a low voice.

"Yes, Nuck is right, Mrs. Herrero," Grady said. "It will be all right." He said it with such conviction that he almost believed it himself for a moment, but the truth was, he wasn't sure just how that proclamation was going to made true.

CHAPTER 6

《》

Beloved and slow-moving . . .

Grady dropped Nuck off at his small home located within a rural farming area to the west of town in an unincorporated part of Timpkin County. It was after 10 p.m., and there wasn't a single light on anywhere on the property. It was a moonless night and pitch black.

"Why don't you take my flashlight, so you don't kill yourself trying to get into your house."

"I don't need it," Nuck responded quickly.

"Alright." Grady watched as Nuck swiftly crossed through a beautifully landscaped area to the right of the driveway. Grady knew his friend spent a lot of his spare time on his gardening and landscaping around his house. Then Nuck crossed his mostly brown, but well-mown, lawn, which consisted of all native grasses and vegetation. He then slipped into the darkness of the front door. Grady heard no key being inserted in the door and doubted very much if Nuck ever locked his doors. He didn't even hear the door open and close. Nuck just disappeared silently into his home in the blackness of the night. After a few seconds, a small, dim, light came on, and Grady left for his own home to see his wife and family. It had been one incredibly long day.

As Grady drove the ten miles home that Monday night, he knew there was little doubt he had hooked into some real trouble with the Marcy Appleton and Linda Herrero story and worried what that might mean for his family life for the immediate future. That familiar tickle of curiosity that had always gotten him into hot water in the past was beginning to work away inside of him. This made him a good newsman, but he knew it was also akin to a sickness, at least as perceived by other, more normal, people, and as sometimes perceived by his own wife and children.

Don't get me wrong, I know for a fact that his wife, Emily, loved the news business, too, and she was a big part of the Tomlin Sands, but she didn't like it when a story completely took Grady over, like it did from time to time. Emily hated it when that look came over his face, that dire, disturbed, unsatisfied, and troubled look that always set him off like a heat-seeking missile, and which always had him gone from her for way too much time. It didn't happen often, only twice before in the history of their marriage, but Grady must have had that look on his face the night he returned home from Waterside at 10:30 p.m.

"What's going on," Emily said immediately after Grady came through the front door. She didn't say it in a nasty way, but in the exact way Grady knew she would. "We've been worried about you." Emily looked at him carefully and saw his troubled eyes. "You certainly didn't tell me much on the phone, and that didn't help any. I knew you had gotten into something pretty serious. What is it, Grady?" she asked.

"I'm sorry, Honey. You know I don't like telling you details over the phone. It's just too impersonal, and it wasn't an emergency. If I had told you, you'd just worry until I got home anyway. In any case, I found out that another young girl, a friend of Marcy Appleton's named Linda Herrero, died recently in Temple Hills. I didn't expect to be gone so long, and I didn't expect to find what I found . . . How are the kids?"

"They're both in bed, but don't try to change the subject."

"I'm sorry I'm so late."

"That's not what has me worried. It's that look on your face. I know that look."

Grady frowned. "Yeah, you're right," he said. "I've waded into the middle of the deaths of two young women, seemingly coincidental, and yet I have the strange feeling that there's a lot more to those deaths than meets the eye. I'm sorry I left without being able to tell you more. You weren't home when I called this morning, so I left a message. What do you know about Marcy Appleton's death so far?"

"I heard a little about it on the evening news," Emily said. Her eyes were still tight with worry. "It's awful. The state police called it suspicious, but they didn't rule out a suicide."

"You're kidding! I don't think it was either of those."

"You don't?" Emily said incredulously. "What was it, then?"

The last time Emily saw Grady all agitated and full of vinegar like he was now had been two years ago. Shortly after seeing that familiar hawk-like look in his eyes, he uncovered a nasty hazardous waste story that caught him up in local, state, and even national politics, and forced him to spend a lot of time at the EPA headquarters in Atlanta. When the case went to trial in a federal court, many powerful people became very upset with Grady. It didn't stop him from reporting on every detail of the story, though, and it didn't keep him from editorializing about it.

Ultimately, his stories and actions raised the anger of some local citizens, as well, who were resentful that jobs had been lost in the area due to the final outcome of the case. Emily remembered very well that that story had come complete with death threats and accusations that he was a ruthless and evil journalist. A medium sized corporation went belly up because of the cover-up of toxic waste dumping, and from the lawsuits that followed the outcome of the federal case. But it was also true that a lot of people fully supported his reporting, because they knew what he had done had literally saved thousands of lives from being shortened by cancer and other diseases that would have accrued from the long-term effects of the illegal toxic wastes. Most people actually cared very much about being able to avoid living in a cesspool.

"I don't know," Grady said. "I don't think it was a murder, and not likely a suicide. When Nuck and I were out there, we noticed something that might suggest her death was accidental. I called Lieutenant James and told him before leaving for Waterside this morning. He's the lead investigating officer of the death. He didn't seem very receptive, but I hope they don't try to make arrests based on a rush to judgment. The police think that three men who were camping in the park last night might have killed

Marcy. I don't believe it, though. And then Marcy's death led me
to a clue that led me further to another young woman, a friend of
hers, who died recently in Temple Hills—Linda Herrero. Nuck
and I spent several hours with her distraught mother in
Waterside. She thinks that Linda was murdered. The police over
there called her death a suicide, which has her mother absolutely
frantic, this on top of the horrible grief she's suffering. So now
we're dealing with two deaths and the possibility that each one
is being declared incorrectly. From what Nuck and I saw while
visiting Mrs. Herrero, I think there's reason to believe her about
her daughter's death, and if that's the case, it's going to lead to a
whole lot more disturbing trails I'm going to have to chase
down." Grady looked at Emily earnestly and then smiled, hoping
to coax her into one too.

"Slow down there, Sweetheart. I understand, but that doesn't
mean I have to like it," Emily said, and then she smiled briefly.

She truly did understand, and she was a big part of the paper,
but she was also a wife and a mother, and she didn't like seeing
her husband being dragged away from home for long periods of
time and becoming embroiled in a lot of nastiness. If he was onto
a real story, she knew that would be exactly what would be
happening during the next several weeks, and she also knew he
wouldn't let go of it until he had ferreted out every detail of it.

"I'm beat," Grady said.

"Will you try to eat something? There's some leftover pizza. I
ordered some when I knew you weren't going to be home for
dinner. I was hoping it would placate the children, at least a
little. The truth is, though, they missed their dad, and they kept
asking me when you were going to be home."

"Yeah, I know," Grady said solemnly.

While Emily was reheating the pizza in the microwave, Grady
went to check in on Krissy and Steven. They slept in separate
bedrooms down the hall. Krissy's was on the right, and Steven's
was on the left. Sometimes, Steven would become frightened,
and he would meekly ask his sister if he could sleep with her that
night. She usually complained a little and called him a big baby,
but then she always relented. She loved her little brother very
much, even if at times little Steven didn't know that.

Grady carefully entered Krissy's room and quickly discovered that Steven was in there, too, sleeping all curled up next to his sister. Grady went over to each of his children and gave them a kiss on the forehead and then adjusted the blankets so that each was covered warmly. He looked down at them with overwhelming affection. He couldn't help thinking about Marcy Appleton and Linda Herrero and the awful pain that Mrs. Herrero and Marcy's parents must be suffering at the moment. Krissy rolled over onto her other side but did not awaken. Steven was dead to the world and didn't budge from his position with his favorite stuffed rabbit held between his arms.

Grady returned to the dining room, where Emily was just setting down a plate with two slices of warmed pizza on it.

"Thank you, Honey," Grady said. "I am hungry."

"You're going to need to keep up your energy," Emily said. "And so am I, to be able to put up with the newsman insanity that's about to take you over."

While Grady devoured the pizza, he told Emily all about the details of the day, about the lightning strike discovery, about the contents of Linda's hatbox, about the contents of the safe deposit box, and what he thought it all might mean, or at least where it was likely to take him with the story. He told her that from what he had already found, this one was going to require a lot of legwork. There were several people he had to talk to before he could begin to get a handle on what had happened to Linda Herrero, which is where Grady believed the real story was. If, indeed, Marcy Appleton's death was an accident, then she was part of the story only because her death led Grady to Linda and because of what the two young women had become involved in.

When he was finished eating, Grady looked at Emily softly, and the love exchanged between them washed away all the anxieties, worries, and tensions, at least for the moment. Emily gently took hold of his hand, and he squeezed back in response and gave it a kiss while looking into her eyes.

CHAPTER 7

《》

Been here for millions of years . . .

"What the hell are they doing in there?" said Joe Hart, spitting out the car window. "I hate this goddamned work. Day after day, watching her goddamned apartment. It's as boring as watching a fly scratch its ass. The woman hardly ever goes out, and when she does, it certainly ain't never to no place interesting. How the hell we gonna find out anything this way? I think it's just the man's way of punishing us for our little screw-up at the Capital last year. He don't never forget stuff like that."

"Yeah well, we did screw up, and royally," said Tom Campton.

"Maybe your right."

"Of course I'm right," said Tom. "How long are the bastards goin' to stay in there. It's been two hours already." Tom stared out at the apartment building across the parking lot. "Hey look, they're leaving."

"It's about goddamned time," Joe said. "Ok, here we go. Maybe this'll turn out to be something."

The two men watched as Mrs. Herrero, Grady, and Nuck walked to the woman's dark blue, 10 year old station wagon and got in. The three drove off, and Tom and Joe followed. They made their way out onto Lansing Drive, and then onto Hemming Street, and then onto Common, which was the main street running through the center of Waterside. After going through two sets of lights, they pulled into the entrance to the Sunset Coast Bank, parked, got out of the car, and went inside.

Tom and Joe also parked, but out on Common Street, and they did some more waiting for the woman and two men to finish their business there. It was certainly of great interest to them, for they were curious and suspicious at what might be going on inside that bank. Forty-five minutes passed before Mrs. Herrero, Grady, and Nuck emerged. Tom and Joe followed them back to Mrs. Herrero's apartment. About an hour and a half hour after that, Grady and Nuck exited her building and left in a white vehicle. When they finally drove out of sight, Tom and Joe got out of their dark maroon luxury sedan and walked up to the woman's apartment. Tom gave three sharp raps on the door. Mrs. Herrero thought it was Grady and Nuck again, perhaps wanting another cup of coffee, or to ask another question, or to spend some more time with her, and she didn't bother to look through the peep-hole in the door to see who was there, because she was hoping it was them. When she opened the door, though, much to her astonishment, Tom and Joe pushed their way unceremoniously into the small foyer of her apartment.

"You're the men who killed my daughter, aren't you?" Mrs. Herrero said, backing up into the living room as they pressed forward into her house.

"What's wrong with you, old woman?" Tom asked. "We haven't killed anyone, and we're hoping we don't have to start now. So, just cooperate, and we'll be on our way, and you won't have anything to worry about."

"What do you want?"

"What we want is this," Tom said. "We want to know who those men were who were just in here, and we want to know what you were talking to them about. We want to know everything. It was about your daughter, sure enough. We know that much, so don't try bullshittin' us any. We'll know right away if you're lying, and that wouldn't be good for you at all."

"Not at all," Joe agreed.

"We weren't talking about anything," Mrs. Herrero said. "They were just here to see how I'm doing. They are nice men."

Joe smiled and looked over at his partner in a knowing fashion. "I can see she ain't gonna make this easy, is she?" Tom said nothing. Joe then pushed Mrs. Herrero back onto her couch and pulled out a leather chord from his back pocket and tied her hands tight in front of her, tight enough so they hurt. "It's gonna get a whole lot worse for you than this if you don't smartin' up."

"I don't know anything," Mrs. Herrero cried out with hysteria beginning to choke off her voice.

Joe slapped her hard across the face, and Mrs. Herrero began shaking in terror with her head slumping forward. After two more of these punishments by Joe's hand, she finally told them why Grady had come. She couldn't stand any more. Tears of pain and humiliation were streaking down her cheeks. She had just slipped into the bowels of hell, and she felt she belonged there. She told the two men about Linda's hatbox and about the safe deposit box. Joe was happy to make it clear to the woman what would happen to her if she ever talked with Grady again, or to the police, and he said, "I didn't kill your daughter, but if you don't show us everything in those boxes, I'll have no choice but to put you in the ground in an ugly and painful way."

Tom found the hatbox on the bed in Mrs. Herrero's bedroom. The two men pawed through it recklessly, throwing letters and papers about as they searched for the particular pieces of paper they were seeking. After they finished with the hatbox, and not finding what they wanted, they untied Mrs. Herrero's hands and accompanied her in her car to the bank, where they told her to go in and retrieve the contents of the safe deposit box. The sun was just beginning to sink below the tops of the buildings, but it was still a plenty hot afternoon. Mrs. Herrero was sweating enormously and was feeling deeply sick to her stomach. She just wanted the men to leave, so she could do what was pressing from inside her to do. She could feel herself coiling up into a place from which she knew she would never return. It was a place that in her heart of hearts she had decided she deserved for allowing her daughter to be killed. She was convinced that from this day forward, she would suffer alone, and in total despair of her failings and of her loss. She had decided that it was her lot in life, her deserved hell, now that everything had been taken from her, including any feeling of self-worth, dignity, or any reason to carry on. She would not be in this world ever again. She knew it, not as a conscious thought, but as something sweeping through her. She was only waiting for those awful men to leave, so she could get on with letting the void of her tragedy completely devour her.

So, she went into the bank, and once again getting the assistance of the same young clerk who had attended to them before, she asked if she could get into her safe deposit box again. He gave her a bit of a funny look, but then he obediently escorted her into the small vault. He asked her with all formality, just as he had last time, if she wanted to use a booth, but she said no. After he left the vault, she opened Linda's box, scooped up all of the contents from it, re-closed it, put it back inside the open compartment in the vault wall, closed the small door, and hurried out of the bank. She returned to her car where Tom and Joe were waiting.

On the way back to her apartment, Tom went through all the contents of the safe deposit box that she had handed him. He looked through the manila envelope, looked at the empty envelope marked "Evidence," looked at everything, and then threw it all on the backseat floor in disgust.

"You'd better not be jerkin' us around any. Is this everything that was in that safe deposit box?" Tom asked.

"Yes," Mrs. Herrero said.

"Everything?" Tom repeated, louder this time. "There seems to be something missing."

"It's everything that was in there. There was nothing in the envelope. I swear."

"If you're lyin' to us, we'll be back, and it won't be pretty. I'm warnin' you."

Joe got in the driver's seat of Mrs. Herrero's car and Tom got in the back seat. They ordered Mrs. Herrero to get in the front seat. They drove back to her apartment complex and parked her car. The two men took Mrs. Herrero back inside, where Joe gave her a few more cuffs on the side of her face. Tom searched the house again but still didn't find what the two had come for.

"You'd better not be hidin' anything from us," Joe said to her. "We ain't people you hide things from. We'll find out as sure as you're sittin' there."

"I'm not hiding anything. I don't have what you want. The envelope was empty, I'm telling you."

"Alright," Tom said. "We're leaving now, but we'll be back if you're lying to us. You can count on that."

As they walked to the front door, Joe turned and gave Mrs. Herrero one last nasty look and pointed a slow finger at her in admonition. The two men then left her apartment, went to the far side of the parking lot, got into their maroon sedan, and drove off.

Mrs. Herrero could still see in her mind's-eye that pointing finger, and she knew exactly what it meant. It meant that evil had gotten loose in her world, and she was defenseless against it. It was evil that had taken her only daughter—evil that could freely enter her own home at will.

She sat motionless in her chair in the living room well into the night. There were no lights on in the apartment, and she didn't bother putting any on. She sat there in the darkness, feeling as alone as anyone could possibly feel. She began crying silently and continued to do so until she finally sobbed herself to sleep.

CHAPTER 8

《》

It's a long time between young ones . . .

Tuesday had been extremely busy at the paper, and the day had flown by without much time to even think about the Marcy Appleton/Linda Herrero story. It had been up early and to bed late, with a hard day's grind in between. Grady and Emily had woven the duties and scheduling demands of newspaper and family into a fast, tight weave of living that day, where every minute was a rush to attend to the moment and move on to the next. They had managed to get the paper printed and out early Wednesday morning, though the delivery people had to wait an hour before they could prep and load up. This edition had Grady's initial Marcy Appleton story in it. Sleep had come quickly and soundly for both of them when their heads finally hit their pillows that night.

Upon waking the next day, Grady went for an early run, which on occasion he worked himself up to do. The sun was spreading gold over the ocean's vast expanse to the east. A few clouds scudded by in front of the fiery globe there. Grady's bare feet padded across the wet sand near the surf's edge, and his breathing was steady, but hard. After finishing about three miles up the beach and back, he plunked himself down on the sand and sat looking out at a distant ship cutting its way along the ocean's horizon line. It was moving ever so slowly to the north. A sailboat was bobbing along about a mile offshore, and the sun lit up its white sails. The wind was blowing from the southeast. Three surfers were trying to catch the fast moving waves, but they weren't having much luck. The surf was choppy and the swells were moving onshore with too much speed to offer good conditions for all but the quickest boards. He had done a little surfing when he was a young teenager, and so he understood some of this.

Grady was enjoying the morning calm and the peace of watching the majesty of the enormous reach of ocean with only a few other human beings around. Sweat was glistening all over his stubbly face, and a few rivulets were working their way down his temples.

He stood up and wiped his face with his towel. It was time to get back to the paper.

When he arrived at his personally marked space on Main Street in front of the Tomlin Sands building, he found that someone had taken his spot. The car had Illinois plates, so it was probably a tourist. The people who did the house-to-house deliveries of the newspaper throughout the community, and to the coin boxes that were strategically located in shopping malls and other high pedestrian traffic areas, had long gone. They had to start very early in the morning to get their routes completed before 6 a.m. A late paper only made for distraught customers.

Grady set about his day's work, which was considerable, since the many elements of the next issue had to be tackled as soon as the last issue was out the door. There were advertisers to call, to update their contracts if they were about to expire or to make changes to their copy; there were wire news articles to go through to see which might be good to include in the paper; there were Reader Opinion letters to read through and select; there were in-house articles to be written and edited; there were several freelance articles to read, some from regulars, some from unknown writers making submissions to the paper; there were a hundred calls to make to attend to one detail after another; and there were a hundred and one problems to be solved, mostly small and merely annoying, but a few of larger proportion.

Just yesterday, the paper supplier said they were disconti-nuing the paper stock Grady had been using for the past three years. This was a major annoyance, since he had very much liked that type of paper, and now he had to decide whether to look for another supplier or choose another type of paper on which to print his paper, and that was no simple decision. Grady would have to see how the print looked on any new paper before putting it into use. He liked to use a three-color printing process, and the quality of the paper was important. It had to have a brightness rating high enough to properly contrast and display the photos and images he put in the paper, but not so bright as to lose its look as a newspaper.

Much to his surprise, around 9:30, Grady received a call from Lieutenant James of the state police. Grady picked up the phone and began with his usual, "Tomlin Sands City Desk." Answering the phone that way had started as a joke one day about four years ago when he introduced himself to a caller that way in front of his staff. He had smiled broadly and looked about the room at them, and they had chuckled quietly, appreciating the irony and the humor. For months after that, they called Grady their "big city" editor. In fact, it had only been partially a joke from Grady's point of view, and partially a wish to be respected as a legitimate newspaper. But Grady had continued to answer the phone that way ever since, and it became a point of pride with him. Indeed, the caller had reached the Tomlin Sands City Desk.

"Lieutenant James here, of the Criminal Bureau of Investigation. I'm just calling to let you know that you were right about Marcy Appleton's death," the lieutenant said. "We strongly believe now that it was an accident. It appears that the young woman was struck by lightning. The coroner found evidence of burns on her neck, shoulders, and right arm. But just to make things a bit confusing, he also did find some evidence to suggest that she might have actually been trying to commit suicide at the time she was hit by the bolt of lightning. Now that is sad, isn't it?"

"What evidence?" Grady asked, caught by some surprise.

"Well, the coroner's office believes she was standing on the railing of the observation platform when the lightning struck her. Not what you would call normal behavior. She then fell into the spring, hitting her head on the submerged stump you mentioned to me a couple of days ago. The Coroner found wood debris from the stump embedded in the wound on her head. After going back out to the scene, and making a detailed survey of everything, we now believe that she must have been up on the railing, perhaps contemplating jumping in, when she was struck.

"We took some very careful measurements. From the distance the stump lies from the platform, we are pretty certain that she could not have been sitting on the railing. She would not have landed far enough out in the water to strike her head that way. She certainly couldn't have been standing on the platform itself. That would have been impossible. Given the evidence we have now, we won't be calling it a suicide, however. It was an accident, no matter what she might have been doing or contemplating at the time the lightning struck her. We have notified Marcy's parents, and we have also told the three boater men that they are no longer suspects. In keeping with their pleasant personalities, they threatened to sue us and all, but I'm sure it was just a lot of hot air. I doubt very much they want to bring upon themselves the kind of publicity such as action would cause to descend on them. They had to be relieved. Anyway, thanks for your help in this. We would have come up with the truth of what had happened sooner or later, but you helped us get there sooner, and I appreciate it."

"You're welcome, Officer James. I'm just glad it all worked out."

"We are, too. Marcy Appleton's death is a tragedy, but I think we can safely put it behind us now."

"Lieutenant?" Grady asked. "When you went through the girl's things at the camp, did you find anything out of the ordinary?"

"No. Just camping gear, some food and drinks, and a few papers she had stuffed in the glove compartment of her car. Just normal stuff, like a topographic map which she probably used on one of her hiking or camping trips—she apparently did a lot of that—a tire warrantee, some papers that looked like they might have had something to do with her lobbying efforts on that manaseal bill she had been working on with Linda Herrero."

"So you know about that?"

"Sure I know about it. We're not the incompetent boobs you may think we are."

"I don't think you're incompetent at all. In fact, I think just the opposite."

"We tracked down Linda Herrero's mother, and I gave her a call."

Grady was suddenly worried that the state police might have found out some of the same things he had, and if they knew what he knew, then they might even decide to go mucking around in the Linda Herrero case. He didn't want that to happen. Not yet, anyway, because if too many people were poking around, they might frighten away any chance of uncovering what was really going on.

"Find out anything?" Grady asked.

"A few things, but mostly that you were headed over to Waterside to see her that afternoon. I guess my question to you is, did YOU find out anything that we should know about Marcy Appleton's death."

"No," Grady said, and he wasn't lying—not technically. Nothing Mrs. Herrero had told him or shown him changed anything about Marcy Appleton's death. The connection between the two young women and what they may have discovered had implications reaching more into Linda Herrero's death. For now Grady decided he would tell the Lieutenant as little as possible, of course always making sure that he stayed within the boundaries of Newmont law regarding the giving and withholding of evidence. The only real evidence he had was no evidence at all—only an empty envelope.

"Mrs. Herrero showed us some of Linda's letters and things and the contents of a safe deposit box her daughter had. She wanted to convince me that Linda was murdered." Telling the lieutenant this was a gamble, but Grady decided it was one he had to make. His instincts told him that it was better to be a little forthcoming, otherwise, he might raise suspicions and worse, he might be jeopardizing the trust he had so far earned with Lieutenant James. It was a tricky bit of business, because he didn't know what the lieutenant knew about Linda Herrero.

"Yeah, I know. She told me the same thing, over and over again, on the phone. The Temple Hills police have closed the case as a suicide, and since we have no jurisdiction over Linda Herrero's case, there is nothing more for us to investigate. None of it changes what we know about the nature of the Appleton girl's death."

Grady said, "I understand." There was an uncomfortable pause in the conversation as both men were thinking. Grady finally said, "Would you mind if I took a look at the items you found of Marcy's at the campground before you return them to her family?"

"Not at all. There is nothing overly personal in any of it."

"I'll try to get over there in a couple of hours, then," Grady said. "Will that be ok?"

"Certainly."

"Thanks, Lieutenant. I'll see you then."

"No problem. I'll be here until about two. If I'm gone, I'll make sure Lieutenant Oakley lets you see the Appleton girl's papers. By the way, is there anything you're looking for that we should know about, Mr. Able?"

"No, I don't think so, but I'm working on a story about Marcy Appleton and her friend Linda Herrero, and I don't want to leave any stones unturned. If I do happen to come up with something the state police should know about, you'll be the first to know, Lieutenant."

"Fair enough. Good luck with your story."

Grady sighed with relief when the conversation ended. The call had caught him by surprise, but it did have the effect of stirring in him an urgency. He had to get on with the Linda Herrero leads. He immediately dropped everything else having to do with the paper and performed a news service search for "Francis Jaimansen" but found only two hits. The first was a straight forward piece in the business section of the paper about Jaimansen's two growing companies, and it offered little in the way of insight into what kind of man he was. The second was an editorial in the Calhoun Zephyr News, from the hometown of Jaimansen's primary residence. It spoke out on a vote by the local City Council and the resulting legal battle that ensued over that decision. Calhoun was a small town on the northwest coast of Newmont. The editorial went on to criticize Francis Jaimansen for trying to thwart the City Council's unanimous decision to not allow his proposed marina, golf course, and condominium development project to be built on a pristine section of old growth woodlands within a sensitive area of habitat where the Tremblyrand River merges with the Lomahassie River. Both waterways are used extensively by a large number of manaseals, wading birds, alligators, otters, and countless other species of wild plants and animals.

The editorial went on to say that Jaimansen, who was well known for owning two different marine manufacturing companies in that area of the state, one specializing in luxury yachts, and the other in sporting boats and jet skis, was once again trying his hand in the lucrative business of land acquisition and development. Apparently, he was also extremely wealthy from an inheritance from his grandfather. The second paragraph of the editorial read:

"Mr. Jaimansen has put a lot of money behind the lobbying and legal effort that thwarted the City Council's decision. His attorneys managed to come by a judge who was willing to overturn the Council's April vote. Unfortunately, the judge agreed with Mr. Jaimansen that the zoning of the property had not been properly done. The matter is being appealed. Mr. Jaimansen is a businessman who, of course, is looking out for his own business interests. There is nothing wrong with that, per se, but there is something wrong when he wages an expensive ad-campaign in the local media declaring himself a friend of the environment and a friend of the community. This cannot go unchallenged. Francis Jaimansen's interests as a developer have proven not to be in keeping with the interests of the community. The Calhoun City Council offered to find another, more suitable, area on the Lomahassie River, where he might build his project without contributing to the ongoing havoc and destruction of Newmont's ever diminishing natural resources.

"Mr. Jaimansen's attempt to force his development on Calhoun goes against the interests of the people who live in this community, and it goes against the quality of life Calhoun is trying to sustain for its citizens."

Upon reading this, Grady immediately decided to call the editor of the paper, Bill Harlan. When Grady got him on the phone, the man was congenial and spoke in a plodding manner, as if he had nothing better in the world to do than to talk to him. Grady found it refreshing.

"Oh yeah, I wrote that one," Mr. Harlan said. "Sometimes you just have to call it like it is. That just happened to be one of those times."

"So what happened with Mr. Jaimansen after his victory over the Calhoun City Council?" Grady asked.

"He got a very big sense of himself, I'm afraid. Since then, he has involved himself more and more in political dealings and behind the scenes power-brokering. He's become a pretty big deal in Newmont politics—all quiet and hush-hush, you know. No one ever mentions him by name, when such things are discussed, but you hear things, and you find out things—not enough to print, of course, but things nonetheless. Jaimansen thrives on the power, and he usually does his manipulating of the system in a way that's kept all neat and legal. Local and state government in Newmont is still often government by political hacks for political hacks. Some things in Newmont never change."

As Grady listened to the editor over the phone, he visualized a sly, knowing smile behind what he imagined to be a large, meaty, and open face, perhaps a bit red from the hundreds of Jack and sodas he imagined the man had consumed. Sometimes, Grady let his imagination run away with him. And in a place like Newmont, that was an easy and natural thing to do. But for all he knew, Harlan was as skinny as a rail and as dry as a desert.

He liked the man right away and suspected he was a very good newspaperman in the stuff that really matters. They talked on for quite some time about the trials and tribulations of the news business in this modern day. They seemed to be of a like mind about the changes the news industry had gone through during the past several decades, and they agreed they didn't much like any of it.

By the time the conversation came to an end with Bill Harlan, Grady thought he knew Francis Jaimansen a whole lot better, but what he found out didn't make him feel one bit better about the story he was trying to scratch together. Grady did more research on the man, and began to fill in some of the details around the broad strokes of Jaimansen's activities.

First, he called a friend at the Manhattan Globe Citizen who, as a favor to Grady, or more accurately as a favor to the memory of Grady's father, helped him track down several of Jaimansen's recent associations to businesses and corporations and their subsidiaries. It appeared that Jaimansen was into a lot of things, and he confirmed the man had accumulated an enormous net worth. Though all of this information was interesting and helpful in gaining a perspective on Francis Jaimansen, unfortunately, it did not give Grady what he was looking for. He needed to find some clue or hint as to what possible reason Jaimansen's name would turn up in a letter written by Linda Herrero in connection with the evidence she had claimed to have in her possession.

Grady decided it was time to try a bluff. He didn't like doing that kind of thing, but he needed to expose that singular thread in the Linda Herrero story that might be given a pull and thereby unravel the truth surrounding the young woman's death. He knew he wasn't likely to find that thread alone, and before he could put his bluff successfully into action, he wanted to find out all he could about Jaimansen. To this end, he used all the connections and resources he could muster.

He called a reporter he knew at the Miami News Beacon, who he thought might be able to fill him in on any shady activities in which Jaimansen might be engaged. The reporter couldn't tell him anything more than Bill Harlan had already told him, but he did know a freelance reporter, a man named Larry Johnston, who could. It turned out that in the past couple of years, that reporter had been tracking and investigating some of the lobbying and big-money campaign contributing that he believed was nothing but influence peddling at its tawdriest. He hadn't been able to come up with any smoking guns, but through it all, he had developed a sense of who some of the main characters were and how they operated.

It was as close to a kick-back scheme as you could find, but a legal one, the reporter told Grady. If you had money, and you could find a powerful politician who was greedy for that money, then you could help grease their campaign onto victory. In return, the politician would then make sure that any legislation passed was favorable to that contributor's business. This would, in turn, put more money into the hands of the contributor, and some of that money was then given back again to the politician in the form of larger campaign contributions to keep him happy and in power. It was a cycle of corruption and crony capitalism that fed upon itself, and the poor citizen was left out in the cold without much of a real chance of say about how his or her government operated, especially if they kept themselves uninformed. He further told Grady that most of these people were untouchable, because there was no way to prove the existence of any quid-pro-quos in terms of money given and legislative votes placed.

At the end of the conversation, and in ominous tones, the reporter told Grady that if he had any sense, he would just forget the whole thing. Grady explained that he couldn't do that. The reporter said he understood, but told him that Jaimansen simply bought whatever he couldn't get through straight politics or through his many high-powered connections. Before hanging up, Grady got the reporter to give him Francis Jaimansen's home address and phone number, a number that very few people had.

Grady sat there for a few moments, wondering how Jaimansen had climbed so high and so fast in the world. In just six short years, he had gone from being the owner of two medium size businesses to walking directly among the high and mighty in Newmont politics. It was also obvious from the reporter's warning that Jaimansen was a dangerous man and not someone to trifle with.

Grady decided on the outline of a plan. It would require another trip to the west coast of Newmont. It would require being away from the paper for more precious hours and again handing off the responsibility for much of the work to others, which he didn't like doing. He sat there for a moment of inaction, thinking and worrying, and then finally getting up the nerve for it, he placed a call to Francis Jaimansen.

He couldn't believe his luck at finding the man there and available to talk to him, and he further couldn't believe his luck in finding Jaimansen so willing to be interviewed by Grady. He told him that he was writing a story about development in Newmont and whether or not it was at odds with protecting the environment. Grady said he was trying to see if there was a balance, some common ground, that could be found. Jaimansen seemed eager to set Grady straight about it all and assured him that environmentalists often overreacted to new development. Grady knew that he had approached him in the proper way to get the interview. A meeting was arranged for the following Wednesday at 1 p.m.

Emily was home with Steven, and so Grady decided to go there for lunch and spend some time with them. Krissy was in school. Grady had been away from home much of the past couple of days, and he was likely to be away more in the coming days. He knew that much now, and he had not been carrying his end of the bargain as a husband, or as a father. Not only that, Emily had to take on some of Grady's duties at the paper when he was gone. He was feeling guilty about it, and he was worried that the next several days would only increase that guilt.

When he reached home and drove in the yard, he saw Krissy's bicycle in the driveway. He couldn't believe she was already six and Steven was four. It seemed like only yesterday he had started the paper, and it seemed like only yesterday that he had met Emily at a 4th of July celebration and had fallen in love with her. He had proposed to her at the Horizon Rivers restaurant overlooking the intracoastal waterway. It seemed like only yesterday when he had held little, cute, pink, bright-eyed Krissy in his arms in the hospital just after she had been born. And then in the blink of an eye, young Steven had come into their lives, and Krissy began growing and talking like she had been born with the English language already inside of her. It all seemed like it had gone by in that blink of an eye.

Grady had a good relationship with Emily, and he loved her more than ever. The busy nature of their lives had been rough on them at times, though. They were often caught without much sleep, and with too much work to get done in too short a period. It seemed everybody's lives were that way anymore—running here, running there, on the phone way too much, grabbing too many meals on the run, or skipping them entirely. But once in awhile, about three times a year, they found the time to go out dining and dancing, when they could find a good rock 'n roll band playing somewhere within the Central East Newmont area. It always left them exhausted because they danced with such relish and vigor, and they danced until the band quit for the night. It was a good kind of exhaustion, though, and it made them feel younger than their growing years.

Grady walked into the kitchen, where Emily was preparing lunch for herself and for Steven. Steven would be starting pre-school next year.

"At last, a chance to look at my wife and my beautiful little man."

"I'm not little," young Steven said in stern protest.

"No, of course you're not. I can't believe how big you're getting." Grady ruffled his son's hair, and the boy looked up at him with a big smile and big blue eyes.

"Long days, lately," Emily said as she stirred the vegetable soup. She had made a huge pot of it the day before, all from scratch. Grady loved it, and Steven seemed to like it, too, especially when it was served with freshly made bread. Emily used an electronic bread-maker for that, and the bread was always delicious and made with healthy ingredients. When they first were married, she made bread from scratch and baked it in the oven. They tried to eat healthy whenever they could, which was not as often as they would like. The healthy eating had to be wedged in between fast food restaurant meals and too much junk food and soda purchased from the local grocery and deli just two doors down from the paper.

"Yeah. Very long." Grady said.

"You were gone early this morning. I have barely seen you at all in the past two days."

"I know. I woke up early and decided to go for a jog on the beach. You were sleeping like a baby, and I didn't want to wake you. By the way, I got a call from the state police, and they said the Appleton girl's death was an accident, just like Nuck and I had surmised."

"Really!"

"Yeah. They confirmed the girl had fallen off the railing after being struck by lightning. Apparently she had been standing on it. Lieutenant James thinks she may have been contemplating suicide. I think it's a strong possibility."

"Why would she be trying to kill herself?"

"Depression. Over her friend's death—Linda Herrero. I think there may be a lot more going on here. I wouldn't get too excited about it yet, but I think we may have stumbled onto something big. I don't necessarily like it, but that's just the way it is."

"Oh you silly," Emily said smiling as she ladled soup into three bowls. "You're always looking for that one story that's going to put our little paper on the map. But we're already there, Honey. I saw us on the map just yesterday. We're in Tomlin Dunes, about one half mile from the Newmont intracoastal waterway."

Grady smiled back as Emily looked over her shoulder at him. She had medium length, strawberry red hair, pony-tailed up with a scrunchy. "I'm serious about this one, Emily."

"I know you are. I can see how you're running around in a semi-wild frenzy."

"Frenzy, huh? I think not."

"I think so."

"Not so. No frenzy."

"Yes, frenzy. Not, NOT so. So not, NOT so." The two frequently enjoyed this kind of verbal banter.

"In any case," Grady said. "I have to run around some more, over to the local state police headquarters. There are some things of Marcy Appleton's that I want to take a look at."

"Well, before you do that, you just sit your butt down here, and eat some of my fine home-cooking. It might be a long while before you get any more."

"Alright, I'm sitting. I'm sitting, Honey," Grady said with a smile. And he did sit, and he grabbed a soup spoon and held it propped straight up on the table to show that he was ready for some serious eating. Emily looked at him and frowned through a smile.

"I told you you were silly. That's why I married you."

"I think it was I who married you, my darling."

Emily smiled. "How you talk."

Emily called Steven in from the living room, where he had been playing on the floor with an old set of "Erect Em" blocks, and the three of them shared a nice lunch together. They giggled and laughed and spilled soup throughout it all, and Grady was glad he had come home for lunch. He knew Emily was right about his running around chasing after the grand-slam story. He would certainly be doing some serious running around until he found out what had been going on with Linda Herrero and Marcy Appleton, and why two young women had died at such a young age. There was definitely something there to dig into.

Grady entered the state police headquarters and asked for Lieutenant James, but he was not there. Instead, a younger officer came forward when he found out Grady was in the building and offered his assistance freely. It was Lieutenant Oakley. He said that Lieutenant James had told him to show Grady the girl's personal possessions, especially those found in the glove compartment of her car. He brought him over to a small table that had books and papers piled up on one end of it and asked him to have a seat. The officer then left and came back shortly with a green plastic bin containing Marcy's things.

"Not much to look at, but here you go."

"Thanks, Officer."

There was only one thing he was really looking for, and he found it almost immediately. It was the topographic map Lieutenant James had mentioned over the phone. He looked it over carefully and found just what he had been hoping to find ever since leaving Mrs. Herrero's apartment yesterday, a small mark, a tiny blue dot, in the upper left hand quadrant of the map. It was a map of Southeast Brunswick County, which included Lake Belquin. The dot was located in a large swampy area emerging from one of two small streams that flowed into the Lake from the north. Emily was right, Grady thought. I'm off on a chase. There would be nothing holding back his manic investigation now. What could be more enticing than possible buried treasure marked on a treasure map. In this case, it was journalistic treasure he was seeking.

He asked the young officer if he could photocopy a few of the documents, and the officer accommodated him. Grady didn't want to tell him exactly what he was interested in, because he had learned long ago that you never revealed the details of a story until you had put it all together. It would only cause problems. He would keep his word to Officer James if he found something the police needed to know, but for now, he didn't want them to begin snooping around again. So he copied the map and a couple of other papers just to make it look good, and then he left.

Upon returning to the Tomlin Sands, late in the afternoon, Grady wrote a small follow-up story about Marcy Appleton's death which was to go in that Saturday's edition of the paper. He quoted Lieutenant James as saying, "We strongly believe that her death was an accident." Grady did not mention anything about how he and Nuck had been instrumental in the state police coming to that conclusion. They had gotten it right, and he didn't feel it served any good purpose to mention their own role in the discovery of the truth of the young woman's death. He was glad they had been able to help.

CHAPTER 9
«»

Delicious water hyacinth and sea grasses . . .

Grady was now itching to get at the business of chasing down some answers to the story. If nothing else, it was a story that had some frightening and far-reaching questions swirling about it, but Grady also had a paper to run, and he had to put his attention there for a few days. The work was piling up, and when Grady returned from the State Police Headquarters, he spent the rest of the day at the paper and then worked well into the early morning hours.

Grady then spent all day Thursday and Friday tying up the many other loose ends that had developed while he had been away Monday. They finally got the Saturday edition of the paper printed by the wee hours of Saturday morning, ready for the delivery people. During the day Saturday, after only a few hours of sleep, Grady frantically continued to play catch-up. He had dozens of calls to make, and he had six columns to begin putting in order for next Wednesday's paper, which meant pressing the freelance writers he used for material on subjects he thought would be of some interest to his readers. He spent Sunday with his family, trying to get some much needed rest. And then, very early Monday morning, he and Nuck headed north to pick up the thread of the story that had begun with Marcy Appleton's death.

Grady had been doing a lot of thinking about the events of the past few days, and he wasn't sure what he had gotten himself into, or rather what his curiosity and sense of fairness had gotten him into. He felt that the Temple Hills police had ignored Mrs. Herrero's fears that her daughter had been murdered, and he knew he was likely her only chance to get at the truth. He felt it was his responsibility as a journalist and as a human being to try to provide her with some answers. And now he was in a canoe with Nuck on Lake Belquin, paddling alongside a local guide he had hired, hoping to find Linda Herrero's hidden evidence, evidence that may, or may not, exist at the location she had indicated on her topographical map by a single blue dot.

After reading Linda's letters, Grady fully believed she had, indeed, discovered something she thought was critically important and even dangerous. He believed that, and because of it, he was now in that canoe paddling in the cool air of a cloudy January day in northern Newmont. And he was afraid of that evidence too, afraid that it might actually exist and that it might press him on to a danger and nastiness he wasn't ready for. He had a feeling for things like that. Of course, he had been wrong about the same such apprehensions in the past, and so he didn't take the feeling too seriously.

Lake Belquin was about fifteen miles southwest of Hasselford, the capitol of Newmont. It was fed by two streams that came wandering all the way down out of the western hills of Georgia. After exiting Lake Belquin as a single stream, the Belquin River flowed to the Flobian sea on Newmont's northeast coast. If I'm wrong about any of this geography, please forgive me. As I say, sometimes my memory of how Newmont relates to other states is flawed, hazy, or missing altogether. In the big picture, it really doesn't matter much.

Nonetheless, much of the Lake Belquin wilderness, including the Belquin and Primlo Rivers that flowed into the lake, had been kept in their pristine natural condition, with no houses, developments, strip malls, or any other kind of civilization anywhere in sight. The area was the centerpiece of the Lake Belquin National Park which included thousands of acres of protected pristine lands. Grady's guide, Big Mountain Bert Campfield, knew the area intimately. He was half Cherokee and half red-neck farmer, and he had generations of knowledge and experience of every river, lake, and swamp in all of Brunswick County.

"How far is it?" Grady asked Mr. Campfield who was paddling along in his kayak next to Grady and Nuck's canoe.

"Oh, not far. A couple of miles or so," Big Mountain said. He had a full graying beard and a long, loosely braided ponytail that reached all the way down to his belt. His head was massive and was a mismatch for his smallish, sinewy frame. Small though he was, his upper body was powerful, without an apparent ounce of fat. His legs were strong, sleek, struts, thinning their way down like thick ropes of muscle and sinew into two smallish feet, which were covered in old, heavily worn moccasins. Grady felt lucky to have two such rugged and capable individuals along with him in the wilds of northern Newmont.

Grady had hired Big Mountain at the recommendation of a college professor he knew at North Newmont University, located in Hasselford. The professor was a bit of a birder and had often hired Big Mountain to take him off into the backwoods, where, with his camera and his powerful birding binoculars, he always hoped he might find that one rare bird that was missing from his life list. And, in fact, he had already found two quite rare birds that way in the five years he had lived in Hasselford—a King Rail and a Wilson's Phalarope.

Along the way, Grady, Nuck, and Big Mountain saw five manaseals swimming and playing together in the clear waters of the Belquin River, and Grady began to realize why Linda had hidden her evidence somewhere along this waterway. It was symbolic for her—gave her comfort and tied everything together somehow in a way that removed some of the fear she was experiencing. He surmised that she and Marcy had probably canoed over these same waters during the period of time they had been lobbying in Hasselford a little less than a year ago. Grady could tell that she truly loved these creatures—and what was not to love? They were such peaceful animals, and so friendly—gregarious by nature, even though they rarely swam in groups for sustained periods of time. Instead they were individualistic in their behavior.

Big Mountain pointed out that one of them was a female, though Grady had no idea how he could have possibly known. She swam directly over to Grady and Nuck and popped her nose up out of the water and pressed it against the front of their canoe. For several seconds she stared up at Grady with her cute face, as if to say, "I like you, and I am curious about you, and I trust you." Grady looked down into the eyes of the manaseal, which were couched within two circles of wizened skin, and he said out loud, "Don't trust us—not even for a second. People are capable of every manner of horrible thing. We are not to be trusted." It made him feel ashamed for the human species, and it made him strangely angry. The extent that human selfishness would destroy all that is beautiful in the world, especially such a special and gentle creature as the manaseal, in the name of the dollar, or in the name of jobs, or just to avoid the slightest inconvenience in life, or just to feel superior to the helpless, made Grady want to just yell at any boater that insisted they had the right to drive their boats as fast as they wished, yell at any developer that would bulldoze down an old growth forest, and yell at any elected official who would neglect their duty to protect all this beauty—and tell them to just knock it off.

As Grady continued looking into the eyes of that friendly manaseal, he knew that no boater, no developer, no politician, no anyone had the right to harm or kill even one of those precious animals. He understood that accidents could happen, and that manaseals could be injured and die from those accidents, even when people were taking great care in their boating habits, but selfishness and apathy were no excuse at all. He had never felt quite this resolute before. That singular experience he had in the wilds of northern Newmont on that day in January had changed his attitude forever. It was manifested by seeing the creatures in the beautiful, unfettered wild, and seeing how wonderful they were. He would never again simply ignore issues of conservation and environmental concern like he had tended to do in the past out of ignorance and apathy, and yes, even laziness. He had always been one of those people who let others take care of the heavy lifting when it came to difficult environmental issues. And environmental issues were always difficult, because they inevitably bumped right up against big money interests and powerful people who refused to let anything stand in their way, especially in a wild, immature state like Newmont.

"It sure is beautiful country out here," Grady said, overwhelmed by it all. "I never knew such a place existed in all of Newmont."

"Yes, it is," Big Mountain said.

"Do you suppose we'll have any trouble finding the exact location on the map?"

"No, not at all," Big Mountain said in a soft but certain voice.

"Professor Ballard tells me that you have a lot of Native American blood in you."

"I am half Cherokee, on my mother's side."

"I guess I couldn't be in better hands as we move into what you call 'the upper swamps,' then."

"No. You are in good hands. Professor Ballard speaks highly of you, too, and says you are an honorable man. He asked me to take good care of you out here, and that is what I'm going to do. You can count on that."

"I appreciate it. I'm not very good in a canoe."

"You're doing just fine."

"Thanks for being diplomatic. I appreciate it. It helps having my good friend here aboard. I know if I had to come out here alone, I'd probably tip the canoe over and drown in about five minutes, and nobody would find my corpse for weeks."

Neither Nuck or Big Mountain laughed or responded to this, which made Grady take his ineptitude even more seriously.

They were paddling over very shallow and swiftly moving waters now. The current tried to twist them sideways whenever the canoe got turned even slightly. Big Mountain, in his light kayak, seemed to be having no difficulty at all. Grady could feel Nuck's powerful paddle strokes behind, not only attempting to keep the canoe going in the right direction, but also propelling it steadily forward. Grady's strokes were not very efficient, and he suspected his inexperienced efforts were actually making a lot of work for Nuck. He kept switching back and forth from one side of the canoe to the other, always trying to correct the turning impact from his previous paddle stroke. He was sure this was not what a good canoeist would be doing. Even though he was bad at it all, Nuck said nothing. His friend simply corrected the canoe's aim when it was necessary and kept them going straight up the narrow channel they were in. The sandy bottom of the river was only two feet beneath them, and Grady kept hitting his paddle against the sand with each stroke. There were massive amounts of long flowing grass growing on the stream bed, and they waved lazily back and forth with the movement of the water.

After quite some time fighting the swift current and shallow waters, the stream began widening. Numerous lagoons spread out from the main channel, some quite large. If they hadn't been on a particular mission, Grady would have loved to enter one or two just for adventure's sake, but there was no time for that now. The stream itself had many offshoot channels winding in and out of the dense grasses and thick hummocks, and it was beginning to appear like a confusing maze to Grady. Big Mountain, though, seemed to know exactly where he was going at all times.

After about an hour and a half, they came to a large turn in the stream, and the channel narrowed to the point where Grady could no longer tell that it was a channel at all. Grady and Nuck's canoe scraped along the bottom quite often. Sometimes Nuck had to dig his paddle into the sand to help the canoe slide over a particularly low area. Grady helped as much as he could. Big Mountain's kayak had no problems in the shallow waters, because he was more skillful and because his kayak did not sit as low in the water.

The forest that lined both sides of the stream now seemed to have invaded the waters. The trees were mostly swamp maples, cypress trees, and a few live oaks on the higher, drier grounds. The Belquin Channel had become a three mile wide swampland now. The birds were chirping and singing in their loud bright tones. A mockingbird was performing its rich repertoire of songs, one right after another, as if to show the two visitors just how magnificent a bird he was. And he was, indeed, magnificent.

There were hummocks and wide stretches of sea grass everywhere, all protected by a broad canopy of overhanging tree limbs. It had been a cold winter so far, and many of the Cypress trees' green needles had turned brown, with many of them having already fallen to the ground and into the water.

Big Mountain negotiated his kayak in and out of each sharp turn in the channel with skill. Grady and Nuck followed along in their clumsier fashion.

After they had gone about a mile into the swamp, Big Mountain turned his kayak into a secondary channel, though Grady again couldn't be sure it was a channel at all. After about another mile or so of difficult paddling in even thicker grasses amongst more numerous muddy hummocks, Big Mountain suddenly brought his kayak to a halt.

"Let's take a look at your map," he said.

"Grady pulled the folded sheet from his back pocket and handed it to Mr. Campfield. The guide opened it and examined it carefully for about a half minute and then handed it back to Grady. "It's just over there," he pointed through a heavily wooded hummock island to another smaller hummock about three hundred yards away.

Grady said nothing, but he had no idea how Big Mountain could be so certain from the map.

"It's the only solid land anywhere near the vicinity of the dot," Big Mountain said. "I doubt anyone would try hiding something in the marsh. It would be too difficult to find again."

"All right," Grady said, peering around. "Let's take a look."

Big Mountain began paddling again—actually it was more of a pushing from the channel bottom than paddling. He worked his kayak around the large mucky, tree-grown island and moved toward the smaller hummock he had pointed to earlier. Within a few minutes, he had powered the front of his kayak up onto its muddy bank. Grady and Nuck followed suit and ran their canoe onto the bank next to their guide. Big Mountain was out of his kayak and onto the hummock in a flash. Grady climbed out carefully onto the mud and then held the canoe steady so Nuck could walk his way down the length of the canoe and get out. Grady had no idea where to begin looking. His legs were stiff, and his hands were sore from paddling. Big Mountain moved past Grady, gliding between the swamp scrub and cypress tree trunks. He had already spotted something and was moving toward it with purpose. "Follow me," he said.

Grady and Nuck followed, looking in the direction ahead, trying to see what Big Mountain had possibly seen to put him on the trail of something of interest. Grady had gained such faith in the man's ability as a guide by now that his hopes rose significantly. If Big Mountain thought he saw something, then you could bet your boots it was something worth checking out.

The guide rounded a tree and suddenly knelt beside a sapling that had been broken over. It was not a fresh break, but one that was browned by some age.

"Someone's been here. That's for sure."

"Couldn't an animal have done that?" Grady asked. "A bear or deer, or alligator, or something?"

"No, no. No bear. No deer. No alligator," Big Mountain said feeling the ground gently with his hand, massaging it with very precise movements of his fingers. He felt here and there. "No this was a human. Feel the imprint in the ground here. You can tell by its shape, even though it's many days old. It was no hoof, and it certainly was no bear paw, and it was no alligator claw. It's definitely human. You feel, and you'll see."

Grady bent down next to Big Mountain and felt the place where his guide's hand was. There was a very slight depression in the ground beneath the leaves and Cypress needles, but Grady couldn't have distinguished it from any other natural depression in the ground. He could feel nothing that could relay any information to him at all. Nuck then knelt and also put his hand in the depression. He said to Grady, "Yep, he's right." Grady looked at Nuck for a moment and then decided it didn't surprise him.

Their guide had already moved on ahead about twenty yards. He was kneeling again. "Better come take a look," he called back to Grady.

Grady and Nuck hurried over and looked down at what Big Mountain was pointing to at his feet. Within an area of muddy, leafy ground, which appeared to have been disturbed, encircled by three medium sized cypress trees, there was a large jar with the cover lying off to the side. The jar had dried mud all over it. Grady bent down and picked it up and looked inside. He then looked over at Nuck and then at Big Mountain. He tipped the jar opening toward each of them so they could see. It was empty. His heart sank. An empty envelope in a safe deposit box, and now an empty jar.

"I guess that's why the footprints are still detectable," Grady said. "Linda or Marcy, or both, must have returned here not too long ago and removed whatever it was they had in that jar. Either that, or someone else got to it first." If it was Jaimansen who had retrieved it, Grady thought, then the game was over. Without Linda Herrero's evidence there was very little he could do.

It was just after 1 p.m. when they got back to Big Mountain's guide camp at the east end of lake Belquin. After Grady paid and thanked their trustworthy guide, he and Nuck said a hearty goodbye to him, and they got in Grady's white SUV and began the long drive back to Tomlin Dunes. Grady asked Nuck to drive. There was one more thing Grady wanted to look into before leaving Hasselford, though. He got on his cell phone and called Richard Jacobs at his place of work. On a hunch, Grady had done a little research during the past few days concerning the unsigned letter he had kept from Linda's safe deposit box, and he was hoping to use this opportunity to set up a meeting with him. Richard was the brother of Perry Jacobs, who was Senator Sarcost's assistant. That was the connection he wanted to pursue. Grady thought, *We have Jaimansen and Sarcost and an unsigned letter from a man who supposedly delivered to Linda the important evidence we have been looking for. And that letter said "I know my brother's boss is not all that clean either."*

Grady couldn't be certain that Richard Jacobs was the one who had given Linda the unsigned note he had found in her safe deposit box, but if the boss he was referring to was Sarcost, then the brother he referred to was likely Sarcost's assistant, Perry Jacobs. If nothing else, he intended to find out for sure.

Richard Jacobs worked in the finance department of a large insurance company in Hasselford, and Grady was hoping he could arrange to meet with him and find out exactly what information he had given to Linda Herrero. Whatever that information was, it might have gotten her killed. Grady couldn't shake that one thought from his mind, because if it was true, he knew he had latched onto the tail of one very dangerous tiger with this story.

The company switchboard operator answered. "H & T Insurance. How may I direct your call?"

"Mr. Richard Jacobs' office, please, extension 412," Grady said.

"Hello," a man answered when the call was connected.

"Richard Jacobs?"

"Yes, it is."

"Oh, good. Hi, my name is Grady Able, and I'm from a small Newmont newspaper, the Tomlin Sands, down near Creighton Beach. I've been working on a story about Linda Herrero's death, and I was hoping you might be willing to help me out. I happen to be in the Hasselford area today and could stop by, if you want."

There was a moment of silence on the other end of the line, and then finally the man said, "How could I possibly help you with a story about this Linda Herrero person?"

"Well, Mr. Jacobs, I wouldn't be calling you if I didn't think you could help. I'm pretty certain you gave Linda some information that was so dangerous that it put her at great risk, and maybe worse."

"The only thing I can say to you, Mr. Able is, you should be very careful what you go poking around in." There was another momentary pause, and then the man said, "I'm afraid I've got nothing that would be of any help to you."

"The fact that you say that tells me that you do have something. I know you tried to help Linda with Francis Jaimansen." Grady was careful not to say too much, careful not to reveal how little he actually knew about Jaimansen and what Linda might have been into.

"I'll say it again, I have nothing to tell you. Nothing at all," The man's voice was now strained, and Grady knew this conversation was about to end.

"I know that isn't true, but I won't bother you about it right now. I WILL be in touch, though."

"That wouldn't be wise."

"We'll see," Grady said. "Thank you for your time, Mr. Jacobs."

A click on the other end of the line ended the call.

Nuck said nothing. He continued to drive down the highway, in his cautious, never-above-the-speed-limit fashion.

"Well, that didn't go very well," Grady said, grimacing. "I guess it fits in with how the whole day has been going, though."

"Not so good," Nuck said. His eyes remained focused on the road ahead.

Grady did a lot of thinking and worrying as they made that long trip home that day. Nuck remained silent for most of it, but it didn't bother Grady in the least. He was glad to have him along. He was entirely used to the ways of his friend by now. Nuck's sure presence always lent a strength to Grady at times like these, even when his comrade in news gathering barely uttered more than a word or two. When Nuck was along, in a strange way it made Grady believe they could handle almost anything together. Grady knew it was silly, but what it boiled down to was, he liked Nuck, and he trusted him implicitly. And Nuck's quiet manner never stopped Grady from talking on about whatever was on his mind. He would exchange glances with his friend from time to time, even if no verbal response was forthcoming, or if the response was only a single clipped word, which it often was.

CHAPTER 10

《 》

Caught up and strangled by fishing line . . .

After dropping Nuck off at his car at The Donut & Coffee Shoppe, Grady drove to the office. It was just after 7 p.m. when he arrived, and he was feeling quite discouraged by the day's events. Emily, Doug Waxell, and everyone else was still there, working hard, attending to all that had to be done to keep the paper on schedule for printing Tuesday at midnight. Emily was in the front office and hit Grady up with four or five questions immediately after he came through the door. The writer for the "How Things Grow" weekly column was late. One of the delivery people was going to be out Wednesday due to a death in the family, and Grady had to come up with a replacement or ask one of the other delivery people to pull a double route. The fax machine had jammed and wasn't working, and Emily had called the company to have someone come look at it. The representative told Emily that their service warranty had run out. So Grady was going to have to deal with that, talk them into covering this current breakdown by agreeing to sign up for another two year warranty stint with them. He had already decided he would tell them he hadn't realized the current service coverage period was over, which was the truth. He had a good business relationship with the representative, so it shouldn't be too much of a problem.

Steven had decided he wasn't talking to his sister anymore. Yesterday, after Krissy had come home from school, Steven asked her to take him along when she and her friends went to the park near their house to play. She had refused. "I don't want you always hanging around with me," she had said. When Steven came running into the laundry room complaining about this injustice to his mother, Emily told Krissy that she should take her brother with them from time to time, that she wasn't going to force her to do it, but it was the right thing to do. Krissy had decided to ignore her mother's advice, and Steven had decided he would never talk to his sister again from that moment forward. So all in all, his return to the office after being away for a day was just about normal.

Unfortunately, he had decided that he was going to have to spend another couple of days away, since the day in the Lake Belquin National Park had proven to be a fruitless venture. Grady knew he had no choice but to spend more time on the Marcy/Linda story. Either that, or he had to let the story drop altogether, and he wasn't willing to do that. It had the potential to be one of those big stories that comes along only once or twice in a lifetime, and he was determined to pursue it, at least enough to see if it actually might lead somewhere.

He was beginning to think he had overlooked something. There had to exist some clue to indicate where Linda may have hidden her evidence, since the dot on Marcy's map had turned up only as an empty jar. Something had been hidden in that jar. That was for certain. It was too much of a coincidence to find it there exactly where the dot was marked on the map. Who had the contents of that jar now was unknown. Maybe Marcy or Linda had moved it to another location before they died.

As he finally settled into his chair at his desk, he looked out the window at the large maple tree in the back lot of the building. All its branches were bare of leaves, and it was looking a bit ghostly in the mellow glow of a nearby street lamp. A songbird landed high in the tree and began chittering out an early night song—a strange phenomenon for this time of year, Grady thought. He then turned around and looked at the work piled high on his desk and then looked out the window again at the bird in the maple tree. He suddenly knew it was an absolute must that he return to Waterside and see

Mrs. Herrero once again. He needed to find out why the hidden jar had turned up empty. He couldn't help thinking he had missed something important in Linda's things. In that moment, he decided on a course of action, a bit ragged though it was. The operation of the paper was going to suffer, if he had to be away another couple of days that week, but it was his philosophy that you sometimes just had to do what you had to do, and let the chips fall where they may. This was one of those times.

He immediately placed a call to Mrs. Herrero. When she didn't answer the phone, he thought nothing of it at first, and in fact thought she was perhaps just out shopping or something of that nature. He tried several more times during the next couple of hours, and when she didn't answer any of those calls either, he then began to worry that she was away, or that something was wrong. When he had seen her previously, she had been desolate and depressed. He worried that perhaps this had been debilitating for her in some horrible way, and this notion began working on his mind. Regardless of whether Grady could get hold of Mrs. Herrero on the phone, he knew more than ever he had to drive over to see her, if for no other reason than to see how she was doing. He also had the meeting with Jaimansen already scheduled for Wednesday afternoon.

He gave over most of the paper's responsibilities to his able assistant, Doug Waxell, and he planned on staying in touch by phone, to make sure everything was going all right. Emily had made it clear long ago that she did not ever want to be placed in charge of the paper, even for an hour. She would help out in a large way, but nothing more. She had children to look after, and that was enough responsibility for her. Grady decided to take his laptop with him so that Doug could email him any articles or columns that needed editing. He had an old-fashioned streak in him, and he certainly didn't prefer doing his work that way, but in a pinch, it was extremely helpful.

Everyone at the paper had gone home by eight, except Emily. She was busy editing a story for the front page when

Grady walked into her office. Their steady, reliable nineteen year old babysitter was looking after the children.

"Honey," he said, and she looked up from her computer screen.

"Yes, my love," she said smiling, anticipating the meaning in his tone of voice.

"You can probably tell from my behavior this afternoon, I've got something that's eating away at me."

"I'd have to be blind not to notice it. What's going on?"

"I've got to go over to Waterside again tomorrow to do some follow-up on the Appleton/Herrero story. I was hoping I could talk you into coming with me. I know you have a lot to do, but the paper can get along without us for a couple of days. I've asked Doug to look after everything."

"What about the kids?"

"Maybe you can get your mother to look after them for a day or two?

"Yes. Sure, I'll go," Emily said her smile growing larger. Grady was surprised at how quickly she had agreed. He had expected her to put up a fight, but he guessed she really did need a break from everything for awhile. She had been grinding away at family and work, non-stop, for such a long time.

"It might be fun to get away for a bit of news sleuthing. I'm sure my mother would love to look after the children for us, and she is so good with those two." There was a lilt of excitement in her voice.

"Yes, she absolutely is good with them." Grady had grown fond of Emily's mother, Doreen. She was always so willing to lend a helping hand. It made him think of the days when his own mother, Martha, had come to Tomlin Dunes for a six month visit right after Steven was born, and she, like Doreen, had been a marvel at helping with the kids. Now his own mother was in poor health in Boston. Grady called her often, but he missed her terribly.

It had been more than a year since Grady and Emily had had any kind of vacation together. The last time they made an escape from the paper, they took a week and went camping in the Blue Ridge mountains with the children. It had been fun, and exhausting. It had rained steadily the first two days, and setting up the tent and their camp had been a soggy disaster. When things finally dried out, though, they had enjoyed the experience very much. They went for short walks on the trails that originated out of the park, and they went for long drives through the mountains on the Blue Ridge Parkway. It had been a refreshing experience, and one that was sorely needed again.

Unfortunately, Grady knew that this trip to the west coast of Newmont was not going to measure up in that regard. It was going to be mostly business, but at least Grady and Emily would be together.

"When do you plan on leaving?" Emily said.

"Early tomorrow morning. I've got to make every attempt to see Mrs. Herrero again. I think I must have missed something in Linda's things, or I didn't ask the right questions when we were there, or something. That empty jar we found up in Belquin Lake sure the hell means I missed something important."

"That's one strange story you've latched onto, Dear. One thing's for certain, though. Whatever was in that jar at one time, Linda and Marcy must have thought it important, and dangerous. Why else would they hide it way out in the wilds of North Newmont like that?"

"You're absolutely right about that," Grady said looking blankly past Emily at the text on the computer screen in front of her. His thoughts were drifting elsewhere, to a place he did not like to go with Emily. He broke himself away from them and said, "I'm a little worried about Mrs. Herrero. I tried calling her several times, but she does not answer the phone. So, if I can't reach her before we get there, we're just going to have to try dropping in on her tomorrow, unannounced. I'll keep phoning her. It's really important I see her again and ask her a few more questions. I'm kind of at a loss with this whole thing, and unless I can get some new lead, I can't see where I can go with the story. I need that evidence that Linda supposedly had in her possession before she died."

"Maybe after you're done, we could go out and have a nice dinner together, tomorrow night, at some good restaurant over there," Emily said.

"That would be nice," Grady said with a smile.

They left for Waterside Tuesday morning at 5 a.m. The rush hour traffic became a nightmare on the new interstate going west, and they encountered an accident near the Hacklee exit that had traffic backed up for ten miles. The traffic remained knotted all the way past Newmont's largest city, Emberly, but then eased some as rush hour started to wind down around 8 a.m. They crossed the crest of Mount Plain just before ten, and after stopping for a quick early lunch, they finally arrived at Mrs. Herrero's apartment complex in Waterside at about 11:30.

Grady knocked several times, but the woman did not come to the door. Grady and Emily could hear the TV droning away inside—it sounded like one of those small-claims courtroom shows to Grady. He tried the door and found it was unlocked. This made him worry, because he knew Mrs. Herrero always kept her door locked and bolted. She had even secured it after letting him in the apartment the day he was there a week ago.

"Something's not right," Grady said.

He opened the door and took a step inside. The powerful stench of spoiled food, urine, feces, and other bodily odors hit him immediately. He walked down the dark entry hall and peered into the living room. Emily followed closely behind, making nervous glances about as she walked. Then Grady saw Mrs. Herrero sitting in her favorite chair, staring trance-like at the television. She did not look at him as he came into the room. He glanced over his shoulder at Emily to see how she was bearing up. She grimaced with a look of pain and compassion, which he knew only too well. Her heart always went out with great ease to the suffering of others. She was a wonderful mother to her own children because of this. They always felt loved and cared for, maybe too much sometimes for their own good, Grady thought, but then just as quickly, he thought, *maybe that's not possible.*

"Mrs. Herrero," Grady called to the woman. She did not respond, nor did she alter the stare she had trained on the TV. "Mrs. Herrero," he repeated. "It's Grady Able, and I've discovered something that I think might help us get to the bottom of what happened to Linda. I think, more now than ever, just as you said all along, she was onto something serious, and that something put her in jeopardy. I came back to ask you a few questions, if you'll allow it. I'm sorry to intrude on you like this." Grady was hoping to stir some emotion in her, to bring her back to the world from her trancelike state.

Mrs. Herrero remained as she had been when they entered the room, and she made no acknowledgment whatsoever of his or Emily's presence in her house. The television flickered away in the dark room. Grady walked over to her chair, reached over and switched on the nearby table lamp and knelt down in front of her. She looked at him oddly, but her eyes were devoid of all emotion. She said only, "Is Linda coming over?"

"No, I'm sorry. Linda is not coming. It's just me, Grady Able—remember, the newspaper reporter."

"Oh, yes, Mr. Able. How have you been?" Her eyes suddenly showed some signs of recognition.

"I'm fine." He smiled at her, and she smiled back, but it was a distant look she gave him with an unreal quality to it. "I want to help you," he said.

"Yes, that would be fine. Please have a seat, and I'll get you some coffee and cookies." There were dishes lying everywhere in the room, most of them with half-eaten cookies, or pizza, or cake, or sandwiches on them. Some even had a fuzzy growth of bluish mold growing on them. The chair Mrs. Herrero was seated in was stained horribly with urine, and she smelled of terrible body odors. There was a roll of toilet paper on the floor, most of its sheets unwound and leading into the bathroom.

"Thank you, but that won't be necessary. What happened to you, Mrs. Herrero?"

"I'm just being punished for all that I should be punished for," she said calmly. "That's all. God has his way, you know."

"And what should you be punished for?" Grady asked.

"For my daughter's death, of course. Everyone knows that. I killed her because I didn't save her from being killed. And I'm being punished because I'm a coward."

"Oh, Mrs. Herrero," Grady said, sorrowfully. "You had nothing to do with Linda's death. Nothing at all. And you're certainly not a coward. You did all you could do to try to warn her. She was her own person, and she did what she thought was right. That's the way our children grow up to be sometimes, and that part's a good thing . . ."

Grady took Mrs. Herrero's hand and gently led her out of her chair and into the bathroom down the hall. He asked her if he could help her get cleaned up some. She said she wanted to be dirty. "Dirty as can be," she said. "I betrayed my poor Linda. I betrayed her completely."

"You didn't betray her, Mrs. Herrero. Here, why don't you close the bathroom door and take your clothes off and pass them out to my wife through the door. I'll find you some fresh things to wear."

Emily came up from behind and said, "If you need some help to wash yourself, please let me know, and I'll come in and give you a hand. Do you have a clean washrag and a towel in there you can use, Mrs. Herrero?"

"Yes," the woman said with some confusion in her voice.

"Let's get you cleaned up, then, and please, Mrs. Herrero, I don't want to hear anymore talk about how you deserve to be dirty," Emily said. "I'm sure you have betrayed no one. You have been only a good mother who has suffered a terrible loss. You need some help right now. We all do from time to time. Who wouldn't need some help, considering all you've been through. We're going to leave you alone in there while you clean up, but if you need me to help you with anything, please just let me know."

"I betrayed her," she said through the door and then she opened it just enough to hand Emily a handful of soiled clothes. "You don't know."

Grady took the clothes from Emily and brought them into the laundry room, which he found next to the kitchen. He went into Mrs. Herrero's bedroom and gathered up some clean clothes for her. He grabbed the first thing he could find in the bureau drawers for underwear, a bra, pants, and a top, certainly nothing that would be considered a fashionable combination, he thought, but he couldn't concern himself with that right now.

Mrs. Herrero was in trouble. Who could withstand the death of their daughter and then find herself all alone in the world to try to deal with her grief. Something had given way inside her, and she desperately needed help if she was ever to be brought back into the world of the living.

"How are you doing in there?" Grady asked, returning to the closed bathroom door.

"She didn't deserve it," said Mrs. Herrero, mumbling to herself mostly. "She was only trying to do the right thing. I told those two men everything about her, about you asking questions, about her papers and her things. I told them everything. It was horrible, and I was so terrified. I'm so sorry. I betrayed her because I was terrified. I'm a horrible mother. I'm a monster. I betrayed my daughter, even after she was dead. I'm a coward."

"What do you mean, Mrs. Herrero? What two men?" Grady asked with sudden concern.

"The two men who came right after you left. They said they would kill me if I didn't tell them everything. I should have let them. But I told them what they wanted to know. I let my Linda be killed, and then I betrayed her."

"That's nonsense, Mrs. Herrero," Emily said in a soft, kind voice. "Again, you didn't have anything to do with your daughter's death, and you didn't betray her." She knew these words couldn't be repeated too often in her state of mind. "You get cleaned up a bit, Mrs. Herrero, and we'll have a talk in a few minutes. I've got some fresh clothes for you."

Grady handed the clothes to Emily, who opened the door a crack and handed them in to the woman. Mrs. Herrero took them and thanked Emily, ever so politely.

Grady thought that perhaps Mrs. Herrero's upbringing and her politeness were now helping her reach out through her despair. When he thought about how she had looked sitting so desolately in her chair, in that trance of despair, he began to believe that the only instinct left inside of her of any use was the one that refused to be discourteous to a visitor. It allowed her to escape for at least as long as he and Emily remained there in her presence.

Grady began clearing all the dirty plates and coffee cups from the living room. He found some household cleaner and began wiping and cleaning every surface. Emily worked on the dirty dishes that had piled up in the kitchen. The smell of the chemical cleaners began to merge with the smell of the rotting food and the ammonia smell of the urine and other body odors. Grady also found some deodorizing spray under the kitchen sink and sprayed it everywhere in the apartment. He cleaned Mrs. Herrero's chair with a sponge and detergent to the best of his ability and dried it with a towel. He could hear the shower running in the bathroom and was relieved that Mrs. Herrero was taking that step on her own. It terrified him to think what would have happened to her if he and Emily hadn't come to see her when they did. She might have died in there without anyone knowing for a very long time. It had become clear from the long conversation he had with her over a week ago that she had no living family members she could turn to. He only hoped he and Emily had provided her with human contact early enough so that she could be spared some permanent psychological damage from her trauma.

"*Two men*," he thought. He worried about the meaning of that.

When Mrs. Herrero emerged from the bathroom, she looked and smelled nice and clean. She had on the pink pants and the purple top Grady had mustered up for her. It was a laughable combination, but Grady smiled at her and said, "You look wonderful. That's got to feel a little better, doesn't it?"

"Yes, it does, but . . ."

"No buts for now, okay, Mrs. Herrero," Grady said gently. "Do you want something to eat?"

"No, but I want to get those cookies and coffee for you that I promised."

"Let's not worry about that right now. We're not really hungry. We grabbed a quick bite to eat on the way over, but thank you. Emily then appeared from the kitchen, still holding a wet dish rag. "By the way, Mrs. Herrero," Grady said. "This is my wife, Emily. I'm sorry I didn't properly introduce her to you earlier."

Mrs. Herrero smiled at her and said, "It's very nice that you came for a visit."

Grady led Mrs. Herrero by the hand back to the living room and over to the couch, which was reasonably clean on the right end. There was a large coffee stain covering the left cushion. He gently sat her down. Her expression had grown very somber again, and she avoided all eye-contact with Grady and Emily. The only remaining clean, dry, sitting spaces in the room were a large mahogany rocker situated in the corner of the room and an ornate love seat, upholstered in a heavy silky material with a broad floral design. Grady and Emily sat next to each other in the love seat, which Grady found a bit embarrassing. This was not the time for even the slightest hint of romance. Emily smiled at Grady, and he beamed back, and then they both looked over at Mrs. Herrero, who continued to look down into her own hands, which she had folded in her lap. She appeared to be extremely tired now.

"Do you mind if I ask you a couple of questions, Mrs. Herrero?"

She did not look up at him, but she said, "That would be fine."

"You mentioned that two men came to see you after my visit with you last week. Do you know who they were?"

"No. I never saw them before, but they were terrible men."

"Did they hurt you?"

"They slapped me a lot, and they threw me onto the couch and then onto the floor when I didn't tell them what they wanted to know . . . they told me they'd kill me . . . and so I betrayed my Linda. I was frightened, and I was weak."

"Of course you were frightened," Emily said. "Who wouldn't be. You did what you had to do. Any of us would have done the same."

"When they were finished going through Linda's things and throwing them all over the house, they left," Mrs. Herrero said. "They told me that if I talked to the police or anyone else about their being here, they would come back and kill me. I don't care anymore if they do. I deserve only to die."

"That is NOT true, Mrs. Herrero," Grady said firmly. "You are a wonderfully courageous woman. You didn't betray Linda or anyone. You have suffered a horrible tragedy, and you have been only brave in dealing with the terrible loss of your daughter. We're going to get to the bottom of all of this. I promise you that. I want you to come back with us and stay with us for awhile. You'll be safer there. Will you do that?"

"No, I could never do that. It would be too much of an imposition."

"Not at all. We would love to have you. Please say yes."

"Yes, Mrs. Herrero, please come stay with us for awhile," Emily chimed in, smiling broadly. She wanted to make sure the woman didn't think she had even the slightest reservation about the invitation offered by her husband.

Mrs. Herrero looked deeper into her hands and said nothing.

"I'm going to take that as a yes. Before we help you pack and get ready to leave, though, I would like to look through Linda's things again. There is something I must check. Would that be alright with you? I know how painful it is to you to have people pawing through Linda's private things, and I wouldn't ask if I didn't think it was important."

"I trust you, Mr. Able. And I see your wife is a kind person I also trust. So you look through Linda's things as much as you like. If there is any way I can do anything to make restitution for my betrayal of Linda, I want to do so." She looked up at Grady and Emily for the first time. They both smiled at her. Emily then got up and went over to her and held her hands in hers and gave her a gentile but warm hug. Mrs. Herrero began crying. Emily then sat next to her on the stained couch and took her hands in hers again and comforted her. She talked to her gently about her lovely home, and about how she must have been proud of Linda. And she talked about grief and about how the living suffer after those who have died. She talked about losing her own sister in a car accident four years ago, about how she had thought then that she'd never get through that. "We never think we have the strength to carry on, do we?" she said. "But we do. It's in there somewhere. Sometimes we just need a little help getting to it." Emily began crying quietly, as she remembered her own painful grieving after the loss of her much loved sister, and she could see some of the same terrible suffering in Mrs. Herrero.

After a few minutes, Grady excused himself quietly and went to what had been Linda's old bedroom. The room gave him a strange feeling seeing it put together the way it had been when Linda was still living with her mother. Grief is a powerful force in life, and it makes people do all manner of strange things. The dead are gone, but the living have to find some way to keep on living. Grady was now keenly aware that Mrs. Herrero had been finding that task almost impossible. The room was neat as a pin, probably the way it had been when Linda had lived there. He imagined poor Mrs. Herrero removing Linda's clothes from boxes that she had taken from her daughter's apartment in Temple Hills and putting them carefully away, neatly folded in the dresser, and tidily hung in the closet, just as she had found them, or perhaps as she imagined they should be in her daughter's old room, in keeping with her daughter's past living habits. How painful it must have been for Mrs. Herrero trying to keep the memory of her daughter alive and always thinking of those fond days when she had lived at home with her while she attended college in St. Pellsburg University in North Trembly Bay the first two years.

He found the hatbox lying open on the bed. He knew that, even in Mrs. Herrero's pain after the abuse by the two men, she must have come into Linda's room and straightened everything up as much as she could after the men had rifled through the apartment. Grady began searching through the contents of the hatbox again. The letters were showing signs of abuse and were stuffed into the box torn and crumpled, apparently damage done by the two men.

After a half hour of pouring over everything again, Grady found nothing new that was of any use to him in his quest to find something that might indicate where Linda had hidden her evidence of wrongdoing. He looked under the bed, and on the shelves in the closet and found nothing. He looked in the drawers of her bedside table and found nothing. He looked on the small maple writing table located beneath the single window in the room and found nothing but a stationery pad. He looked in the center table drawer and found nothing. He looked in the single dresser in the room, starting with the top drawer, which contained socks and scarves and a decorative box of earrings. Nothing. In the second drawer, he found underwear and bras, but nothing else. He opened the drawer wide and felt around through these most personal of clothing items, feeling more uncomfortable with each passing second, and found nothing. The bottom drawer also offered up nothing. His discouragement rose.

There was only one place left to look. He opened the sliding door to the closet and began searching through the pockets of the clothes, as a last resort. He found nothing in any of the pockets of the pants or shirts on hangers. On the floor was a small pile of clothes, half-folded, presumably left just as Linda had placed them in her own apartment many months ago, just before her death. Maybe the men had rummaged through it all, and maybe Mrs. Herrero had replaced everything as close as she could to the way she had found it in her daughter's apartment.

In the pile on the floor he found a pair of jeans, a pair of white Capri pants, one pink blouse, and a T-shirt with a mother manaseal and baby calf on the front of it. Grady felt through the pockets of the pants first and found nothing. He then checked the pockets of the blue jeans, and much to his astonishment, he found an envelope stuffed in the right rear pocket! It was folded in two and was addressed to Marcy Appleton. "Insufficient Postage" was stamped on the face of it. Apparently Linda had sent the letter, and it had been returned. Perhaps this had happened just before she died, and she never had the chance to resend the letter.

Grady took the envelope and returned to the living room. There, he found Emily and Mrs. Herrero still talking quietly. He could see that the communication between them, however, had become far deeper than anything words could convey. Emily understood grief, and she knew how it had to be released so that it didn't become so bottled up inside, and so surrounded by guilt, that it became an entirely self-destructive thing. Certainly, a single outflow of emotion wouldn't do the trick in Mrs. Herrero's case, because her loss was so great, but as Grady listened and watched in silence, he knew that Emily's caring presence was doing the troubled woman some real good. There were tears running down Mrs. Herrero's cheeks. Grady could tell that Emily, too, had been crying. He smiled inwardly, and felt a sudden rush of love for her. He wondered how he had ever been so lucky to find someone as wonderful as her to enter his life and make it full. It sent a shiver down his spine, because he also thought about the consequences to his life had he not been favored so fortunately with Emily's love. He truly believed there was no other woman on the planet that could love him and make him happy like Emily did. And his own love for her frightened him at times.

When there was a break in their conversation, Grady interjected, "Mrs. Herrero, I found this in a pair of pants on the floor of Linda's closet." He held out the letter for her to see. "It was returned by the post office because it had no postage on it. I was hoping to see what's inside, but I thought you should be the one to open it and read it first. And then you can decide if you want anyone else reading it."

That poor girl, Grady thought, so frightened, and so determined to continue on with her mission to face down a wrong, no matter the cost, and not having any idea of how to actually do that. She must have been in such a tortured state of mind, with nowhere to really turn, possibly being pursued aggressively, and as a result of her fear and confusion, she had simply forgotten to put a stamp on the letter. Grady had made that same mistake himself, more than once. Linda must have gone down to the mail boxes in front of her apartment complex and found the returned letter there with the other mail for the day. She had folded it and put it in her back pocket, probably fully intending to resend it.

Grady handed the envelope to Mrs. Herrero. She gently tore it open and removed the letter. There was not much written on it, and she read it quickly. Tears were forming in her eyes. Without saying a word, she handed the letter over to Grady."

It said:

> Marcy,
>
> I had to re-hide it. Do not try to contact me now. They are following me, and I think they mean real business. I'm really frightened, Marcy. Please stay away. I don't want them coming after you, too. In a few days I'll get back to you and tell you everything I know. Maybe I've just become paranoid.
>
> If anything happens to me, I want you to go to my website at *www.LindaHLovesManaseals.com* and read what I have posted there. You are the only person with the password to it. You know what to do then.
>
> Love and Friendship Always,
> Linda

This was it. Grady had found what he had come looking for. It was dated December 19th. This letter remained in limbo because Marcy had never received it. Grady couldn't help thinking how odd life can be sometimes. It might have changed everything if Linda had simply remembered to put a stamp on the letter in her stressed-out state and Marcy had received it. Maybe she would have gotten some help for Linda. Maybe she would have talked her into giving up whatever it was the young women had in their possession that had brought such vile and nasty people to chase after them. Who knows where the letter might have led. It might have led nowhere, too. Everything might have still happened just as it had. The road of such lost possibilities is never clear, no matter how one wishes to travel it out in one's mind using hind-sight as a guide. One thing was certain, though. The fact that the letter had been returned, and that Linda had put it in her back pocket, probably in frustration, and that those jeans had been put on the floor of her closet, probably ready for the laundry, and that Linda had then died the very next day after that, and that those same jeans in her closet along with all her other clothes had then been transferred by Mrs. Herrero to Linda's old room, were all events that were likely the reason the two intruders to Mrs. Herrero's house never found the letter.

Grady recognized the stationery that the letter was written on. It was from the same stationery pad he had seen on top of Linda's writing table. It had the same delicate blue, yellow, and white wildflower design in its top right corner and along its left border.

It took Grady and Emily another hour to finish cleaning up Mrs. Herrero's apartment and to get her things ready so she would have everything she needed to move to their home in Tomlin Dunes. There was no way she would be safe in her Waterside apartment anymore, especially since the men who had threatened her may have been watching her every move and may have seen Grady come for a second visit. They were after Linda's secret evidence, and that evidence was obviously something so dangerous as to get people killed over it.

Grady could have never imagined that the death of Marcy Appleton that morning a little over a week ago could have led to such dire circumstances being pressed upon him now. He feared for his own family even, but it was too late to do anything about that. His only hope was to find the hidden evidence, secure it in a safe place, and make it clear to those who were after it that it would be made available to the greater press and the authorities if anything happened to Grady, his family, or Mrs. Herrero—that was the immediate plan, anyway, at least until he could figure out what he should do. He knew it was a desperate plan, and that he was dealing with desperate, ruthless people who had likely already killed once. He had to make sure, and quickly, that they knew there was a great price to be paid for any further violence they might be contemplating. He was completely convinced now that Linda's death had been no accident at all. He also knew he couldn't go to the

Sheriff or to Lieutenant James of the State Police with what he now knew. It would only put his family and Mrs. Herrero in further danger.

Grady and Emily packed Mrs. Herrero's things in two large suitcases they found in her bedroom closet and then loaded everything into the car. Grady still had business to attend to here on the west coast of Newmont, so he had Emily drop him off at a car rental agency. Emily drove back to Tomlin Dunes with Mrs. Herrero, and Grady rented a car and checked into a cheap hotel for the night. He then called Nuck on his cell phone and asked him if he could drive over as soon as possible to meet him. He told him what he had found and that some photography work might be required of him. Nuck was on his way.

Grady then looked up the number for the Temple Hills Police Department and placed a call to them. The desk sergeant answered, and Grady told him he was a reporter and asked him if he could be put through to the 911 Emergency Services Department. The sergeant asked why, and Grady told him there was a particular 911 tape he was hoping to listen to involving a story he was working on. When he was connected to that department, a woman answered in a very pleasant and accommodating voice, which surprised Grady, because he always expected people working in such high stress, high demand jobs, to be ornery and short-tempered with people contacting them who did not have legitimate emergencies. Grady told the woman that he was hoping he could listen to the tape of the 911 call made by Linda Herrero the night she died. He gave her the date of the call. The woman said it would be all right for him to listen to the tape of the call anytime he wanted, as long as he could prove he was a reporter. She made it very clear, though, in a very polite way, that he could not copy the tape of the call, nor could he broadcast it, publish it, or play it for the public in any fashion whatsoever without permission to do so from the department, or unless he obtained a court order to do so.

As soon as he got off the phone, he drove the hour trip to Temple Hills and had a listen to the tape. He went through it three times, and each time, it put a cold chill in him, but as far as he could tell, it could have very well been a suicide call. In fact, it sounded every bit like one, and he was having a difficult time convincing himself otherwise. Linda had cried out in a barely conscious voice, "It's time to put an end to all of this. I canNOT live this way any longer. I'm sorry. Please tell my mother that I'm so, so sorry. She'll want to blame herself, but don't let her." It was very similar to the note she had left. Then there was a slight pause, a dog could be heard barking in the background, and when Linda spoke again, in a barely audible voice, she said, "Don't bother rushing over here to try to help me . . . It's useless . . . It'll be over by the time you get here." The fright and despair in Linda's voice was clearly evident, and the sleeping pills had taken their toll. It left Grady with a cold chill, because he knew that it was shortly after those words were spoken that Linda had died.

CHAPTER 11

《》

Released back into my home—I think the wound has healed . . .

Back in the hotel, Grady decided to give Anders, Grebes, and Williams law firm a call, the firm where Linda Herrero had worked part time before she died. A legal secretary answered and began giving Grady a bit of a run-around, but when he told her he was a reporter, and he wanted to speak with either Mr. Anders, Mr. Grebes, or Mr. Williams, and upon hearing mention of Linda Herrero's name, the secretary excused herself and said she would be right back. Upon her return she told Grady that Mr. Anders and Mr. Williams were out of town but that Mr. Grebes was working late in the office that day and would be glad to set aside a half hour at 5:30 to see Grady if he wanted. Grady said that would be fine. He knew that Nuck would not get to the hotel before he had to leave, so he left a note for him.

Grady arrived at the firm promptly on time, and the secretary was polite but cool and sent him directly into Mr. Grebes' office.

"Mr. Able," said Grebes as he entered. "Come in. I understand you have some questions about Linda Herrero?" He spoke with a down-home, good-old-boy, Newmont accent. He had a large squarish face that was rather rough looking and red, but which exuded only friendliness.

Mr. Grebes stepped forward from behind his desk to shake hands with Grady, smiling broadly at him.

"It's a pleasure meeting you. What can I do for you?"

"It gets down to this," Grady started. "Linda's mother told me that you terminated her about a week before she died. Can you tell me why?" Grady wanted to get right to the heart of the matter. He was only sniffing around the edges of something here, if there was anything at all to sniff around, and he was looking for reactions to his questions as much as he was looking for answers to them.

"Unfortunately, she just wasn't working out here," said Mr. Grebes, his smile now gone. "She was calling in sick way too much, and she wasn't getting her work done in a timely fashion. I just don't think she was cut out for the kind of hard-nosed, and rather boring, corporate law we do around here. Perhaps she would have been better suited to some type of environmental law work."

"Did you know that she died a week after you fired her?"

"Yes, I read about it in the paper. It sure was a tragedy, and I feel real bad about it. I do."

"Do you think that losing her job had anything to do with her committing suicide?"

Mr. Grebes paused for a moment, as a troubled look came over his face. "How could I say? No one is happy when they're fired. But if it helps you any, she didn't seem like the suicidal type. She was angry and disappointed about the situation, but she didn't strike me as the kind of person who would harm herself over something like this. Actually, she struck me as being rather mature emotionally."

Grady watched the man's eyes carefully and decided to pursue his line of questioning a little further. "One of my sources tells me that she was fired because of what she had been digging around in, and because you might have received some pressure from some very powerful people who expressed their wish that she not be working for you anymore. Is that true?"

"Don't be silly, Mr. Able, and what's more, I take real offense at the implication. I'd say that it borders on a slanderous allegation," Grebes said sternly. All the friendliness had gone out of his demeanor in an instant. "Who was your source, Linda Herrero's mother?"

Grady hardened. "My source is confidential at this point, and as a journalist, I have every right to ask you any question I want. You are under no obligation to answer, of course. It's just a question, though, and a question alone cannot be slanderous, as you well know. So, you received no outside pressure to fire Linda?" Grady asked again."

"That's right. Absolutely none."

"Ok. I think that's all I wanted to ask you for now. Thank you for your time," Grady said. "I appreciate you talking to me on such short notice."

"No problem," Grebes said, seeming relieved that this talk was brief. "And I truly am sorry about what happened to that poor girl. Suicide is always a sad thing." The friendly, down-home look had returned to Mr. Grebes' face, along with the friendly tone of voice.

Grady turned and walked to the door, and just as he was placing his hand on the door handle, he turned around and faced Grebes again. "Have you ever thought that Linda's death was not a suicide at all, but perhaps a murder?" Grady asked.

Mr. Grebes smiled and said, "No. I'm afraid I'm obliged to trust the judgment of the authorities in these matters. The County Coroner declared it a suicide, and I have no reason to believe otherwise."

"So, you know of nothing that could possibly make you question the finding of the coroner's office or the police?" Grady asked.

"No. Nothing I know of."

"You didn't know that Linda had discovered something that could prove to be very damaging to certain prominent individuals?"

"No. What kind of something?"

"That'll be made known when the time is right."

"And you think she was murdered over it?"

"It's a possibility that I don't think has yet been given proper scrutiny. The only thing I know for certain, Mr. Grebes, is I'm going to do my job and get at the truth of the matter. Sometimes the truth is not easy to find. So, if you change your mind, and you remember anything that might be helpful, please give me a call." Grady stepped forward and handed Grebes his business card. He was a strong believer in casting a shadow of fear over those who might be hiding something. The man knew a lot more than he was telling. That much was certain.

Grady left the building and got in his rental car. As he drove back to the hotel, he called Francis Jaimansen on his cell phone to confirm that his appointment with him was still on for the following afternoon. The time had come to confront the man mentioned by Linda in her communications concerning the evidence she had found, evidence which implicated not only Francis Jaimansen, but perhaps others in the political world.

Mr. Jaimansen's personal secretary answered the phone and told Grady that Jaimansen was not in and asked what he wished to speak to him about. Grady told the man that he was the owner of a small newspaper called the Tomlin Sands on Newmont's east coast, and that he had arranged an interview with Mr. Jaimansen about a week ago. Grady mentioned Linda Herrero's death, and just as with Mr. Grebes' secretary, Linda's name immediately brought a whole new level of attention from the personal secretary. And just to make sure he had the man's full attention, so he wouldn't try to dismiss him too easily, Grady added, "I know that Linda had bumped up against Mr. Jaimansen indirectly over the manaseal protection bill she had been pushing. I'm just calling to confirm our meeting time, which Mr. Jaimansen scheduled with me for one o'clock tomorrow afternoon."

The man quickly said, "Oh yes, I do see your appointment here in my book. Yes, one o'clock is still on for you, Mr. Able."

Grady thanked the man, and the man thanked Grady with an over-politeness Jaimansen's secretary likely used with anyone he considered worthy of it. It seemed that just the mention of Linda Herrero was getting a lot of nervous reaction out of everyone Grady wanted to talk to, and he was a believer in the old saying, "Where there's smoke, there's probably fire," and he had already taken in enough whiffs of it to set him doggedly on the trail of the source.

Grady returned to his hotel room, and Nuck arrived about an hour later. The two men went to get something to eat at a small diner just down the road. It was mostly a silent meal, with Grady interposing a few comments here and there about the food, about the Linda Herrero story, and about the day. Nuck grunted an occasional "yes" or "no" through forkfuls of broiled salmon, vegetables, and baked potato.

After dinner, Grady took Nuck to a miniature golf course he had noticed during his trips around Waterside. It happened to have lights and was open until 11 p.m., and it was very busy. They relaxed and played twice around. Grady knew Nuck loved the game and actually became quite animated at times over shots that went awry, and likewise over shots that came off as planned. He'd sometimes even mutter four or five words at a time, such as, "Can you believe that one?" or "Here she comes," referring to the blades of the windmill turning across the path of the putt he was preparing to strike. And believe me, Nuck refused to play any miniature golf course that didn't have a windmill. "It's not a proper course," he would say when he found one that didn't have one. Nuck beat Grady in both games, by three strokes, the first round, and by seven the second.

They then returned to the hotel, and Nuck sat in the big easy chair in the corner of the room, put on the light next to it, and began reading a book he had brought along. It was a novel called *Where the Seas Meet*. Grady busied himself by looking over all the information he had gathered about Francis Jaimansen to prepare himself for tomorrow's interview. At about eleven, both men decided to retire for the night.

CHAPTER 12

《》

Waters rising, temperatures falling . . . must get somewhere safe and warm . . . must get there fast . . .

Marcy had become despondent over the death of her best friend, and the wildness of the night seemed to blow right past her. She knew very well that Linda had been murdered, and because the police had labeled it a suicide, she had become quite depressed and filled with feelings of futility. She had fought bouts of clinical depression most of her young adult life. Though the various psychologists she had seen during the past years had assessed its causes differently, she had always suspected that the bulk of it derived from her tendency to care too much about all that is vulnerable in the world, and how that which she cared for always seemed to take a horrible beating in the end. For example, when Marcy was a senior in high school, she had spent most of the year working with a group of activists trying to acquire basic help from local businesses and local and state governments for the homeless— more housing, more temporary shelter, more food, more medical care, and more job training and assistance. What she had seen in response, however, was city after city, town after town, community after community in Newmont showing only that they didn't want the homeless around, didn't want them to be seen. More laws and regulations were continually being passed and enforced against them. A few cities even had programs whereby they would pay bus fare for the homeless if they would leave their city and go to some other location, any other location. It was this blame the down-and-out-victim mentality that crushed Marcy's spirit on a daily basis.

And then she had turned her caring to the manaseals, primarily because of Linda's enthusiasm for protecting the species. Even with manaseals, there were plenty of people who were willing to blame the victim. These people, out of their own malicious reasoning, came up with all kinds of rationalizations why manaseals shouldn't be protected, such as the animals were eating all the sea grasses, which was not true, or they were polluting the water more than people, which was certainly not true, or the long-term health and size of their population was sufficient for the species to not need protection from the ever-growing threats in Newmont, which by any objective measure was most definitely not true.

Marcy was finding it more and more difficult to stand the injustices she found in life. Some people responded to injustice with anger or with steadfast resolve, but Marcy responded to it with depression. It had been hard on her, and she didn't understand why it had to be this way. She felt as if all the battles she had ever chosen to fight had been losing ones, and feeling that way, the death of her friend, Linda, had begun to be too much for her.

That January night she had been camping at Warm Springs Park and had hiked the short distance from the campground down to the observation platform at two in the morning, wanting to die among the manaseals who were in for the night from the cold waters of the Hopkins river. She had carried with her a large camping flashlight.

She had been standing on the railing of the observation platform, with her arms down by her side, looking out into the ink black waters below. Every few seconds she could hear a manaseal coming up to take a breath. The sound brought a peace to her, but that peace only hardened her resolve. There were at least 200 manaseals in the spring that night. Many hours ago, they had known that cold weather was approaching from the North, and they had moved in for protection. Manaseals had a wonderful sense for changes in weather, especially when severe cold weather was approaching. It was a matter of life and death for them.

The cold front had arrived, and the atmosphere had become unstable. A large, fast moving cold air mass was beginning to move its way over the warmer, moisture-laden air mass that had been over all of Newmont before the night began. The jet stream had dipped well to the south so that it was sweeping across Newmont just to the north of Suntree. Many strong and quick moving thunderstorms had come into the area, accompanied by a lot of heavy lightning, rain, and winds. A tornado warning had been in effect that night for all of North and Central Newmont.

Marcy knew that Linda Herrero had died only because she and Marcy had learned something that was too dangerous to handle, and now Marcy stood staring into the water with no will to continue her own life. There was thunder all around, and flashes of lightning were frequently illuminating the night sky.

She had been standing there on the railing for fifteen minutes already, and she had decided she would stand there for as long as it took to accomplish what she had come to do. Before another ten seconds could pass, though, she heard two manaseals rise and take a blow, almost simultaneously. One was right beneath her just to the right of the observation platform, the other further out in the water. It distracted her momentarily. Only a few seconds after the sound of the manaseal breaths had blended back into the night's silence, a bolt of lightning, which Marcy never heard in any meaningful way, and which was not a very powerful discharge in relative terms, struck the tree above the platform, rocketed straight down to the platform and to Marcy and then expended all its energy into the spring waters below. It had to go somewhere, and she had, by pure happenstance, become part of the best possible route for it to go to ground. She fell off the platform and into the water, striking her head on an old tree stump that was lurking just beneath the surface. She was knocked unconscious by both the lightning strike and the blow to her head, and she drowned shortly thereafter, her body to never again take in another breath of fresh air.

During late fall of the previous year, Marcy and Linda had signed up as volunteers with the Nature Protection Foundation to help with a lobbying effort the organization was mounting over a bill being introduced by Senator Hinsdale in the spring Newmont legislative session. Senator Hinsdale was from Linda's district in Trembly Bay, and she had always been a strong manaseal protection advocate. Linda and Marcy were lobbying several representatives on the Environmental Resources Committee that Friday morning, hoping to make sure Senator Hinsdale's bill made it out of committee without any difficulty, and they were reasonably certain they had the votes, although it was going to be close enough to keep them nervous right up until the committee members actually voted.

That morning, they were in the state house waiting in the hall for an appointment they had made to see Representative Melanski, a vote they were quite sure of, but one they wanted to nail down with certainty. The two young women were talking softly and looking out toward the north which presented a view of the corner of the beautifully treed east lawn of the capitol building. Everything was in fresh bloom, with the light-green hues of new foliage putting a blush on every tree. The two women were enjoying the view and discussing their victories of the morning, and their failures, such as their meeting with Representative Johnson, which became contentious when the man began challenging every single aspect of the bill as being too intrusive on the rights of boaters and industry. He had said, "So as to not waste your time and mine, I have to tell you that it'll be a cold day in hell before I'll ever vote for that kind of nonsense." The two women held their tongues, realizing the futility of any further discussion with the man. They thanked him politely for allowing them the chance to try to change his mind, as they always did with every legislator who opposed the bill, whether they were friend or foe.

As they were standing there in the hall, looking out the windows, their conversation had turned to where they might want to have lunch after their morning meetings. There were several very good choices within walking distance of the state house. Just as they began talking about whether they wanted to go for a pizza, to a sandwich shop, or to an Italian restaurant, they overheard two men whispering loudly just down the hall from them. Their attention was captured immediately when one of the men said in a slightly louder voice, "That damned Hinsdale is gonna be trouble. You know she is."

When the two women heard their senator friend's name mentioned, their own conversation immediately ceased, and they listened.

"That stupid bill of hers is starting to get some momentum," the man continued. "It's those goddamned manaseals. Jaimansen isn't going to be happy about it one bit."

The other man then whispered back, "Come on, Tom. You worry way too much. Jaimansen is meeting with Sarcost on Monday. It'll be handled. That, you can count on. There ain't going to be no Hinsdale manaseal protection bill." As this man finished this pronouncement, his eyes made a sweep of the hall area to his left. He noticed the two young women standing not too far away, and he gave a poke to his comrade. Marcy and Linda pretended not to pay the least attention to the conversation between the men. Even though they were listening intently, they had continued to look out the hallway window and had started up some chatter about the spring greenery on the trees and how they loved this time of year. It was all they could think to talk about, and they were hoping it didn't sound forced.

The men ceased talking and slowly walked away, with one of them glancing back just before turning the hallway corner. Being the curious type, and possessing a very resourceful and determined mind, Linda followed the men when she thought it was safe to do so.

"I'll meet up with you around noon at the Capitol Sandwich Shop," she said to Marcy. "I'm going to see if I can maybe find out who this Jaimansen guy is. We need to let Senator Hinsdale know what we heard, too, but first I have to find out a bit more."

"She'll probably know who he is?" Marcy said.

"Maybe, but I'm not taking any chances. I'll catch up with you later."

Marcy knew that Linda was a bit of a worrier and could become quite intense over something like this. When she made up her mind to do something, there was no changing it, so Marcy just let her go, even though it was against her best judgment.

Linda quickly made her way to the hall corner and spotted the men just making the turn at the end of the hallway leading to the elevators. She hurried down the corridor, and she carefully peered around the corner just as the men were getting into a down elevator. Even before the elevator doors had closed, she quickly made her way to the stairway and ran down the three flights of stairs and waited in the lobby over by the drinking fountains near the women's restroom on the ground floor. The elevators in the building were notoriously slow, mostly because they were constantly forced to bear too much traffic. People were always complaining about them. She was hoping the men were leaving the building, because she knew if they stopped on the second floor, she would probably lose track of them completely. She could see that the elevator had stopped at the second floor momentarily, but it would soon be arriving at the ground floor. A man and two women had pressed the up button, and they were waiting for the elevator to arrive. The bell went off, and Linda bent over the fountain to get a drink of water so the two men would not see her, if indeed they did come out of the elevator.

Sure enough, there they were, and they were in a hurry. They pushed quickly past the two people trying to enter the elevator and walked swiftly toward the doors at the rear of the building. They were in the South building, which was connected to the main Capitol chambers by an enclosed walk-over that was accessed on the second floor. The South building housed the state senators' offices, and the north building housed the state representatives' offices.

Linda went to the doors and watched the men go to a small parking lot across the street from the rear of the Capitol building. Her car was parked on the street itself, and she hurried to it, while still keeping an eye on the men, who were well down the street now and just entering the parking lot. She started her tan, two-door compact car and watched as the men got into a large maroon luxury sedan. They drove out of the lot, worked their way over to Collins St, and then turned left onto Crenshaw Parkway which is also State Road 340. They went down the long sweeping hill leading away from the Capitol. About ten miles outside of Hasselford, the men made several turns which made Linda's task of following them without being noticed somewhat difficult due to the sparse traffic on the road.

She was sure they were going to see her, and she hung back as far as she could while still keeping them in sight. Finally, the men turned onto a road that led to a private drive with a security gate. Linda was forced to drive on by the large estate, hoping not to be noticed. She made note of the address, 83 Branson Road, and then headed back to the Capitol.

Later when she met up with Marcy for lunch, she told her where the men had gone. Marcy suggested they go to the Taxation and Property office and see who owned the estate. They both agreed they shouldn't bring any of this to the attention of Senator Hinsdale just yet, not until they knew more. They didn't want to worry her unnecessarily.

They ate quickly and went to the Hammond County Court house and found the office where they could look up 83 Branson Rd in the plats and maps and deeds to see who owned the estate. The clerk helped them find the proper book for the deed, which also contained the registered survey map for the property. The owner was in fact a man named Francis L. Jaimansen, just as they had heard from the conversation between the two men.

While Linda and Marcy were tracking down the identity of the man who was supposedly about to see to it that Senator Hinsdale's manaseal legislation would be stopped in its tracks, Joe Hart and Tom Campton were inside Jaimansen's Hasselford estate reporting back to him about their morning's efforts. Jaimansen, a small man with a bum left leg that he kept outstretched when he was sitting, was working on his coin collection, which he always took very seriously. Joe and Tom told him what they knew of the progress of the Hinsdale bill as it was making its way through the statehouse, and Tom made mention of the two women they had seen in the hallway outside of Representative Melanski's office.

Tom said, "They might have overhead some of our conversation." As soon as the words had left his mouth, he knew it was a mistake. He took a certain amount of pride in his job, and his instinct was to tell his boss everything, and that instinct sometimes got him into trouble. When Jaimansen immediately pressed him for further details, and when he then put the beam of his intense eyes upon Tom in a way that let him know that this was no trifling matter, Tom said, "Sir, I really don't think they heard anything of any consequence. They were busy talking about something between themselves. I watched them pretty carefully—that I can assure you."

"You assure me of nothing, Tom," Jaimansen said contemptuously. "I have only a feeling of uneasiness whenever I put you two on a job, no matter how simple it is. All I can say is, you had better hope they didn't overhear you, because if they did, you will have to worry about a whole lot more than just your jobs. I won't tolerate this kind of carelessness. I just won't." Jaimansen continued working on his coin collection, which was an avocation very dear to him, and one which took his mind off the stress of his daily business concerns. "I don't want to ever hear that you had a conversation in the presence of others about things that require complete and utter privacy. Let me be very clear about this. You'll both rue the day, if I hear of that kind of foolhardy incompetence again."

Jaimansen then opened an envelope that he had in his lap, along with several others. He carefully removed a coin, examined it with a powerful magnifying glass, and delicately placed it into a protective plastic sleeve. He would later mount it in his collection under glass.

"This is a bit of a beauty," he said casually without looking up. "And I certainly was able to purchase it at a reasonable price—only $18,000. It's a 1911-D Saint Gaudens double eagle $20 gold piece. It's definitely gem grade, MS-67," he said, studying it thoroughly under his magnifying glass. It's just barely up to the standards of what I would allow into my collection, mind you, but I have always had an affinity for the St. Gaudens, so I'll have to keep this one. Ever collect coins, Joe?"

"No, Sir."

"No? Well, that's too bad. Anyway, do you have any idea who these women were, who 'might' have overheard you?" he asked. He continued looking at the coin through the magnifying glass.

Tom, who always did most of the talking for the two, said, "Afraid not, but I really don't think they'll pose any kind of a problem. I'm sure they didn't hear us."

"As I've said, you'd better hope they didn't." Jaimansen did not look up at the two men as he spoke. They remained standing throughout the entire conversation, as they were never allowed to sit while in Jaimansen's presence. They knew the rules and followed them to the letter. Jaimansen's dark, simmering countenance and his unforgiving temper were well known among the people who worked for him, and among those who had dealings with him.

Later that day, Linda and Marcy did some research on the internet and found out that Francis Jaimansen was one of the wealthiest and most powerful businessmen in the entire Southeast. His enterprises included land development, but he only dabbled in that from time to time. Just as Grady later discovered, much of his wealth came from investment speculation and from an enormous inheritance left him by his grandfather. His main source of current business reputation came from marine manufacturing, however. He had two companies: One called "Ocean Horizons," which exclusively manufactured luxury yachts; the other called "Jaimansen WaterCraft" which made large, powerful pleasure craft and jet skis. They found out that the name, Jaimansen, in fact was a big name in the boating industry, and to have a "Jaimansen" was a bragging point among many boaters. His boats were not cheap, but they were well made and had a good reputation for quality. Linda, who did most of the research on Jaimansen, began by tracking down his current development projects by checking permit records from the Corps of Engineers, calling county court houses in areas where a development had been proposed, or was finished, or was still pending. She found only two current projects identified as his, both in Newmont. One was a commercial office complex near a marina in the East Merriman area, and the other was a large condominium and golf course resort on the Lomahassie River in Calhoun, in northwest Newmont.

At about 6 p.m. Linda and Marcy went to Senator Hinsdale's office and caught her just before she was leaving. She invited them to dine with her at Martino's, a popular Italian restaurant not far from the Capitol building. She was a well-known patron there and was seated right away. The Martino's staff made a point of knowing most of the legislators at a glance. A lot of lobbying went on over antipasto, salad, pasta, seafood and wine there. The three ordered one of Martino's specialties, a large pasta salad that came in an enormous bowl and which was served with two loafs of garlic bread to be broken or sliced by the diners as they wished. Senator Hinsdale ordered a rose water, Linda a Chianti, and Marcy a Merlot.

As they sipped their drinks, Linda and Marcy told the senator what they had overheard and what they had found out about Jaimansen. She knew who the man was and said that his name had come up once or twice concerning other pieces of legislation during her three terms in office. She said she would ask around to see if she could find out anything more about what he was up to. When they left the restaurant and the company of Senator Hinsdale, Linda and Marcy were feeling quite distraught. The dire look they had seen come over the senator's face when they had told her about Jaimansen and his plan to kill her bill made them worry all the more that the rug was about to be pulled out from under their efforts and the manaseal protection legislation for which they had been fighting so hard.

Sunday afternoon, Linda called Marcy and asked if she would meet her at Chamberlain Park in southeast Hasselford, where they had been a few times before to walk and talk and to relax. Marcy, of course, agreed that it was a good idea. They met there and fretted between themselves some more and finally decided it might be a good idea to hang around the vicinity of Sarcost's office on Monday morning to see if Jaimansen showed up for the much worried-about meeting. They had no idea what they would do, if he did, indeed, show up, but they had some vague idea of alerting Senator Hinsdale and perhaps even the press about the meeting and what they had overheard Jaimansen's two men saying on Friday.

On Monday morning, Marcy met Linda at a bagel shop not far from the Capitol building. They ate and talked anxiously about the events of the past few days. It was a dark, cloudy day, with rain already beginning to spit from the sky. Both women had their umbrellas with them. The rain was supposed to come down heavier as the day progressed.

At half past nine, the women paid for their breakfast and headed for the Senate Office building. It was already raining harder, and the wind was picking up. Just before they entered the back entrance along Prainey Street, a loud clap of thunder came crashing down from the black clouds hanging ominously from the sky over the northwest corner of the city, only a couple of miles away.

The rain was coming down hard by the time they got their umbrellas folded and entered through the large glass doors of the state house. The building was bustling with activity. It was the second week of the legislative session, and it was a Monday. There were more than a dozen people waiting for the two elevators. Most everyone was dressed for the rain, and lots of umbrellas and dark rain gear were in evidence. Linda and Marcy moved with a group of eight others into the left elevator which had let out seven people. The buttons for all three of the upper floors were pressed, and up they went. Linda and Marcy got off on the third floor and headed slowly down the hall to the right toward Senator Sarcost's office, number 317. When they were in eyesight of it, around the second turn in the hallway, they stopped and waited there. Marcy bit nervously at her fingers. Linda took out some papers from her briefcase and pretended to be discussing details about them with Marcy. As long as the two men didn't accompany Jaimansen to his scheduled meeting with Sarcost, there shouldn't be any chance of being recognized. That was their nervous hope, at least.

As the minutes ticked by, Linda and Marcy became more and more anxious. They knew deep down that their plan was not a very good one, in that they had no idea what they might accomplish by it, other than to see if Jaimansen actually showed up and met with Sarcost. But they also knew that discovery, alone, was important. It was important for a lot of reasons. For one thing, if he did show, then Linda and Marcy knew they were going to have to take action. Maybe Senator Hinsdale could do whatever maneuvering she might think necessary. The senator was very adept at handling difficult political and legislative situations—she was well known for this. Linda and Marcy had seen her in action aplenty when she was in the process of forging the language of the bill. She had made quick deals with other legislators on various key points in the bill, avoided all the landmines that had the potential to explode on any piece of new controversial legislation, and she had worked the minority leader of her own party to get him to back the bill, thus offering some real clout.

The two women conscientiously kept a close eye on the hallway at every moment, but ten o'clock came and went without anyone going in or out of Sarcost's office except for a young man, who Linda recognized as Sarcost's legislative aide. He left once for five minutes and returned in a hurry with a document of some kind in his hand. At half past ten, the two women were about to abandon their watch and assume that the meeting had been changed or canceled. That would have left them without knowing anything, and that would have been particularly bad considering their anxious state of mind. But at 10:35, a well-dressed, very short man with perfectly coiffed grayish white hair walked past them in the hallway and moved swiftly to Sarcost's office door. He was using a cane and had a pronounced limp. There were many people walking to and fro in the hallway, and there were many people standing outside of offices talking. A senator's aide was leaning against the open door of Senator Carmichael's office, not far from where Linda and Marcy were standing, and he was chatting away with a woman, and quite loudly, about some legislative minutiae. He laughed boisterously about something, just as Jaimansen knocked on Sarcost's door and was let inside.

A few minutes later, Sarcost's aide came out of the office again and went down to the end of the hall and into the Men's restroom. Linda and Marcy noticed that he had left the office door slightly ajar. They cautiously approached and stood next to the door, trying to see inside, but nothing was visible through the small available opening. They listened carefully, trying to look as nonchalant as possible as they hovered near the door. They could hear faint muffled voices within the office but could not make out any of the words spoken.

Linda looked at Marcy and said, "I'm going in. The hell with it. It doesn't matter now whether he finds out we're here or not. I don't give a damn."

Marcy said nothing and only stared back, fighting off an urge to bite her fingers by tightening her jaw. Linda recognized the fear on her friend's face, but as in the past, when she was determined to do something involving some risk, when Marcy would try to talk her out of it, she called upon the strength of her own determination.

"I'm sorry, Marcy. I've got to go in. Maybe I'll hear something that can be useful. Who knows." And without waiting for another moment to pass, she gently pushed the door open and entered Sarcost's office. There was no one in the main part of the office, but Linda could hear the rumbling voices of Sarcost and Jaimansen behind a closed door of an inner office. She moved closer to the door, hoping to hear something of the conversation. She was worried that the aide might return at any moment, but she steeled herself against her nervousness and continued to listen. She would deal with the aide if, and when, she had to. She had her ways. She bolstered herself with this self-assurance. As she came right up to the door to the inner office, she began to hear some of the conversation taking place within.

"I don't want this getting out of committee one," a voice said. It had to be Jaimansen's. Linda was familiar with Sarcost's deep voice and knew it wasn't his. "I don't want any momentum developing over those damned sealcows, or manaseals, or whatever they're called these days. It's gone too far already. So, how soon can you kill it?"

"Well, Francis, you do realize I have campaign monetary concerns, and just plain fiduciary concerns, overall. These concerns have to be at the top of my agenda. It's all very expensive, as you know. Re-election requires money. Getting the Environmental Resources Committee to vote against Hinsdale's bill will require substantive monies to grease the machine. And, in fact, my lifestyle requires money, as well. But you know that, Francis."

"Yes, my friend, money is important, and that is one thing I have plenty of. We're both on the same page when it comes to that. I'm willing to pay what you are asking, and even more, and it can be done in a way that'll draw no suspicion. But having said that, I want results, and I want them immediately. I don't pay for inaction. The Ocean and Sun Resort is on schedule to begin ground-breaking, and I don't want it held up, not for any reason, not even for a single day, especially not because of that ridiculous manaseal bill. If I can't put in the marina, then there is no Ocean and Sun Resort. I won't have that. I don't mind paying my way in life, but you'll discover very quickly that I have little patience for lack of results. Do we understand each other?"

"Yes, I believe we do. You won't be disappointed."

Jaimansen then softened his tone. "I don't expect any more or less than what you do for any other big interest when they come asking for your assistance. They bring their army of lobbyists and bags full of campaign money—but lobbying is not my style, and legalities can get too messy and take too long. I like to get to the point more directly. I like cold, hard, cash because it can be used in a more efficient manner. I like it a lot, and I like being very generous with it. I'm sure you understand what I mean."

"Of course. This could be quite an expensive one. There are a lot of people in the way, and getting them out of the way is not going to be cheap. Maybe we should ask for some help from The Group on this one."

"If it becomes necessary. We have some new members, and we might just want to test out their resolve. I've left a list in an envelope on your assistant's desk but you needn't concern yourself about that right now. I'll let you know if you should be making contact with any of them. Don't worry, though, I'll provide you with whatever you need."

As Linda listened, she looked about the room and cast several nervous glances at the door. And then she looked at the assistant's desk. She saw a plain manila envelope lying there, on top of everything else, and in large black letters in the upper left hand corner was printed "Jaimansen Development Corporation." Linda decide it might be important to take a look inside—just a quick peek—and so she did. Inside the envelope, she found a single list of names, of which she instantly recognized one as a state senator and one as a state representative. There were seven names in all. "Only If Necessary" was scrawled in heavy black ink above the names.

A sudden rush of panic swept through Linda's mind as she read down through the names on the list. She knew she had stumbled onto something important and something that might prove to be useful to Senator Hinsdale in her fight to keep their manaseal protection bill alive. Then in a panic, and without thinking it through carefully, she quickly stuffed the sheet of paper inside her suit jacket pocket and replaced the envelope on the desk where it was originally lying. She could hear laughter from within the inner office and decided she had better get out of there, for it well could be finishing-up-business laughter.

Just as she began walking toward the door, the assistant returned and walked swiftly into the office. He eyed Linda sternly and then glanced about the top of his desk. "Can I help you? Senator Sarcost isn't scheduling any appointments this morning."

"Oh, he isn't?" I was hoping to speak with him about some environmental legislation that is being drawn up by Senator Hinsdale. I was also hoping we could count on his support."

"Well, I'm sure he would be glad to speak with you about it, but you will have to schedule an appointment in the proper fashion, just like everybody else does."

"Oh, yes. Certainly," Linda said, wanting only to get out of there as fast as possible. "I'm very busy today and tomorrow, so I'll have to give you a call later." She was just grabbing for the door handle to leave, when Sarcost and Jaimansen emerged from the inner office. Sarcost looked at Linda for a moment, and she stared back with frightened eyes.

"Is there something I can do for you?" Sarcost said in a pleasant enough voice.

The assistant then spoke up. "She's a lobbyist for the Hinsdale bill. Said she wanted to speak to you about it, hoping to persuade you to put your support behind it."

"Oh my, well that's going to have to wait until later in the week, I'm afraid," Sarcost said, now looking Linda over very carefully.

"Yes, that's what I told her," said the assistant.

Jaimansen had also fixed a stare upon her. The way he looked at her with those stone cold eyes frightened her right down to the marrow. She had a nearly irrepressible urge to turn and run out of the office, but in a state of sheer terror, she somehow managed to hold her ground. Jaimansen's lips were tightly pursed, and his eyes were unflinching.

"I'll be on my way then, "Linda said after a brief uncomfortable silence. "I'll call back in a day or two, to see if I can schedule some time with you, Senator. Thank you."

She was wearing her official lobbyist badge, which allowed her to roam the statehouse halls without a problem. She was certain that both Sarcost and Jaimansen had taken note of that. They could easily find out who had been admitted as official lobbyists for the manaseal protection legislation.

She walked swiftly down the hall toward Marcy, wanting nothing more than to be away from that office and those men within. She knew she should not have taken the list of names. What could she have been thinking? She knew very well that Sarcost wasn't anyone to mess with. He had a lot of power in the capitol, and she had none, and who knew what Jaimansen might be capable of. When she saw that list, however, after hearing the conversation between the two men, an instant of fury had come over her, and for one quick instant, she wanted only for them to know that she knew what they might be up to. So she took the list. She had also some vague hope that when they found it missing, it might give them some pause before trying to scuttle the Hinsdale bill. All of these thoughts had become a collision of nonsense and foolishness that had formed a single impulse to act. Linda was disappointed in herself. She knew she had done everything wrong and had acted in an utterly foolish manner. Without saying a word to Marcy, she grabbed her firmly by the arm and ushered her quickly away down the hall.

When they were around the corner and out of sight, Linda said, "We've got to get out of here." From her dire tone, Marcy knew immediately that something had gone horribly wrong in Sarcost's office.

"I tried to delay Sarcost's aide when he returned to the office," Marcy said. "I asked him a series of questions about every piece of frivolous nothingness I could think of. He was all business, though, and in a hurry to get back in, and so I wasn't able to keep him long."

"It's okay, Marcy. You did well." Linda reached inside her suit jacket and said. "I found this on Sarcost's desk." She withdrew the list from an inner pocket and held it up for Marcy to see.

"What is it?"

"It's a list of names, some of them important. Jaimansen was talking about it to Sarcost. He mentioned something he called 'The Group.' The seven people on the list are apparently new members. Unfortunately, there's nothing about the list itself that would directly implicate either Sarcost or Jaimansen in anything illegal, but from what I heard them talking about, I'm sure it's very dirty business they're engaged in. We've got to be very careful with this, though. Frankly, Marcy, it's got me shaking. Come on, let's get out of here."

After returning to the temporary apartment both Marcy and Linda had rented for the legislative session, Linda told Marcy all she had heard inside the office. Then Marcy made some tea, and they sat, and with concern on their faces and sipping now and then, they talked quietly, trying to figure out what they should do next. As they talked, at first they decided they had no choice but to go first to Senator Hinsdale and then probably to the press with what they knew. The problem was, they had little hard evidence—only the list, which was nothing but a piece of paper with names on it. What they had overheard of the conversation that had taken place between Jaimansen's henchmen and what Linda had just overheard between Jaimansen and Sarcost wasn't likely enough to get anything done. They had no idea, in fact, whether it would be enough to get someone in the press even marginally interested in doing a story.

The more they talked about it, the more Linda began thinking it was a bad idea, and so they talked about it some more. Finally, they hatched up a new plan, a much more dangerous one. They decided they would approach Sarcost and see if they might frighten him with what they knew and perhaps get him to at least back off with respect to derailing Senator Hinsdale's manaseal bill. They also decided they must keep Senator Hinsdale out of it and not tell her what Linda had found or heard.

If only they had known the full scope of what that list represented, such thoughts would have never crossed their minds. They were soon to find out, because when Linda took that list, she unknowingly set into motion events that would catch them both up and pursue them right to the end.

Not long after that day, Perry Jacobs, the brother of Senator Sarcost's assistant, Richard Perry, contacted Marcy by phone, and that's when things really began to heat up.

Perry sounded agitated, and he said to Marcy, "I've got some important information and a document that I want you and your friend to have. I happen to know you have a list that Linda took from Sarcost's office, and I have decided to put an end to all of it. My brother has gotten himself wrapped up in things that will surely lead to his downfall. He's a very talented man, but I'm afraid he's going to throw it all away. He does tell me things he shouldn't. Anyway, I have a document I found in my brother's home office when I was there visiting last week. I knew he was into something really bad. This document fully explains your list, and more."

Linda had gone out to do some grocery shopping and Marcy was alone. She was suddenly gripped with fear and didn't know how to respond, so she said only, "I don't understand what you're talking about Mr. Jacobs. What list?"

"I won't play games. I won't. Within the hour, I'm going to slip the document under your door. I had better warn you, though, your life is in danger, and I hope you will somehow be able to use the information to help yourselves. What I'd really like to have happen is to get my brother away from Sarcost, or even get him fired. He's ruining his life. I can't bear to watch him being drawn further and further into Sarcost's and Jaimansen's web of corrupt activities."

"I don't know how to respond," Marcy said.

"You don't have to," said Perry Jacobs, and then he hung up.

Good to his word, he slipped the document and an attached note under Linda and Marcy's apartment door within the hour. Linda still wasn't back, but Marcy was there to collect it. She tried to rush to the door and open it, hoping to have a word with Mr. Jacobs, hoping that in doing so she could put herself onto some kind of solid ground, but he was gone by the time she got there.

CHAPTER 13

《》

I trust them, but momma says I shouldn't . . .

Grady had called Emily Tuesday night, to make sure she got home with Mrs. Herrero without problems. She assured him that all was well, and she also told him not to worry too much. They were on schedule to get the Wednesday edition of the paper printed on time later that night, though it was going to be a bit hectic at the office. She was hoping to drive in and help out during the last three hours of crunch time. Grady told her to not knock herself out over it and to not worry if the paper got out a little late.

Grady needed to get a better feel for Jaimansen and what he was involved in, and so he wanted to take a look at just where Jaimansen's Ocean and Sun Resort development was scheduled to go. To this purpose, on Wednesday morning, as he and Nuck drove the two hours north to Calhoun, he called Claude Donovan, a man who had written a strong Reader Opinion in the Calhoun Zephyr. He was retired military and was now a boater, fisherman, and a hunter, and he was full of angry attitude toward Jaimansen's development plans. Grady reached him at his home and told him he was thinking about doing a story on Jaimansen and that he wanted to know more about the controversy that continued over his project. Mr. Donovan was more than willing to tell Grady how he felt. "I despise these developers who are ruining all of natural old Newmont," he said to Grady. "Somebody's got to do something to try to stop them. Now, I don't much take to environmental organizations in general, but if they're the only one's fighting the Jaimansen's of the world, then I have no choice but to support their efforts." He made it very clear that he wanted manaseals protected, and he also wanted to preserve pristine areas of Newmont and not have them trashed and despoiled by people like Jaimansen.

Grady and Nuck met the man at a Little & Quick convenience store on Gessel Road at about 11 a.m. From there, they all drove to the development site, which occupied a rounded triangle of Newmont land at the corner of the mouth of the Tremblyrand River where it merged with the Lomahassie.

When they arrived at the site, they parked by the side of the road and got out of their cars to look at Jaimansen's handiwork. "This used to be one of the most beautiful places in Newmont," Mr. Donovan said. "Not any more, though, as you can see."

If you live in Newmont, or you have driven through it, you've seen similar developments everywhere you go, so I won't describe this one to you, other than to say that there wasn't anything left of the original vegetation. Everything had been laid to waste by the bulldozers that had worked over the area—gouging and dragging every square inch. For Grady, what had been done to the land was instantly disgusting at some elemental level that reached right down into his guts and his instinct for survival, and it made him outwardly wince. At the north boundary of the actual site, Grady could see what little was left of the old forest that had existed on the land for millions of years and how beautiful it had been. Now it looked decapitated. There was little doubt that the forest remnant would also soon fall victim to further development, since the first gouging had already been done.

As he watched, he knew in his heart of hearts that if such destruction continued unabated, there would be no natural beauty left in the world, and without such beauty to sustain the spirit of the human species, he believed humans would go the way of the dinosaurs, but unlike the demise of other species, human extinction would be entirely self-inflicted. Grady wasn't against all development, but there was good and bad development, responsible and irresponsible development. He knew that some developers made at least a minimal effort to fit their projects into the environment without destroying everything in sight. At a glance, it was easy to see that this was not the case with a Jaimansen project. It was obvious that bottom-line profit was the only consideration that ruled his plans and designs.

Some of Grady's previous research had turned up information that Jaimansen hired only architects and engineers who would not give him a hard time about his intentional recklessness with the environment, and there were plenty of those types of professionals to be found. In fact, they were a dime a dozen, these days in Newmont.

Mr. Donovan, the boater fellow, talked on at length about how the city had fought and fought to stop Jaimansen but had failed on legal technicalities and dishonest politics at every turn. He said, "The Jaimansen's of the world always get away with almost anything, and all the professional people he has hired to move his development forward are nothing but whores." It had been Grady's experience that Mr. Donovan was at least partly right, that there was little doubt some people would do anything in the way of lowering themselves ethically and morally if it would stuff a few more dollars in their already full pockets. Not only that, they were the very people who would be the first to use The Ocean and Sun Resort, because they would be the people who could afford to do so.

Grady was glad to have had the chance to receive Mr. Donovan's perspective, one that came from the point of view of one of Calhoun's citizens. There weren't many such citizens who dared speak out with such vehemence and determination against the rich and powerful. Grady knew there was an ugly tradition in Newmont of developers getting most everything they wanted, whenever and wherever they wanted it.

Nuck was busy taking lots of photos. The more they lingered near that site, the angrier Grady became, but of course he didn't allow any of the anger to show outwardly. Claude Donovan steamed on about all the corrupt politicians, bureaucrats, and "money grubbing" businessmen who were responsible, in his opinion, for all the destruction of Newmont. And of course, as a native Newmontian, he had plenty of blame to place on those "Yankees"—never stopping to realize that Francis Jaimansen himself was a Newmont native and had come from five generations of Newmontians. But in Claude's mind, the Yankees had brought all that was bad to Newmont. Grady knew that many natives felt that way, and he couldn't deny that the charge was true to a large extent, but its sweeping strokes also ignored a lot of history and reality that spoke to the fact that greedy, selfish people were present in all places, at all times, and they were more than willing to take advantage of every opportunity in the name of that greed and abuse of power. Beauty and conservation never entered into any calculation with such people, whether they were Northerners or Newmont natives.

"Are you going to the public hearing today on the DEC's proposed manaseal protections along parts of the Lomahassie and the Tremblyrand River?" Grady asked Mr. Donovan.

"Yep. I'm gonna be there. I'll probably speak out in favor of the protections. Something needs to be done to protect the manaseals."

"I hear these meetings can get pretty wild."

"Oh yeah. It'll be a wild one. You can count on that. A lot of boaters are going to show up to oppose the new speed zones. Some of those people happen to be friends of mine, but they can be a very mean bunch when they're all gathered together in a room. It doesn't matter. I'm gonna be there, and they're not going to intimidate me none. You know, I've been a hunter and fisherman almost all my life, but I'll never understand these people who live in their fancy homes, and drive their fancy new boats and don't give a damn about what's in the water beneath them. Not one damn. If you could ever hear them talkin' when they're alone together, you wouldn't believe the crap that comes out of their goddamned mouths. I've heard it all. They call themselves fishermen, but they're out there with their fish finders and all manner of other modern gear to make sure they catch their fish, to the point where they've taken all the sport right out of it. Most of 'em aren't real fishermen, because they have no respect for the fish and the wilds they're fishin' in."

Grady couldn't help thinking as he listened to Mr. Donovan that when Donovan, himself, went out to hunt, he probably used, as many of his friends bragged to him about using, the best and latest rifles and scopes. Some of Grady's friends had even admitted they lured deer with feed and pheromone scents. Even if they hunted the so-called "natural" way, with bows, they had the latest increased mechanical advantage bow machines that hardly resembled bows at all, all rigged up with pulleys and tackle, and some of them even had scopes mounted on them. Grady also couldn't help thinking that what many a hunter and fisherman referred to as sport, he had always called "play-acting the primitive." On many occasion, he had wanted to say to his hunter friends during conversations about such topics, "It's real hunting when you go out and live in the woods, and you have an empty belly because the only food you ate last was your last kill, and the only weapon you have is one you fashioned for yourself out there in the woods. That takes all the hypocrisy and bullshit out of it, don't you think. That's real hunting. And if you are trying to prove your primitive manhood and prowess in some way, in a world that doesn't allow much of that anymore, then you won't resort to phony-baloney hunting as it is done today in the modern killing world." That's what Grady wanted to say to his hunting friends, but he never did. And he wanted to say the same thing to Mr. Donovan, but he didn't. He knew the man wouldn't understand, and he knew his hunting friends wouldn't understand either, and he knew they would become all defensive and angry at the insinuation that their manhood wasn't being properly tested by their hunting and fishing. In fact, he knew some of them would want to demonstrate their manhood right there on the spot by punching him right in the nose. He handled such friends with care, because he knew their male egos were delicate, and usually their instinct for violence was strong.

Despite all these thoughts, as he listened to Mr. Donovan rant on effusively about every manner of thing having any possible relation to the evils of the Ocean and Sun development and Francis Jaimansen, Grady liked the man. He liked the look in his eye, and he liked the man's direct honesty, one which revealed a lot of heart. There were a lot of honest and direct people who Grady didn't like, because they didn't have any heart. Mr. Donovan had an especially gruff exterior, but shining just beneath the surface was a gentleness and caring that touched Grady, and so he listened to the man, and he tuned into what he had to say and even enjoyed how he expressed himself. He was trying to figure out if in that voice and spirit that exuded both ignorance and wisdom there was a sign, either positive or negative, for the fate of the human race. Grady often went wandering off with thoughts such as these, thoughts that always ran out into a desert of emptiness all loaded up with promise, then trailing off into a fading question mark, and finally disappearing into a philosophical nothingness. Those kinds of answers he sought never came, and because of it, Grady's cynicism continued to grow a little harder every year in the land of Newmont. His only saving grace from becoming lost in all that cynicism was Emily and his beautiful children, which softened him on a daily basis.

CHAPTER 14

《》

*I saw one of those manatees once—I wonder where it was going.
I know I wouldn't ever dare leave my own shores, like it did . . .*

Grady turned onto Windsor Avenue. It was lined on both sides with very large estates, each property accessing one of the many canals that branched off the large main Blue Hascal Canal which ran out to the nearby Straights of Flobia. Expensive yachts were moored at nearly every dock.

"That was 405, so we're close," Nuck said.

"Yeah. I wonder how much trouble we'll have getting in. It doesn't look like the folks 'round here are much used to seeing a beat-up old white SUV driving down their street. The phones are probably ringing off the hook at the local police precinct."

"They're just people, like you and me," Nuck said.

Grady was getting nervous, and Nuck's down-home bit of wisdom, stated so matter-of-factly, helped. The super rich had always made him nervous, and there was good reason for that. They usually protected their possessions and privacy behind massive walls of stone, dogs, electronic security, and secrecy. It was a world completely foreign to him, and though he had entered it a few times to do stories in the past, it always left him feeling cold. Most people were enamored by the lifestyles of the rich and famous, but to Grady it all looked like a prison, though indeed, a nice one. Once you entered that world in a real way, you would never escape the life it engendered, one far removed from all that was natural in the world and the common struggle for the essentials of living. And in time, that lack of wanting would likely kill off the more vigorous instincts for life. Grady thought perhaps that is why greed flourished among certain of the wealthy. It was the only vigor they had left. One could always strive to have more and more, no matter how unnecessary, and one could always strive to control the lives of others, no matter how oppressive. Greed and a lust for power were usually close relatives.

As Grady drove by estate after estate, he wondered what kind of prisoners were developing within each. He tried to tell from the look of the mansions and the surrounding posh landscaping, but each was so ostentatiously beyond that which was truly human that they failed to reveal anything significant beyond a display of wealth.

In light of what had happened to poor Mrs. Herrero, the terrifying visit by the two men, this interview with Francis Jaimansen was taking on more importance than it had when Grady had first called to schedule it last week. At that time, he had only a single mention of Jaimansen in connection with Sarcost and in connection with the "list" within Linda's things. He didn't know who had hired the two men, but he had his suspicions, and he was determined to find out for certain. Mrs. Herrero was now under his temporary care, and that meant the situation had become personal. Maybe, he thought, it was someone other than Jaimansen who was behind the thuggery. He ground his teeth in anxiety as he and Nuck came to the estate at 517 Windsor Avenue.

Grady pulled up to a pair of enormous iron gates, which had a center column of stonework with an intercom and security dial-pad for both incoming and outgoing cars. He rolled down his window and pressed the green button on the intercom device. The massive stone wall that enclosed the property extended off to the right and the left. The wind was howling, and it was making such a rustling of the dense leaves within the giant magnolias and oaks lining the street that Grady was afraid he wouldn't be able to hear anything coming through the intercom. He spoke loudly, too loudly he feared, identifying himself and declaring that he had an appointment with Mr. Jaimansen. He glanced at the stones that made up the wall and noticed they consisted of granite and quartz for the most part, which meant they had been transported at great cost, since there is very little granite or quartz to be found in Newmont. Such an odd thing to notice, Grady thought, but then again, he was in the business of noticing things.

"Mr. Able, please enter," came a most proper voice through the speaker. "You are expected."

The gates opened, Grady rolled up his window, and he drove through. He took a breath as he made his way along the luxurious winding drive that was overhung with the lush foliage of many grand trees. It was a warm day, in the low eighties, and it felt especially warm considering it had been in the fifties just a week ago. With the wind blowing, though, and the blanket of shade that covered the drive, it was quite comfortable in the car without the air-conditioner on.

Grady parked directly in front of the large gardened walkway leading to the pillared front door of an enormous mansion. He fully expected, and had prepared himself for, what he would be facing, and he knew that it would be extremely intimidating and daunting in terms of the wealth the surroundings oozed. The mansion and the grounds were exactly what he would have expected of a man like Jaimansen. It was all newly built and ridiculously overdone—completely lacking in elegance, subtlety, and taste. It was designed intentionally to be too much, too opulent, or perhaps that was just Grady's opinion in the light of what he knew of the man who had built it and who now lived in it. There was no sense of history, antiquity, or tradition in any of it, except for maybe the old trees the builders had left on the property.

It struck him as thoroughly ironic that Jaimansen had preserved quite a bit of natural beauty at his home, and yet the man made certain that everything in sight was destroyed and bulldozed to a fare-thee-well in his Ocean and Sun development. Grady knew it was because Jaimansen was convinced that it was far more cost-effective that way, at least the way he operated. And it seemed he took personal satisfaction in the destruction he brought upon the land. Perhaps he saw it as a symbol of his power. That morning, Grady and Nuck had talked with some other local citizens, in addition to Mr. Donovan, who also opposed Jaimansen's latest development in the area. One woman had said he liked to stand proudly in front of his projects with a white construction hat on, lording over all in his domain, including any protesters that might show up in a futile effort to stop him. He, in fact, loved it when protesters showed up. He would make a special appearance in that case, just to rub it in all the more, and then he would have his bulldozers grind everything into an unrecognizable, ugly rubble. He loved the stump burning permits he obtained, so he could add copious amounts of smoke to the scene of his destruction. The protestors had no chance to stop him, once he got his legal permits, and he made certain they knew he would do as he pleased with his land despite their horror. Preserving old trees didn't fit into his bottom-line picture, except when it came to the land of his own home. And the word "home," in this case, made a liar out of language. Jaimansen was not the kind of man who would ever truly live in a "home."

Grady and Nuck were ushered by the personal assistant into the library where Francis Jaimansen was seated in a vast leather chair, smoking a cigar and reading a newspaper. A Scottish terrier was lying on his lap, barely visible beneath the newspaper. Grady wondered if this was staged, if Jaimansen had planned to be smoking and reading a newspaper, with his pet dog in his lap, when Grady arrived, just to demonstrate to him how comfortable he was.

Grady began to really fear he had made a huge mistake in coming there, but if there was a chance of getting something out of it, if there was a single chance he might loosen up even a fragment of information from Jaimansen, then it would be worth it. His suspicions about the man were driving him, but he had no evidence to prove anything. All trails leading from the murder of Linda Herrero had been well-covered.

"Good morning, Mr. Able," Jaimansen said looking at his watch. I'm glad you could make it—and prompt you are, too. I like that in a person. I've no respect for people who are late for appointments." He held his hand out over his newspaper and offered for Grady to have a seat with a gesture towards a chair adjacent to him. "Make yourself comfortable. By all means." He simply ignored Nuck, as if he didn't exist.

Grady sat in the large chair, but he did not settle back into it. He kept himself toward the front of the seat, with his hands resting as casually as possible in his lap. He nodded for Nuck to take a seat nearby. Nuck shook his head no, and Grady let it go immediately.

"Do you smoke?" Jaimansen asked Grady.

"No. Afraid not."

"Now, that's a shame. You're missing out on one of this world's most relaxing customs. I've always thought the ritual of it helped two men have a chance to get to know each other a little better. But we'll make due. By the way, I want you to meet my good friend, "Cracker," here. He's been with me for eleven years now, and he's the best damn dog a man could have."

"Hello, Cracker," Grady said, raising his eyebrows questioningly as he said the dog's name.

Jaimansen took a long drag from his cigar. "So, you said you were thinking about doing a piece on me?"

Grady looked at the dog and found something disturbing about seeing it lying in Jaimansen's lap with such arrogance and stern affection in his eyes. Grady wondered if the dog was the only thing in the entire world that Jaimansen actually loved. He imagined that Jaimansen was the kind of man who poured all his love into his dog, love which might have otherwise gone into his family, had he had one, or into friends, or into those close to him. Grady had developed a bad opinion of the man, mostly from second-hand information and speculation, and he knew that it might be unfair, but it strengthened him now as he looked at him.

"Yes," Grady said and pulled out his tape recorder from his tan jacket pocket and showed Jaimansen. "Do you mind?"

"Oh—I'm sorry, but in fact I do mind—very much. I never allow anyone to put my private words on tape. I guess it's my shyness. You understand, don't you." Jaimansen stretched his bum left leg out to reposition it.

Grady put the recorder away, but he clicked the "on" button, anyway, as he put the device in his jacket pocket. He didn't want to leave any of the conversation to memory. The terrier then growled at Grady and let out two sharp barks.

"It's alright, Cracker," Jaimansen said. "He gets a little excited whenever there are strangers in the house."

Nuck glanced nervously at the dog, and Grady looked too, just for a moment. Then he said, "Okay, so, where do I begin with my questions? I guess I'd like to know a little about your latest venture, the Ocean and Sun development you want to put in at the mouth of the Tremblyrand River. We were down there this morning, taking a look at it. My sources indicate you might have run into a bit of financial trouble with some of your other enterprises, and perhaps this project has become all the more critical in getting you back in the pink. Is that correct?" Grady had made a decision to try to stir things up right away, even if it had to be with a falsehood. He could see that Jaimansen was a hard, cold, man, and he knew he had to rattle him as quickly as possible to maybe shake something loose. He could tell he was already close to accomplishing just that because of the darkening look that suddenly came over Jaimansen's face.

"That's some mighty faulty information you're choosing to start off your interview with, Mr. Able. Might even say unfriendly."

"It's just what my sources say. Is there any truth to it?"

"Hell no, there's no goddamned truth to it. That Tremblyrand River project is going to be a big success, but I certainly don't need it. It's just a good investment. That's what I do, you know—make good investments."

"Oh, I'm sure you do. But I'm also sure a man such as yourself, doesn't make those investments without knowing the tilt of every inch of the playing field, even to the point where you might have to adjust an elevation or two to your advantage."

"Of course," he said with a chuckle. "Every good businessman knows the lay of the land before making a potential deal or investment. Wouldn't be much good, if he didn't, would he?"

"On a related matter," Grady pursued quickly. "Other sources have given me to understand that you had a private meeting with Senate President Sarcost, in his Hasselford senate office in March of last year. Can you tell me about that?"

"I don't remember the meeting. But I meet with hundreds of people during the course of a year," Jaimansen kept an even expression on his face, but his eyes looked as if they might spit fire at any moment.

"So, you have no memory of the meeting, one which dealt with an important matter, a matter which I doubt seriously anyone would ever forget?"

Jaimansen looked sideways at the arm of his chair for a moment, as he collected himself. Grady could see that his irritation was beginning to harden. And that was Grady's intent—get some anger going in him and maybe even some worry. It was the only way he would ever get anything he could actually use out of this so-called interview.

"I don't remember it," Jaimansen said looking up, his eyes now burning straight at Grady.

"If you did indeed have a meeting with the Senate President, however, what might have you discussed? I have a document in my possession with a list of names, contributors to Sarcost and other key political figures in the state government. And the funny thing is, none of their contributions have been registered as official campaign contributions. I have it on pretty good authority that this list of names was hand-written by you on a piece of paper that was taken from Sarcost's office."

"I don't know what you are talking about," Jaimansen said flatly.

"Do you know Linda Herrero?" Grady decided that it was time to fully unload on him and see what came of it.

Jaimansen began smiling at him in a rigid, hate-filled fashion. Grady could see he had hit a nerve with the unexpected mention of Linda Herrero.

"I do recognize one thing, Mr. Able. I recognize a small-time, muck-raking journalist when I see one, and this interview is over."

"Yes, well," Grady stammered back in cold anger. "Nonetheless, maybe you can tell me something about your connection to the groups that have organized and that are fighting the proposed manaseal protections that would shut down your entire Tremblyrand development. And of course there is your boat manufacturing enterprise that is also directly affected if people in the state actually decide to go ahead and protect the environment from the growing number of boats in the water and the marinas and developments that support the boating industry. That wouldn't be a good thing for you, now would it, Mr. Jaimansen? Not for you or your boat manufacturing business, or for your lucrative development business." Grady was pressing hard now with anything he could think of, whether it made substantial sense or not.

"Don't you worry yourself about any of those matters," Jaimansen said. His tone had become more unyielding, and all the pretense of friendliness he had laid upon Grady just minutes earlier, had gone from it. "You come here apparently looking for some truth, as people like you quite often think you are doing in your tiny world of delusional self-importance. So, I'm going to give you a piece of the truth you are seeking, because I'm hoping it will serve you well." He paused for a moment as if analyzing Grady like he might some gold coin under his magnifying glass, as he scoured it for a flaw.

A few tense seconds passed as he stared, and then he said casually, "I've made a decision about you." He was still eyeing Grady. His tone had changed back to a more soft and subtle one, almost like that of a dad talking to a son. It made Grady feel all the more uncomfortable. "And I can assure you, it's a decision I never thought I'd be making today," he continued. "And it only came about when I heard within your questions a naiveté I never expected. I can see that you need to learn a few things about how the real world works. Where do you think some of the organizing money comes from for some of those groups? And without money, they would be only a whining bunch of self-interested yahoos, wouldn't they? Just listen to them go on and on about their boating rights—like it was bigger than life itself, like a child throwing a tantrum because it didn't get its way. It's good, though, because I take that emotion, and I use it for my own purposes. That's all. And they're happy, because they get to go on being angry."

"It's most definitely not that simple," Grady interjected, his ire getting up. "I'm sure the members of those groups believe very strongly in their positions about their boating rights, even if some of those positions may seem wrong to many others, including me. But they certainly don't need the likes of you to pursue their political efforts."

"Of course they believe their own rhetoric, but regardless, it's all extremely useful to me, and I can hardly contain myself when I find causes such as this, with people who are willing to protest against a helpless creature in favor of the powerful. We live in rare times, indeed. This wouldn't have been possible thirty years ago in Newmont.

I'm insulted, Mr. Able, that you would give such plebeian groups any credit for what I have accomplished. I, and others with position and money, get things done because we want those things to be done. I'm a patient man when it comes to public policy. You have to work it a bit, bide your time, but in the end, if you spread enough money around, including to groups who oppose what you are trying to defeat, you get what you want, and it's all as legal as lawyers. It's democracy!

"You must know in your heart of hearts, there's no stopping me," Jaimansen went on, obviously enjoying himself greatly now. "Why? Because I know how to use money and power, and in this country, people are more than happy to let the powerful do pretty much anything they want. They are afraid and stupid, and that, in itself, gives me more power. It took several generations to mold them properly, but the job has been accomplished, especially here in Newmont. What a great state it is. Money is power. The Supreme Court had it right when it put forth the money-is-speech notion, but of course they missed the point—it's not just speech, or free speech, but in fact, it's ALL speech. If you don't have money, you won't be heard, not anywhere that counts, at least—no matter how much you have to say. I get a kick out of people like you who actually still believe you can preserve what you think of as the egalitarian, independent press. It doesn't exist anymore, my friend, at least not in any fashion that carries the slightest amount of weight. The media is owned by businessmen like myself, you see."

"Yeah, well they're not all businessmen like yourself," Grady said with cold anger.

"Close enough, though," Jaimansen responded. "And Mr. Able, you also seem to care about what people like you call 'natural beauty,'" Jaimansen went on. "Understand one thing, and you'll sleep better at night. That natural beauty is mine to do with as I please. It belongs to me and anyone else who has the money and power to take ownership of it. And I will develop it any way I please—turn it straight into gold—because that's all it really is—gold."

Grady looked at Jaimansen, completely unnerved by both his own rising anger and by his surprise at Jaimansen's arrogance and outright audacity. He had wanted to rattle the man, but the exact opposite was now happening. He knew the man was doing what he always did with his "prey." He was playing with Grady—intimidating him in a most demeaning fashion—deliberately diminishing everything Grady held dear.

"You must know by now that I can frighten the average citizen into giving me anything I want," Jaimansen continued. "All I have to do is get the politicians who do my bidding to frighten their constituents with words such as 'jobs' and 'terrorism,' and the public will cower so low people like me can get almost any legislation we want passed with hardly a fight. Have you seen some of the ridiculous things they've been willing to pass lately. It's quite funny, actually. It's sad to say that much of the challenge has gone out of it. I don't get the high from it I used to get, because it's become so easy.

"Frankly, Mr. Able, my power is growing, and I see no limit in sight. It won't be long before a very small group of people in this country will own everything—lock, stock and barrel. If you don't believe me, then just go to the public hearing down at the Benoff Wildlife Management District Chambers on 3rd Avenue this afternoon. It should be an education for you. My Ocean and Sun project lies within the Benoff district. The meeting starts at four, and you won't want to miss it, because it'll give you a taste of what I'm talking about."

"You may be right," Grady said when Jaimansen finally paused to take one final drag from his cigar. "But I'm going to get the truth out anyway."

Jaimansen stubbed out the cigar energetically in a nearby ashtray as he watched Grady, and then he smiled.

"We'll bring you down in the end," Grady added, but all the confidence had gone from his voice, and he knew it. His rage was nearly choking the words off before they could come out. He now felt impotent in front of Jaimansen. He looked at Nuck, who had drawn into himself, not from fear, but to keep himself as calm as possible. He was giving off no signs of emotion whatsoever. Grady had seen him do that before, to the point where he became almost statue-like. He wished he could do that, too, but he didn't have it in him.

Jaimansen laughed at Grady with outward contempt and bravado, and after he was finished laughing, he smiled and said, "I doubt that rag of yours will be in business a month from now. I'd be willing to place a friendly wager on it, in fact. You see, Mr. Able, you've attracted my attention, and that's something you should have never done. Here you are—actually in my house, in my castle. The minute I begin to take you even a little seriously as a possible threat, I'll have no choice but to see to it that you are shut down. It's just a simple matter of business. Don't take it personally."

Grady glared at Jaimansen, but he knew the man was having the precise effect on him he wanted. Grady was intimidated, though he tried desperately not to show it.

Jaimansen looked at him, and Grady looked back, and in that exchange of looks, Grady knew what Jaimansen wanted him to know, and because he also knew there wasn't anything more to be accomplished by talking to the man, he said, "Oh, I do take it personally, Mr. Jaimansen. Now if you'll forgive me, we'll be on our way. I think I've got what I came here for, and then some. No need to get up. We can find our way out."

With one quick look, Nuck followed Grady's lead, and they both hastily left the Jaimansen mansion.

CHAPTER 15

《 》

Too many necropsies—the cause of death is merely a symptom

The Jaimansen interview had been a harrowing experience for both Grady and Nuck, but they both refused to let it put a damper on what they knew they had to do.

After grabbing a bite to eat at a restaurant in downtown Calhoun, Grady and Nuck drove to the municipal building, parked in the one vacant space they found in the lot on the south side of the building, and went inside.

Grady was now determined more than ever to attend the public hearing on the manaseal protection issue. The two men followed the signs indicating where the hearing was to take place within the Benoff Wildlife Management District meeting chamber on the second floor. Benoff is the eight county region in which Calhoun is located.

They talked with a few people outside the meeting room in the hallway, read a few handouts from advocacy and opposition groups involved, and read the details and history on the District Commissioner's agenda sheet.

More than a year ago, a group of citizens in the state had sued the Newmont Marine Species Preservation Agency (NMSPA) over their failure to enforce upon the Benoff Wildlife Management District (BWMD) their duty under state law to come up with a Manaseal Conservation Plan (MCP), this modeled loosely after what Florida had done in conjunction with the manatee issue. This was also tied up in federal species protection laws. The circuit court judge sitting on the case had ruled that the state had failed to meet its obligations under state and federal laws regarding the manaseal. The judge could see no possible justification for such failure, in light of all the available science that pointed to a serious situation for the future health of the manaseal population, especially in Benoff Wildlife Management District. In his ruling he had added, "This is particularly egregious in light of the fact that there are over three quarters of a million registered boats on Newmont waterways already, with close to an additional 300,000 out-of-state boats. Add to this an ever growing number of people moving into Newmont every year with all the pressure such growth brings for increased development in manaseal habitat, and the general degradation of that habitat from that increased population. Combine these facts with the record manaseal mortality rates in the District, and I can't see any wiggle room for you in carrying out your lawful duties, and carrying them out in a timely fashion."

In its defense, the state had testified that the manaseal would be protected with just as much vigor, whether BWMD came up with a Manaseal Conservation Plan immediately or not, and that in fact, it made no actual difference, whatsoever, in their duties. The judge upon hearing this immediately said, "Am I to assume from this then, as part of your duties, you will be strictly enforcing the state's law requiring every Management District with a significant manaseal population to adopt an effective Conservation Plan?" The answer was a prompt "Yes" by the NMSPA officials, which put the state in a bind, because the judge then ordered NMSPA to show speedy progress in enforcing this law upon the Benoff Wildlife Management District. In his final ruling, Judge Samson added, "The science demonstrates the exact opposite of what you have argued here concerning the merits of allowing management districts more time to come up with MCPs, and since you say it makes no 'actual' difference in your enforcement of manaseal protection laws, then I am ordering you to continue to protect the manaseals in an 'actual' way, and not delay in enforcing action upon the BWMD to submit their Plan. They were originally given a deadline, and they defaulted, and since that time, they have gone many years past that deadline. If within a year from this date, you have still not received a proper Manaseal Conservation Plan from Benoff Wildlife Management District, one that will actually protect the manaseals from the numerous human-related threats to their survival as a species, then it is your duty to take the appropriate punitive action against the district and localities contained therein, as specified in Newmont's own state laws, and to enforce the manaseal protection yourself."

It was a scathing ruling and a complete rebuke to the state, and it had some of the boater groups, some developers, and parts of the marine industry, namely the Jaimansen part, in a tizzy.

So, ordered to do so by the state, the Benoff Wildlife Management District was finally getting around to putting together a Manaseal Conservation Plan. They had been dragging their feet for so many years because of the opposition of many special interest groups and because of politics in that management district. The BWMD Commission meeting that Grady and Nuck were attending was the final part of the process under the judge's strict edict and was supposedly to take into account the opinions, science, and expert testimony on the manaseal protection issue in the Benoff District.

Grady had no idea how contentious and disorderly such meetings could be. It was as if the BWMD Commissioners, either out of cowardice, vindictive mean-spiritedness, or pure politics, allowed at least one gathering of anti-manaseal protection advocates to yell out insults at will at those citizens brave enough to take the podium to declare their support for the protection measures in the District's Manatee Conservation Plan. It was the first time Grady had attended one of these meetings, even though there had been a whole series of them in his own Lassert Management District several years ago. He had sent Doug Waxell from the paper to cover them.

In the middle of the hearing, one poor nervous woman got up to speak, and she could barely get her words out. The commission members at first seemed to take some pity on her and listened patiently and intently to her as she spoke in a quiet voice. But as she quoted a few facts from one of the recent scientific studies that had been done concerning the trouble the manaseal population was in, a group in the audience began booing her and yelling for her to sit down. She paused and courageously waited for District Commission Chairman, William Pollardy to say something to the crowd so she could continue. He didn't say anything, though, and she was forced to simply wait for the boos to subside, so she could continue. With great spunk, she asked for her time to be restored, and it was. Some in the crowd began booing her again, and a few yelled out insults at her.

Grady was amazed that the commissioners didn't stop these disruptions. He thought for sure the Chairman would have the Sheriff's deputies toss out those who continued to disrupt the proceedings, or at least rap his gavel several times to stop the commotion, but he did nothing but watch.

Grady noticed that Nuck had turned and had put one of his deliberate, incomprehensible stares on the group of men behind them, a group who had been doing some of the shouting and booing. The men stared back at Nuck, entirely unable to determine just what Nuck's eyes were saying. The men said nothing in response, either to Nuck or between themselves. They only stared back. Grady turned too, and glared at the men with anger and scorn, and he knew that they would have no trouble instantly reading the look on his face. He also instantly knew he had to rein in his emotions. He was at the hearing to get background information on the Linda Herrero and Marcy Appleton story and so was there only as an observer. It would not be good to become embroiled in a fracas and wind up in a news story himself. So, he stared at the men, and they stared back with an anger of their own, and they mumbled some more nasty things among themselves. Grady calmed himself, turned around, and kept his eyes trained forward on the commissioners.

He also reminded himself that some of the nastier people in that meeting hall didn't represent all, or even most, boaters or citizens in the state. He knew that, in fact, from every poll that had been done, a significant majority of boaters favored protecting the manaseals. The disruptive people who showed up at such meetings and yelled down other speakers were obstructionist, and for very selfish reasons. It was obvious they opposed any kind of rational solution to protecting manaseals if it included any restrictions on how fast they could operate their boats. Only two of the people sitting with the most disruptive group actually got up to speak, and neither of them had anything to offer in the way of a solution. They only reiterated their view that there were already enough manaseals in the waters. What went unspoken was their utter disdain for the marine mammals, as evidenced by one T-shirt he saw with a manaseal on a barbeque spit. Grady found it to be disgusting and vile on so many levels. Some of those who had come to this particular hearing had also demonstrated quite clearly that they were bullies, at least when in a crowd.

Grady also noticed that not all those who got up to speak against increased manaseal protection behaved in a vile way at the hearing. On the contrary, some of them behaved very respectfully to the others at the meeting. In fact, Grady knew that there were boater groups in the audience, but in most cases, he could not tell which people belonged to which group, or who had come to the meeting as individuals. Grady was very careful in his thinking to not lump every bad-behaving person into one boater group or another, or into any group at all. To do so wouldn't have been fair to those organized groups, and he was quite sure it also would not have been accurate.

The woman struggled to finish her three minute talk and then returned to her seat.

A man from a seat in the far left front of the chamber then came forward to speak, and he said, "I'll keep what I have to say brief. I've been fishing the waters around Calhoun for over thirty years, and I've never seen more manaseals than there are today. I can tell you, there are more than enough of them. They're everywhere. Have you been out on the waters lately?" he asked the commissioners rhetorically. "I bet I saw over five hundred of them together this past winter over near the power plant where they congregate in the warm effluent there.

There's plenty of manaseals. That's all I've got to say." He received a thunderous applause from a substantial number of the people present in the chamber. It was the kind of speech they loved, short and to the simplistic point they wanted to hear, despite the fact that it ignored all the real science that had been done on manaseals and on the health of the population in certain areas of the state, including Benoff Wildlife Management District waters.

The man's anecdotal observation was typical of what some of the opposition groups tried to put forward as scientific fact, even though it sidestepped all real science—and likely because it did so. Grady was to learn all about this widely used Newmont tactic as he delved into the Herrero/Appleton story more. He discovered that as the political pressure against manaseal protections grew in certain areas, this tactic was put to use more and more frequently by some who were just ignorant of the real facts, or worse, by those who absolutely knew better.

A biologist named Dr. Calvin Hamstead from the Newmont Marine Mammal Science Trust then got up to speak. He was a large, well-dressed man, athletic in build, and he sported a full, well-trimmed, beard. He spoke in a deep voice as he introduced himself. To counter the comment's of the previous speaker, he said, "Manaseals are migratory mammals, and so they do not permanently stay in one place. They often roam widely throughout a wide range of the state's waterways during the course of a year, so when one finds them congregated in one place, especially during the winter months, it doesn't indicate anything about the size, or more importantly, the health of the manaseal population. Manaseals go where they know they can find refuge from the cold water.

"The District should NOT, as it seems you are proposing in your Plan, arbitrarily change the criteria used when looking at needed protections of a species such as the manaseal without giving proper consideration to the fact that rational criteria used for one species does not apply to all species. For example, the protection criteria used for evaluating the status of deer cannot possibly be the same as used to evaluate a marine mammal such as the manaseal. The state of Florida learned this awhile back, and I'm confident the state of Newmont will do likewise.

"So, please, I ask the District Commission to properly evaluate the needs of this marine mammal for the long-term survival of the species and apply the proper protections that will actually accomplish that in this management district. Someone has to speak up on behalf of the manaseals here. They can't speak for themselves, and they are being killed in record numbers every year by speeding boats and habitat degradation."

The man was roundly booed for this by a large group of activist boaters, and a few derogatory personal attacks were also yelled out, as usual.

The man remained on topic, though and refused to let the hostile crowd deter him from putting his knowledge and facts on the record in support of the need for stronger manaseal protection in Benoff Wildlife Management District waters. He continued laying out the scientific case for incorporating stronger protections in the conservation plan they were considering. He then concluded by saying, "There are plenty of people, as we can see in this hall tonight, who are willing to speak out against protecting manaseals. It is sometimes easier to NOT protect a vulnerable species, because it requires no immediate sacrifice. But for those who care about the future of manaseals in Newmont, and there are plenty of people present here today who do, we must ask that everyone care enough for these beautiful animals to protect them for all future generations. If we don't, they won't be around for our grandchildren to see, and the finger of blame will point directly at us for failing to do the right thing."

This was met with more loud boos and nasty comments from the same group of rowdy and disrespectful people. Grady found himself getting angrier by the minute, and he couldn't wait to leave that overcrowded room. He couldn't begin to understand how people could be so self-centered in their opinions. How could they be so vile and so aggressive against protecting manaseals? Grady could understand how differences over the details of those protections could arise, but many of these people, had no interest whatsoever in providing any further protections for the animals. It seemed they just didn't want to share the waters with the manaseals or with anything else that might inhibit their speedy boats. To them, that was "freedom," and to hell with anybody else's freedom. But that was Newmont for you, right out of the worst of the wild west in some ways. It upset Grady further that he was becoming so disturbed over an issue that hadn't even been on his personal radar screen much until two weeks ago.

Through it all, the commissioners just sat there and said nothing with each disruption. At one point, an elderly man had gotten up to speak on behalf of stronger manaseal protections, and one of the boaters yelled out, "Shut up and sit down." The commissioners did not come to the old man's rescue, or have the trouble-makers ejected from the hall, but instead one of the commissioners then actually challenged the poor man on one of the points he was trying to make about the need for increased manaseal protection. The man responded well, but the commissioner stayed after him, and finally after the man left the podium, the same commissioner made his own opinion known that he wasn't "buying any of it." It was obvious to Grady that this commissioner was cow-towing to the anti-manaseal-protection crowd in the worst kind of way, and it was disgusting to watch.

After three-and-a-half long hours of hearing speakers, including Claude Donovan, Grady and Nuck's new acquaintance from that morning, the Commissioners finally voted on several changes that were being considered in the BWMD Manaseal Conservation Plan. One of the proposed sections had language that would put limits on the number of new marinas that could be built, how many boat slips they could have, and where those marinas could, and could not, be built, all in an effort to preserve manaseal habitat. Grady knew that this was the particular section Francis Jaimansen most wanted to kill. Another section was written to create boat speed limits in certain critical habitat waterways, particularly in areas where manaseals do most of their feeding and breeding.

In their pre-vote discussion, three of the seven commissioners openly agreed with the opponents who had spoken that there were already enough manaseal protections in place. Grady understood politics enough, especially Newmont politics, to know what was going on. In the disappointment and anger that had overwhelmed him from the meeting, and the pressure that was working on him from the intractable Linda/Marcy story, a petulance overtook him. Though he knew it to be folly, he angrily thought to himself that the unspoken attitude of the management district commissioners who were lining up against any strong manaseal protection measures seemed to be, *"Who cares about a few dead manaseals. We care about the money boaters generate; we care about the boating industry; we care about developer's needs. They are the milk-blood of politics in Newmont; they are the milk-blood of campaign contributions that flow in to keep us elected."* As soon as the thought rushed out, he knew it was only his frustration speaking, a "polemical endemical" as he coined the phrase to describe such personal rants, so he quickly cautioned himself about characterizing these people without knowing anything about them. He was a journalist, after all, and that required him to maintain his objectivity and to stick to the facts.

One of the commissioners spoke out strongly in favor of the new protections and said, "They really don't go far enough, but it's the best this particular commission is going to do, so we should vote for them." The three other commissioners asked a few rhetorical questions but didn't reveal how they would vote. These three more seemingly moderate commissioners were in a political bind and were hoping to placate the well-financed and powerful forces in the district that were pushing to stop any manaseal protections from being enacted.

When the discussion ended, the vote was taken, and it came out four to three against incorporating the stricter protections in the Manaseal Conservation Plan. It remained the watered-down plan that had been put together before the hearing. The state would not likely be able to accept it as a valid plan, and it would come back to the commissioners for improvement, but for now it soothed the angry beast that was the powerful special interest political machinery that didn't want manaseals to get in their way. And Jaimansen, as one of those cogs in that machinery, knew that by the time it was rehashed, his Ocean and Sun Resort project would be nearly completed, and no one could stop him at that point. It would all be "legal as lawyers," as Jaimansen had said to Grady that very morning. The meeting was adjourned with the wrap of a gavel.

On their way out, Grady and Nuck saw Jaimansen talking to a small group of well-dressed men in the lobby area just outside the Commission meeting room. When Jaimansen saw Grady, he winked at him as he passed. The Commission's vote would leave Jaimansen's development project completely intact, and he knew that once again the majority of the citizens of the city of Calhoun had lost another battle to stop the man from running rampant over their wishes.

Grady came away from that meeting understanding some of the ugliness that Linda and Marcy had been up against in their attempt to protect manaseals. It was a difficult mission. The only support you could get for an endangered species was from thousands of individuals who cared enough to send in their small checks to organizations committed to protecting the animals, and who sent in their letters to the editor in hopes of convincing other people of the need to care, hoping that someone would do something for the creatures. There were no large sources of money such as those provided by the Jaimansen's of the world to funnel enormous funds their way. Nearly all the money of special interest businesses went to oppose new regulations designed to protect manaseals, because those businesses felt they had a direct impact on them. It was difficult to take the side of a creature that couldn't speak for itself about the suffering and injuries it sustained at the hands of developers who built in their habitat and boaters who drove their boats too fast so manaseals had no chance of getting out of the way. Broken bones, ruptured lungs, trauma to the head from hull impacts, strangulation from carelessly discarded fishing line, the polluted waters they had to live in, were all things that the manaseals experienced, but they couldn't speak about any of it at meetings such as the one the Benoff Wildlife Management District had just had. The manaseal's long-term fate teetered in the balance.

Many an elected body had chosen to run right over the manaseals and other endangered species in favor of those who would fill the politicians' coffers. It was an ugly system when it came to protecting the weak. The weak had very little say in Newmont politics, whether it came to endangered species or homeless people. Just as Jaimansen had said to Grady earlier in the day, the Supreme Court had ruled in essence, that "money was speech," and in so doing they had unleashed even more ugliness onto the American political landscape, especially in a place like Newmont, opening up the kick-back susceptible campaign funding system to even more abuse by those with all the money, even if it hadn't been the Justices' intent. Grady would never understand how a majority of Supreme Court Justices could come to the conclusion that the millions of dollars given to candidates by wealthy and powerful interests could be, in any way, equated to the few dollars a working person could offer up to an opposing candidate. Fairness alone made their argument seem specious, and Grady was definitely of the opinion that it turned the democratic principle upon which the country was founded entirely on its head, because it turned the notion of free speech right on its head. To Grady's way of thinking, it was probably the single worst ruling the Supreme Court had made in more than a hundred years, but of course he wasn't a lawyer or a constitutional scholar. He could, however, see how the ruling was playing out in practical terms. In effect, it was turning the republic into a free-corruption zone and had made that corruption legal.

Grady had watched the angry crowd of boaters during the hearing, and he had seen people who seemed to be wholly without any sense of fairness, people who seemed to care only about themselves and their own opinions and pleasures. Grady knew many boaters, but they were nothing like the people who came to this particular hearing. For one thing, they would never turn their disagreements into an intimidating mob at a public hearing. They understood that manaseals had been around for many millions of years, they were precious to the state and its image, and they needed protecting. They also understood some of the horrible growth issues that Newmont was facing and how those issues affected vulnerable species, as well as the quality of their own lives and their children's lives.

In short, Grady's boating friends were reasonable people who could look at an issue in a reasonable way. They were willing to discuss ways to accomplish the protection of one of Newmont's precious natural resources, even if they had to go a bit slower in manaseal areas and take a few minutes longer to get their boats where they were going. They understood that life had gotten way too fast, anyway, and that slowing down was not necessarily a bad thing—not just for the sake of manaseals, but for the sake of people too.

In an angry moment, Grady believed these nasty people he had seen at the hearing, were of the same ilk as people who insisted they owned the highways too. They were the ones weaving in and out of traffic going twenty-miles per hour faster than everyone else, because they felt they were superior to those others. They were the ones yelling and screaming when another car slowed them down even for a few seconds. They were the ones throwing trash out their windows, because they couldn't be bothered to wait to dispose of it properly when they got back home. They were the ones tossing beer bottles off their boats when out on the waters. To Grady they were incredibly bad citizens. He had no time for people like that. And frankly, neither did his boating friends. Grady realized, though, that you could find nasty, selfish people in all walks of life. He only hoped they didn't represent a large percentage of the population, because in the long run it would spell ruin for Newmont.

At times like these, when he became a little hot under the collar, he found he was sometimes wrong about his judgments, and painting with too broad a brush was not wise. There were plenty of people who did actually take some responsibility for their actions and did give a small damn about the world around them and about a sense of community. Appearances could fool you. Unfortunately, what he had seen and heard by some of the rowdy and strident people at the District Commission meeting went well beyond appearances. He sometimes despaired that it was an exercise in futility trying to get people like that to understand that to be good citizens, they had to live on this planet with other people and other creatures, and they had to at least care a little about those others around them. Unfortunately, he felt there weren't enough hours in the day to get such people to understand they couldn't run around willy-nilly destroying everything in their path that they found the least bit inconveniencing.

When Doug Waxell had gone to all of the Lassert Wildlife Management District MCP meetings three years ago in their own district, he had come back saying to Emily, "I've never seen anything like it. Some of them even have the audacity to claim that they, too, are environmentalists, but when it comes to actually protecting ANYTHING in the environment, many of them fight tooth and nail against it, and not only that, they're downright nasty about it." Grady was now witnessing firsthand what Doug had meant.

He doubted that most of his readers had any idea how horrible these meetings were for those who came to them in support of the manaseals. Now he knew why it was so hard to turn out people to these meetings who supported manaseals, even though every poll ever done had shown that Newmontians overwhelmingly supported strong protections for the beloved creature.

The meeting had been demoralizing and exhausting.

CHAPTER 16
《 》

Can stay under for twenty minutes before coming up for air . . .

It had been a long couple of days for Grady, and he and Nuck headed home immediately following the meeting. He was now feeling pressure to get back. He had been away for two days, and spending another night in a hotel and driving back tomorrow was out of the question. Though he had talked often with his wife on his cell phone during the time he was running around the west coast of Newmont researching the Herrero-Appleton story, he was always aware that Emily was home alone tending to all the needs of the children and to the devastated spirit of the fragile Mrs. Herrero. Not only that, but Grady's absence had left a hole in the workforce at the paper, which meant that everybody there had to put in extra hours and take on extra stress to get the Sands out on time. There had been a lot of last minute editing to be done, and it was too much for Emily to do alone. Certainly, Doug Waxell could also handle some of that work, and Grady often relied on him to edit a story, and the man was very capable in that regard, but with Grady gone, Doug would have so much other work on his plate that he would have little time for editing columns or stories.

Grady and Nuck stopped at a Burger Swift along the way to grab something to eat. They were quickly on the road after gulping down a bag full of less than healthy fast food and drinks. Their metabolic furnaces were stoked, though, and they settled in for the nearly five hours of driving that still remained ahead of them.

It was about 9:30 p.m. by the time they got onto the Plain Mountain Highway headed east. Both men were dog tired by then, and they remained mostly silent on their drive back to Tomlin Dunes. At one point, Grady did engage in an energetic flurry of talk, however.

"You know I'm worried about Mrs. Herrero, and I'm also worried about the safety of Emily and my family," he said.

"I know," Nuck said, and nothing else.

Grady was then quiet, too, for a few more minutes, but then he opened up a rant about how the nation's leaders, both political and corporate, had lost all moral direction. He went on about how they lie about everything, they poison everything, and then lie about that, how they crush down on the weakest in society and lie about that, too.

"They have everything, and yet it's never enough," Grady said. "And most of them aren't willing to share anything."

Nuck looked at Grady a couple of times as he spoke to show him that he was paying attention, but he said nothing in response to any of it. Grady went on venting for a little while longer, feeling more foolish with each new rant. Nuck knew that the meeting with Jaimansen and the Beneff Wildlife Management District hearing had gotten to him in some deep way, and Grady knew that Nuck would have no response to any of the venom he was spewing. It was just the way the two men were. Nuck realized it was good for Grady to have a chance to vent from time to time, and he didn't mind listening to it—so long as he wasn't expected to participate in any of it. And he wasn't. To Nuck, expressing such frustrations and anger openly only solidified them within him and gave them a substance and power he refused to allow them.

After a few more minutes of sputtering complaints about other injustices in the world, Grady knew it was another of his "polemical endemicals," and he fell silent once again. He remained that way until they reached the small city of Sienna, well past Mount Newmont and only about an hour away from home. He became caught up in his own thoughts, as he continued to go over everything that had happened during the past two weeks. Every aspect of it seemed to be troubling. And the deeper he dug into the circumstances surrounding Jaimansen, the manaseal issue, and the deaths of Linda and Marcy, the more troubling it all became. His mood darkened.

He decided to stop for gas at Sienna's easternmost exit. He pulled into the nearest gas station. It was a small four pumper with the usual convenience store attached. It appeared to be a family owned station, and Grady liked to support those whenever possible. It was quite late, and there was not a sole around as he got out and began pumping gas. It was an unseasonably warm night, with a pleasant southwesterly wind blowing through his hair. It felt good.

As he filled the tank, Grady absentmindedly looked at a large Rasterman Hotel sign across the four lane highway. He could feel the flowing gas cooling the nozzle in his hand. Something about the sign, the quiet of the hour, the breeze blowing steadily and gently, the gas pump ticking, and Grady's mind working away on some subconscious problem, all combined in that dark early Wednesday morning hour to stir a memory that flitted at first across his mind as a mere tickle and which then came back as a sudden rush of concrete thought. The memory attached itself to, or sprung from, the large first letter "R" in the hotel sign and then suddenly jumped whole into Grady's conscious mind.

It was strange how the mind worked sometimes. It was a silent investigator, searching and prodding images, memories and thoughts, working away steadily in the background until it came up with a solution for that which was troubling it beneath the surface. The solution here was a single word. Grady suddenly recalled having seen it on the note he had found at Warm Springs the morning Marcy had died. How precisely it had come to mind was a mystery, but it had suddenly popped up. The word was "Rantle." A strange word, indeed. Perhaps, he thought, it was some made up word coined by Marcy and Linda. Only later would he learn what it meant to the girls, when Mrs. Herrero would use it offhandedly in a conversation and Grady would inquire about its meaning. Only then would he learn that it was a cross between a rant and a ramble, as they sometimes engaged in themselves in the form of long-winded ventings of their emotions and frustrations. It was, in fact, what Grady had engaged in just an hour or so ago, a "*polemical endemical rantle*," he thought with a smile. The word "rantle" had significance for Grady beyond whatever meaning it might have had for the two young women, though, and at that moment at the gas station, it struck Grady that it might, in fact, be the password Linda had mentioned in her letter to Marcy, the password she used to protect her personal website.

Grady finished pumping the gas, paid the attendant and returned to the car. He got back onto the highway and drove with new excitement and determination, and he drove fast. He was wide awake now. He told Nuck his theory about the password, and he was now anxious to get home. Maybe this was the breakthrough he had been looking for. Now, more than ever, it was crucial to get hold of the evidence Linda had hidden, especially after having met Francis Jaimansen and witnessing firsthand what kind of a man he was. And having the sense he was on the verge of tracking down that very evidence made him all the more aware of the danger that was beginning to creep heavily into his life, danger that was sure to affect those he loved.

They pulled into Tomlin Dunes around 2 a.m. Grady dropped Nuck off and told him he would let him know first thing in the morning if he was able to get into Linda's website. He drove home bone-tired but still in a hurry. Emily and the children were in bed and asleep. In calls to Emily earlier in the day, she had told him that they had gotten the paper out on time. It had been printed a little late, but they still had managed to get it out for delivery early Wednesday morning, just barely. She had said they had everything under control. Grady was so proud of her and all the people at the Sands when he heard this. He had prepared himself for the possibility that the paper might be late that day.

When he arrived home, Emily was sound asleep in their bedroom. Grady was still restless and determined to scratch the itch that was his curiosity about Linda Herrero, and so after checking in on the children, he went on the internet, typed in the URL to Linda's website, and at the User/Password prompt, he tried to get in. After typing in several words for the user ID in combination with the password, "rantle," and failing to access the site, he finally typed in "LHerrero" on another hunch, and then the password, and sure enough he was able to enter the site. He stared at the page that came up for a few seconds waiting for it to load fully, but then he realized it had loaded, but unfortunately it was a completely blank, black screen.

His spirits sank, and all the excitement and energy he had carried with him since leaving the East Sienna gas station suddenly drained away. He was left feeling only tired, exhausted, in fact. In the past three days, he had looked in two promising places, and though it appeared he had come close to finding the hidden evidence, he had come up empty. It seemed all his leads were going nowhere.

He dragged himself off to bed, too tired to think about any of it anymore.

CHAPTER 17

《》

Catching a few winks at the bottom of the river . . .

Grady awoke the next morning and found another bright day streaming through the bedroom curtains. It was after ten o'clock. Emily was already up and was on the computer. She had just started editing an article for the entertainment section that had come into the Sand's email account. She hadn't dressed yet. The kids were off to school, and Mrs. Herrero was sitting in the Newmont room, sipping a cup of coffee and staring out at the holly tree and the many clusters of bright red berries it displayed this time of year.

Grady mumbled a good morning to Emily, gave her a quick kiss, looked into her eyes, and said, "Thank you." She knew he wasn't much use in the morning upon first waking, not until he had a couple of cups of strong coffee in him, and definitely not until at least a half hour had passed. Having any kind of real conversation with him at that moment was out of the question.

Grady then opened the sliding glass door to the Newmont room and poked his head through. "Good morning, Mrs. Herrero," he said. "How are you doing?"

"Oh," she said, coming quickly out of that other distant world she had been in and turning her head toward Grady. "I'm doing fine, Mr. Able. Thank you for all your kindness and for letting me stay in your beautiful home for a couple of days. I think I'll be going back to my home today, though," she said.

"Oh, please don't even think of that right now, Mrs. Herrero. We would love to have you stay with us for a few days longer, at least. It's not safe back in your own home. Why don't you just have a nice vacation over here on the east coast for a little while. When was the last time you were over this way?"

"Oh goodness, it's been many years. We came over to spend a weekend in Perryville a long time ago. Thank you, Mr. Able, for your generous hospitality."

"No need to thank me, but right now, I hope you will excuse me. I've got to take a shower and then get a cup of coffee in me." He smiled at her.

Mrs. Herrero smiled back, but not surprisingly, she didn't seem in the mood for humor. Grady retreated to the bathroom and took his shower. He hoped it would help him feel like himself again and to feel like he was home. He got dressed and went to the kitchen, where he poured the last of the coffee into a mug and then made a fresh pot. He then called Doug at the Sands and thanked him profusely for his heroic efforts during the past couple of days while Grady was away. He told him he wanted everyone there at the paper to put everything aside, no matter how pressing it seemed, and take the rest of the day off. Doug began to protest this, saying there was so much to get done, but in his coarse morning voice, Grady said, "No, Doug. I don't want to hear it. I don't care what has to be done. I'm coming in, and I'll do it. You've got the day off. Everyone does. It's an order." Doug did not protest further and only said, "Whatever you say, Grady."

"That's what I say. I'll see you tomorrow morning."

Grady clicked off his cell phone, finished his first mug with two large gulps, poured himself a second mug from the freshly brewed pot, and sat in one of the dining room chairs, sipping more slowly.

"That goes for you, too, Emily," he said, looking over at her.

"What does?"

"I don't want you doing any more work today."

"Alright," Emily said with a smile. "I can live with that." She quickly finished up what she was working on, came over to Grady, took his hand, and led him out the front door. He was still clutching his coffee mug. They went for a long walk around the block before returning home for a breakfast of English muffins and jam.

Grady began on his third mug of coffee and sat and talked casually with Emily, asking her how things had been going with Mrs. Herrero. Emily assured him that she seemed to be doing reasonably well, considering what she had been through.

"She still seems quite lost," she said.

"Yeah, I know. It's very sad."

After breakfast, Grady drove to the office. At about nine, he gave Nuck a call and told him the bad news about Linda's blank webpage. He then dug in and worked hard all day. It felt good to be back doing the tasks his paper demanded.

The day passed quickly and uneventfully, and Grady felt like he had gotten a lot accomplished in the way of catching up. And by the end of the day, he was beginning to feel less dispirited. In fact, he was beginning to think things were going to work out. Maybe Jaimansen's veiled threat was only a bluff.

He returned home at about 7:30 and took Emily, Mrs. Herrero, Steven, and Krissy out to dinner. They all had a very good time, talking and laughing together. Even Mrs. Herrero emitted a restrained laugh or two when Krissy did her imitation of her stodgy bus driver who sometimes chided the children about their noisiness. Apparently, there was a certain level the children's voices rose to, at which point the din always set the bus driver off on a scolding tirade. All animated, Krissy explained he would look in the mirror and say, "'I want you all to sit still in your seats and keep the noise down. I'll pull this bus over right now, if you persist, and that won't be good for some of you, because I'll report you to the principal and have you banned from the bus. You don't want that, do you? You know who you are.'" In the deepest voice Krissy could manage, she did her best imitation of the bus driver. As she did, she turned and pointed at the imaginary students with her best scornful, threatening finger.

It got a good laugh out of everyone, even young Steven giggled heartily.

That day ended, and another day arrived, and the first signs of real trouble showed up. Grady noticed it as he left his driveway that Friday morning. He noticed it as he turned into the small parking lot of The Pastry Palace on Green Street. He saw it again parked on the other side of Main Street as he pulled up in front of The Tomlin Sands building. It was trouble that came in the form of a late model, dark maroon, luxury sedan with two men seated in the front.

He was being followed, that was for sure. And the only people he could think of who might possibly be doing it were surrogates of Francis Jaimansen. If Grady was right, he had plenty to be frightened about, because it meant Jaimansen hadn't been just blustering and bluffing when he threatened Grady during their conversation in Calhoun. Perhaps the man was already beginning to apply the very pressure he had promised, but in a much more sinister way than Grady had imagined. And it meant that Grady's pursuit of the Linda and Marcy story had stirred up some powerfully negative reactions in Jaimansen, more than he had expected. He started to think that perhaps Jaimansen was afraid Grady might actually have, or come up with, whatever Linda had found. And though Grady fully intended to come up with exactly that, if it was at all possible, he was frustrated by the fact that he had no idea how he might actually accomplish it. And if that was at the heart of Jaimansen's worry, then it meant Linda had stumbled across something very important, indeed. Grady also thought that the men in the sedan were probably the same men who had ruffed up and bullied Mrs. Herrero in her apartment.

Grady made another quick glance toward the sedan parked on the other side of the street just before he entered the Sands, and the creeping fear he had been experiencing since he first noticed he was being followed suddenly gave way to a sudden burst of anger. He had a powerful urge to turn, march straight across the street over to the sedan, and confront the men in the car, but he did not give in to the impulse. It was obvious that the men were following him so out in the open, without fear of detection, to make a point. They had been sent to intimidate Grady. A confrontation would accomplish nothing other than to let them know that they were succeeding. He refused to give them that, and he restrained himself from taking any precipitous action. He had a lot to figure out, and he had to bide his time. He would just ignore the men in the sedan and pretend he hadn't seen them. This strategy was problematic, though, because Grady couldn't help but think about what the men had done to Mrs. Herrero. They were capable of far more than just following him.

As he sat in his office, getting nearly nothing done on the new advertising layouts for next Wednesday's paper, his thoughts continued to be dominated by the dire situation into which he and his loved ones had fallen. For the first time in a long while, he truly didn't know what to do. He knew of no way to fight these people. If he could only find the evidence that Linda had hidden somewhere, he thought that it might give him some leverage in the situation. If he had something to bargain with, maybe he could use it in some way to make his family and Mrs. Herrero safe. But then again, if the evidence was so damaging that Linda had been murdered over it, Grady worried about what lengths Jaimansen was willing to go to keep the truth from coming out, if in fact, Jaimansen was behind it all. The man wouldn't likely be satisfied until he was certain Grady couldn't be a future threat to him, and there was no way he could be certain of that. These were ruthless people, and Grady was beginning to think they weren't ever going to be satisfied until they had Linda's evidence in hand and were certain it couldn't do them any harm—and maybe not even then. And maybe, Grady thought, he was just letting his imagination run wild.

If for no other reason than for peace of mind, he had to find Linda's evidence, so at least he would know what he was dealing with. He was a newsman, and he hated being in the dark. Jaimansen thought Grady knew what Linda had on him, even though the truth was, Grady actually had acquired nothing specific. In his interview with the man, Grady had tried to imply that very thing, hoping to unnerve him, but maybe it all had backfired. It was a horribly debilitating feeling that settled into him as he stared at his computer screen.

He thought of calling Marcy's parents to see if they might know anything that might give him a clue as to where Linda had re-hid her evidence, but he rejected that notion immediately. It would only bring danger to them, and they were not likely to know anything that would help, anyway. Linda's unsent letter made that quite clear.

He also thought of calling Lieutenant James of the State Police but quickly rejected that idea, too. It could do no good to have the police poking around. And they wouldn't be able to find anything more than Grady already had uncovered. It would, in fact, bring only more danger to all concerned. It might put desperation into the man who sent the two thugs and cause him to react in a deadly manner.

He pulled himself out of his funk and spent the day trying to absorb himself in the duties he had to attend to. They were many, and they couldn't be sloughed off on anyone else. Either Grady would do them or the next issue of the paper wouldn't get out on time. Everyone else was out straight struggling to manage their own duties and playing catch-up after being shorthanded during the last few days and after Grady had given them a day off the previous day. When it got down to crunch time, there was little leeway for anyone. Every task attached to Saturday's edition and to next Wednesday's edition that fell behind on Friday would cause more of a crunch as print time approached for each edition, and that was tonight for the Saturday edition.

Emily had stayed home on that Friday and had been editing three local stories that were going in this edition of the paper. She called Grady at around 6 p.m. and told him there was hardly any food left in the house and that she was going out to the supermarket and was taking Krissy, Steven, and Mrs. Herrero along with her. She didn't want him to come home and find nobody there.

The thick, black clouds Grady saw rolling in from the northwest on his way home only added to the tension that had been building in him. The forecast had called for a nasty cold front to arrive late that afternoon. Grady had developed a healthy respect for bad weather in Newmont, especially this time of year when conditions could come together to produce severe thunderstorms and tornadoes. It had been an especially warm January, and the jet stream was trying to push its way down into that warm air-mass. Sometimes that spelled trouble. The squall line was headed this way.

Grady drove home around 6:30, and as he parked his vehicle in the garage, he wondered if Emily had shut the windows in the sunroom before she left. He was always conscientious about closing up the house when storms were approaching. He didn't want to have to deal with the damage that could result from the wind and rain making a mess of everything.

When Grady entered the house, he found the sliding glass door to the sunroom was halfway open and the windows wide open. It wasn't a big thing, and under normal circumstances, he wouldn't have thought much about it. That's one thing Emily paid close attention to, though, keeping those sliding glass doors closed tightly. She didn't like bugs, especially cockroaches, and open doors were only an open invitation to every manner of bug and lizard in the vicinity. The sunroom was anything but bug-tight with all its windows and not-so-tight fitting screens. Maybe Mrs. Herrero had been in the room and had left the door open, Grady thought, but even then, he was sure Emily would have noticed the door was open and would have closed it. Still, it was no big deal.

A flash of lightning lit up the dark sky as the first bolt snapped sharply to the ground about two miles away. This was followed by a loud boom of thunder about ten seconds later that rattled every window in the house. The open door to the sunroom had gotten Grady's attention, but it was another detail he noticed that suddenly put a real fear into him. On his way to shut the windows in the sunroom, and to secure the sliding glass door to prepare for the impending storm, he noticed that a favorite photo in one of the beautiful and elegant frames Emily was always so good at finding was lying face down on the small desk located next to the sunroom. The frame held a wedding picture of Grady and Emily standing together on the beach. This was a photo that had been taken shortly after they had celebrated their wedding with what they jokingly called their "wedding pizza and wine" at a nearby beachside restaurant. They had joked about it ever since.

Their wedding had been a casual ceremony of vows in front of Emily's chaplain. Grady had no affiliation to any particular church or religion, but he hadn't minded the chaplain. The celebration following the wedding had been full of fun and love, the kind of afternoon that settled deep in the memory in a lasting way. The wedding day picture had been on the desk every day since they got the photos back from the developer. Grady knew Emily loved seeing it there. She commented on it occasionally, even after several years, and she always laughed jovially at the foolish grin Grady had on his face in that picture. She loved reminding Grady of it, because she knew it made him blush and that it agitated him slightly. Emily had placed pictures of that day of marriage and celebration all over the house.

As he stood there looking at that photo frame lying on its face on the desk, the hairs rose up on the back of Grady's neck. He immediately suspected that an intruder had been rummaging around in their house. Maybe it was just paranoia building in him from being followed. Maybe Mrs. Herrero or Emily had knocked the frame over without noticing it.

After closing the windows securely, Grady made a careful search of the rest of the house, looking for any other suspicious signs. He became certain that, indeed, unwelcome visitors had been in the house, when he found several pieces of Emily's underwear stuffed unceremoniously into one of his drawers in the bedroom bureau where they didn't belong. He had little doubt as to who the intruders were. They had tried to cover their tracks so that their snooping wouldn't be noticed, but they were clumsy in their efforts, and Grady was very observant.

He was sitting at the dining room table when Emily, Mrs. Herrero, Krissy, and little Steven came hurrying through the door and stomped off the rain that had gathered on their shoes. It was still raining heavily. The thunderstorm had been strong with lightning and wind for about a half hour but had not developed into anything severe. Emily and Mrs. Herrero shook out their umbrellas and hats through the door and leaned them against the hall wall to dry.

Emily walked into the living room and saw Grady with his down-in-the-mouth look. He was staring off into the dark storm outside, but he turned to face her. The look she saw in his troubled eyes frightened her.

"What's wrong?" she said.

"Everything's wrong—ever since I decided to find out more about Marcy's death. I should have known better. I should have just let well enough alone. And now, it turns out that I have involved you and the children."

"What do you mean?"

"Krissy, can you go clean up your room, and take Steven with you," Grady said. "I was in there, and it's a mess. You do that, and I'll take you both out for an ice-cream later, after this storm quiets down."

"Goodie, goodie!" Steven cried out.

"That's not fair," Krissy said. "Every time you and Mom want to talk about something, you send me off to clean up my bedroom, and you make me take the little bug."

"I know, Darling, life is so unfair, isn't it?" Grady smiled at his daughter, and she smiled back in her shy manner, but it was easy to see that she was annoyed.

"Yes, it is," she said, but she shuffled off reluctantly to her bedroom. "Come on Bug, let's go."

"And don't call your brother 'Bug.' It's not nice. Please close your door, Darling. Your mother and I have some adult things to talk about that aren't meant for six-year-old ears. It's more of that unfairness thing."

Krissy turned her head back toward Grady as she was walking away, and she mumbled, "Yes, I know." Steven followed his sister eagerly, hoping some fun might be in the offing.

"If you don't mind, I think I'll go lie down for a while," Mrs. Herrero said. She was being polite, as usual. She sensed that Grady and Emily wanted to talk alone, and she immediately headed off behind Krissy and Steven toward the guest bedroom, which was hers for now.

Grady got up from the table and walked over to the living room area so he could make sure his daughter actually went into her room and that she shut her door completely. She was a very curious child, and he loved her for that, and he knew that she was not above a little deception to circumvent a parental command when she felt that it was unjust, which indeed applied to almost all parental commands, to most six year olds.

When Grady was satisfied that Krissy's door was shut, and that she and Steven wouldn't hear what he had to say, he turned to Emily and in a low voice said, "Someone broke into the house while you were away shopping." His face was drawn tight with worry. "Probably they were waiting for a time when everyone was out of the house. In any case, they were in here, and I'm afraid for our safety, now more than ever."

"You're kidding, aren't you," Emily said.

"I wish I was. I'm sure they think I have Linda's secret, and they are hell-bent on getting their hands on it. It's apparent they are so afraid of whatever she had in her possession at the time of her death, they will do anything to get it. But they are also afraid of having the evidence remain on the loose, and right now it is definitely on the loose, if it exists at all."

"It must exist, if what you are saying is true," Emily said. "Or at least someone thinks it does."

"Yeah. Jaimansen does. I believe he truly is a man without a conscience. You should have seen him when I interviewed him. He's as arrogant a man as I've ever met. If he didn't have money, and hordes of it, he probably would have been locked up long ago for his sociopathic instincts. Who knows what he might be capable of."

"What can we do about it?"

"I don't know . . . Nothing . . . Except be careful. I'm sick to death with it all. Sometimes I wish I had never answered that call from Deputy Myers."

"Oh, come now, Sweetheart. You know as well as I do that you are incapable of not pursuing a lead if there is a story to be reported, or if there is some hidden truth to be exposed. You're a newspaperman, and a damned good one. We'll just have to find a way to stay safe. I married you because of the way you are. I don't like it when you talk like this. It frightens me as much as anything. We'll just have to deal with it somehow."

"Sometimes your ideals have to be sacrificed when they are beginning to directly affect your loved ones. I couldn't bear it if anything happened to you, Krissy, or Steven, or to Mrs. Herrero, for that matter."

"I know. But we'll be alright."

"I wish I could be certain of that. Two men were following me this morning. I saw them watching me from a maroon sedan on three different occasions. They had no interest in hiding it from me, either. I'm sure they're the ones who broke into our home. They're probably the same men who beat up on Mrs. Herrero."

After their talk, and after they called Krissy and Steven back out from their bedroom cleaning duties, they all had a quiet Friday evening together. Shortly after Mrs. Herrero heard Grady release the children from their sequester, she emerged from her room to join the family. Grady felt for her, because she seemed so lonely, and it was obvious she felt out of place.

He ordered two large pizzas to be delivered, and when they arrived, they all sat around the TV eating away. They watched a nature show about elephants, and when that was over, Mrs. Herrero and the children continued to watch more TV. Emily removed herself to a large soft bean chair on the floor where she curled her legs up beneath her and read a novel she had picked up at the library.

After about an hour of lounging in the living room, Grady announced, "I think the train is just about to leave for the ice-cream parlor. All aboard." After a few "Yippees" and "Yays" from the children, joined in by Emily and Mrs. Herrero, Grady made good his earlier promise to Krissy and Steven, and off they went.

Upon their return, and after everyone settled in again, Grady made some excuse to go out into the garage—said he had some tinkering to do. What he really was doing was sanding a plywood Santa Claus he was making for the front door for next Christmas. He was trying to keep it a secret, and so far, he had been able to, but now the Santa figure was cut out and was taking on more of a Santa Claus form, he knew that if anyone walked in on him while he was working on it, the secret would be out. He didn't mind, though. He had begun to make it into a kind of a game he was playing with himself to see just how far along on the project he could get before he was discovered.

When he was finished working on it for the night, he tucked it away behind a large ceiling-high wooden casement of storage shelves which housed paints, tools, and a whole host of other odds and ends Grady thought he might be able use at some time in the future. In it, he had stored parts from an old non-working mower he had cannibalized before throwing it out. He had parts and belts from a washing machine that had quit working that might be of use in a newer machine of the same make he had bought just recently. He had electrical switches he had taken from various devices, and lots of wire. Grady liked to tinker and repair things whenever he had time, and he was quite good at Jerry-rigging things when they broke down.

It was a bit of a mess around the storage-shelf casement, with lawn tools, a weed-trimmer, a shovel and a sledge hammer resting against its end. Dust and spider webs were always trying to take over the entire thing. Wolf spiders especially loved it. Every couple of months, Grady would make an attempt to clean it all up, and he would clear the spider webs with a broom. Inevitably a spider or two would run off behind the casement. He had made a pact with the spiders and bugs that as long as they stayed hidden, he would let them live, but if they showed up in the house, they were certain gonners. He didn't like using pesticides, but he wasn't above breaking out the spray can, if a wolf spider the size of a tennis ball showed up in one of the bathrooms, which they did on rare occasion when they found a way to sneak into the house.

Grady had wanted to be by himself with his project for a little while, because he was feeling worried, and he didn't want his children seeing the trouble on his face. He had needed some time to be alone to think things through.

He then returned to the paper, because it was print night, and there was much to do in the final hours to make that happen. The paper was printed and was loaded on the delivery vehicles nearly on time, and Grady went home to get some much needed catch-up sleep.

The family spent Saturday mostly at home. Grady mowed the front and back yards. It was wintertime, and he hadn't had to mow the lawns for over a month. He needed to stay busy, though, and it was a good excuse. There was also plenty of work that had to be done for the newspaper, but he stayed home and did it on the computer.

In the afternoon, Grady suggested they all go out to the Tomlin Dunes park, which had a beautiful, two mile boardwalk that wound its way through a naturally preserved area of sand dunes. It stretched all the way to the beach, and during warmer weather, you could see many tortoises, birds, an occasional snake, and other wildlife all along the way. Grady wanted to leave the house, in fact viewed the act of doing so as something akin to a test of his will. He wanted to do something to say to himself, and to Emily, that *we are going to continue on with our lives.* If the two thugs wanted to return, let them. There wasn't anything to find.

Grady was working on a strategy in his mind to maybe use Jaimansen's henchmen to retrieve more information about what Linda Herrero had been onto. He wasn't sure how he was going to go about it yet, but a plan was beginning to form. The first shades of it involved something like planting fake evidence for them to find, and using some kind of recording device to hear the reaction from them when they were conveniently led to it by Grady, a plan that seemed so ridiculous and futile on its face that Grady kept searching in his thoughts for something more realistic. Even a ridiculous plan, though, was a hope, and it was an act of strength, a movement in the right direction. It was a small way of beginning to fight back. He couldn't just sit on his hands and do nothing. With Emily's moral support, he had become determined to dig and dig until he got at the root of the Marcy Appleton, Linda

Herrero, and Francis Jaimansen story. There was something very big there, and he couldn't walk away from it.

They returned home from the park, and Grady did a quick search of the house but found nothing at all out of place. The evening passed without incident, and he started feeling a little more secure. Maybe it would all blow over, Jaimansen's men would give up, and Jaimansen himself would begin to feel safe in the knowledge that Grady had found nothing. As long as he didn't feel threatened by anything, perhaps the man would just lose interest in intimidating Grady. These thoughts did not, however, form without him noticing the denial and contradictions they contained within them.

Sunday morning came, and with it also came Emily's usual breakfast of waffles, orange juice, and strips of a delicious non-meat, vegetable protein bacon she had found in the supermarket two years ago. Though the Ables were not vegetarians, Emily was nonetheless very health-conscious, and she was trying to cut back on the amount of saturated fat and cholesterol in her family's diet, as were half of the mothers in the country. Grady loved those breakfasts, and so did the children. In fact, Grady had invited me over on several occasions to share in them, this after first telling me how fun they were once during a round of golf in our Tuesday Summer League. We had played together as a team in that league for the past five years. We weren't much good, but we did have a lot of fun together.

I knew Grady loved those Sunday breakfasts, not because the food was more delicious than other breakfasts served, even though it was in his mind, but because it was a time when the whole family got together in a relaxed way and shared a common experience. It had become an Able family tradition, and it was not easily abrogated, not unless very serious circumstances rose up to get in the way.

That Sunday morning, after filling their tummies, they all moved into the living room, as was also a kind of tradition, where they lounged for quite some time. As usual, each member of the family settled into their own preferred Sunday morning living-room activity. Even though they weren't still sitting around a common breakfast table now, they were all still gathered in the same room and were talking and laughing together. And no one ever thought of putting the TV on during that time.

Normally, as was also part of the Able Sunday morning tradition, this went on for about an hour, and then gradually everyone drifted out of the living room and onto other Sunday activities. Usually Emily took Krissy to church. Steven had refused to go when Emily first thought he was old enough to ask, and it wasn't her parental style to force her children to participate in such an activity, if they really didn't want to. On some Saturdays or Sundays, there was a family trip or event planned.

Weekends, and especially Sunday mornings, were a time when they all bonded as a family, and Grady and Emily refused to let that time go by the wayside. The children loved it, too. I saw this during the several times Grady had invited me. Despite this, Grady was always saying to me in a doubtful voice, "They're growing so fast. It won't be long before they'll think it's too gorky to hang around with the goofy parents anymore, at least if it requires being around us for more than a minute or two at a time. Gotta enjoy it all while it lasts."

Steven was playing with his handheld computer game, but he seemed capable of concentrating on the game and on the conversation, too. Whenever something of interest to him came up, he threw in a comment of his own, like when his mother began talking about how the city was preparing to re-pave their street, Steven said, "Yeah, I saw the yellow and white marks on the street down by Billy's house. He says it's to mark the pipes and stuff underneath."

Mrs. Herrero chimed in to say, "I saw a big paving machine on one of the side streets on Friday while we were driving to the market."

"Yeah, and they're real big," Steven said. "I saw one, too, when I was riding my bike."

"You didn't see one," Krissy said. She was sitting on the couch, reading a children's book. "You're just saying that. You don't know what you saw, you little bug. You probably saw a dump truck or a bus or something stupid like that."

"It wasn't those. It was a paving thing," Steven insisted.

"Alright, Krissy," Emily said. "You don't have to be mean to your brother. And don't call him a bug."

"But he's always wanting to tell everyone that he knows something, when he doesn't."

"Well, Honey, you were the same way when you were his age, so try going a little easy on him, okay?" Emily pleaded with a look and a smile that put Krissy's legs into a barely perceptible bouncing motion on the couch as they dangled over the edge of the cushions. Emily looked back at the A-section of the Sunday Emberly Times and continued to smile inwardly at her children and their infighting.

"Well, it'll be nice to not have to maneuver around all those potholes in the street," Grady said as he worked his way through the sports section of the paper. "I thought I destroyed the entire front end on the car last week, when I was forced by an oncoming truck to drive right into one of those god-awful things," he added.

Steven giggled in response to this, as if the image of his dad driving into a big pothole was the funniest thing in the world.

"It seems like they've repaved every other street in the town now, except ours, so it's about time," Grady continued.

When Emily was done with the main section, Grady would take it over and begin scouring it in detail, but for now, he was onto reading about the Saturday night game between the Boston Celtics and the Philadelphia 76ers. The Celtics had lost by four points, breaking an eight game winning streak. Grady had remained a Celtics and Red Sox fan after leaving the Boston area, and of course he continued to get a lot of crap from some of his friends about it. Grady had just started absorbing the stats for the game, when Emily said with some concern, "Take a look at this." She handed the main section of the paper to Grady, which she had folded over to page six. She pointed to an article called, "Senator's Aide Dies."

Grady read the article quickly and his stomach tightened. It said that last Saturday night, State Senator Sarcost's assistant,

Perry Jacobs, died in an automobile accident. The police did not officially offer a statement as to the cause of the accident, but they did say there was a suspicious nature to it that was being investigated. "The officer in charge would not elaborate," the article said. "Mr. Jacobs was in Carpoli, in Soutwestern Newmont, at the time of the accident, where he resides for most of the year."

Grady looked at Emily, and that same frown of worry had returned to his face that she had seen Friday afternoon after the break-in. "I'm going into the office. I've got some things to do," he said abruptly, and he got up to leave.

He grabbed his jacket from the hallway closet, as it was a cold and windy day. The front had passed through, leaving bright sunshine, freezing nights, and blustery days in Central Newmont. It had gotten down to thirty-one degrees in Tomlin Dunes the previous night, and in the northern part of the state, they had reported a low of twenty-four. It was much like the cold front that had passed through the night of Marcy Appleton's death. Grady thought about the manaseals and how they would all be gathered in the spring run at Warm Springs County Park, just like they had that fateful morning.

He had learned quite a bit about manaseals during the past couple of weeks, much more than he had known previously. He learned that they did poorly in waters with a temperature below 64 degrees, and during cold spells such as this one, most inland waterways in Northern and Central Newmont did drop below that level. The manaseals had no choice but to swim into warmer waters, such as the waters of Warm Springs, which stayed at 71 degrees year round. There was little food in the spring for them to eat, and so they had to hope the waters in the river warmed up enough so they could venture out into it and fill their hungry bellies with water hyacinth, sea grasses, and other delectable vegetation to their liking.

On his way to the Sands, Grady thought of the manaseals, and he thought of Marcy Appleton, and how her body had looked on that morning, and he thought about Linda Herrero and her mother, and he thought about the manaseals again, peaceful, gentle, always curious, and always in danger in their own home. And he thought about his own home and his family and the danger that had befallen them. And then he thought about Francis Jaimansen. His anger rose.

At the paper, he opened up his office and sat in his well-worn swivel chair and stared out the window. He wasn't even sure why he had come in. When he heard about Sarcost's assistant's death, he knew he had to get out of the house. His worry and fear were threatening to explode on his face, and his children were certainly going to notice. And now, he sat, having no idea why he was there. He absentmindedly spun himself back and forth with his feet. Each spin took him part way around and was then stopped as a foot came up against the leg of the desk in one direction, and a push-off sent the chair turning swiftly in the reverse direction, and then the other foot came against the other leg of the desk, and he gave himself another push-off. His thoughts were spinning confusedly and listlessly in keeping with the movement of the chair. He felt like a child, spinning there back and forth, as he did sometimes, when he became bogged down in his work. Now he was bogged down with this turn in his life. He wondered if he had the stuff to be a real newsman, like his father had been—to get the story, no matter the cost, and to tell that story, because it needed to be told. Or was he too willing to waffle, and too willing to be frightened away from a story when it brought possible danger his way.

He couldn't risk his family. He wouldn't. But Jaimansen and his thugs didn't care about any of that, and so the decision to move on, or not, had been taken from him. There was nothing he could do. He had nothing to bargain with, nothing real, at least. He had nothing, but the trouble he had stirred up in digging into Linda Herrero's death. And there was Mrs. Herrero. She would never be safe, as long as Jaimansen thought she knew something or might have access to something that could harm him or the power he clung to. The chair spun to the left— *I have nothing*, Grady thought. It spun back to the right— *Nothing at all*. Then back to the left—*That's what I have.*

CHAPTER 18
《 》

Some waters are safer than others . . .

It had been three rough days of worry and uncertainty for Grady, and he was having difficulty concentrating on his work. He had to look over the advertising layouts for the week, making sure that all the allocated spaces were properly filled. He also had to work on his weekly editorial and choose an opinion from one of the five syndicated columnists he used frequently, and he had to choose from one of the three political cartoonists he also used. He decided to go with the Freeley Sanders column and the Kip Hartell cartoon. The Sanders column was about the growing social security crisis, and how the president and the politicians continued to ignore the enormous problem, and that was sure to bankrupt the program at some point if intelligent action wasn't taken fairly soon, action to stem the tide of red ink that was sure to develop, and to stop Congress from raiding funds that were supposed to be earmarked only for social security.

Hartell's political cartoon showed a very fat cat pawing a strand of yarn from a ball and unraveling it. The cat's face, large ears and all, was a caricature of the president, and the yarn of ball was labeled "programs for the people." Grady had just finished downloading the image file of the cartoon from Mr. Hartell's site, a service Grady paid for on a per use basis. He had just begun copying and pasting it into the desktop publishing program he used to do the layout and typesetting for his paper, when his cell phone rang.

"May I speak with Mr. Able?" The man asked.

"You are speaking with him. How can I help you?"

"This is Bob Stevens, State's Attorney General. There's an issue of some importance I would like to speak to you about. Do you have a few minutes of free time now, or would you prefer I call at another time?"

Grady had heard the attorney general speak several times before, back when he was covering his campaign two years ago, and it sure sounded like the man. He couldn't be certain, but in that moment, he decided it really didn't matter if it was him or not, for if he did turn out to be an imposter working for Jaimansen, then Grady would just have to see where it led. The call had stunned him momentarily, but he quickly recovered. He was determined to not let paranoia take him over.

"Oh . . . Hello, General Stevens," he responded. "No, no, now is fine. What's on your mind."

"I'm afraid it's a serious matter, and I'm sorry to trouble you with it. I'm heading up a task force, at the direction of the governor, to investigate a suspicion of widespread corruption that may be going on in Newmont state government. Why am I calling you? Well, we have received word from someone who must remain anonymous for the time being, that you are working on a story about the death of a Linda Herrero and that you may have discovered some evidence that would be helpful to our investigation. Is that true?"

"Yes, it is true that I'm working on a story about Mrs. Herrero," Grady said. "But unfortunately, I doubt I can be of much help to your investigation, because frankly I have no substantive evidence per say. I must tell you that I have run into one roadblock after another in that regard and have come up empty-handed, so far." Grady approached this conversation with great caution, because he wasn't sure where it was going.

"I know," Stevens said. "We know quite a bit about Francis Jaimansen and what he's been up to. However, until we have completed our investigation and have filed indictments, should any be called for, there's not much I can speak to you about.

Have you received any threats from Mr. Jaimansen, or from anyone under his employ, so to speak?"

Grady thought for a moment, not sure how wise it was to say too much about the disturbing things that had been going on, but then following raw instinct, he blurted out, "I'm being followed, and I think my home was broken into last Friday. Two men also forced their way into the home of Linda Herrero's mother and questioned her in a rough fashion and then rampaged through her apartment in Waterside a couple of weeks ago. She was terrified, and so I brought her back here to stay with me and my wife for awhile. She doesn't want to involve the police. Apparently, somebody really wants to find what Linda claims she had in her possession."

"Yes, I know. We have been monitoring Jaimansen for several months, ever since we received an anonymous call from someone who gave us enough plausible information to warrant our attention. I can't go into any details, but the information was substantial, and when we began to look into the circumstances surrounding Linda Herrero's death, we began to worry very much that it had been something other than a suicide."

"Well, I have to tell you, It's a relief to me to know that you are investigating it," Grady said, and he truly did feel a load lift from him. Someone else knew what was going on, someone with the power and resources to do something about it, and he was now convinced that the man was truly the state's attorney general. "I thought I was in this thing all by myself. If I can help in any way, I will," he said.

"Thank you, Mr. Able. That is much appreciated, and that is what I called to ask you. The governor wants me to assure you that if you feel you need any kind of protection, it will be provided for you and your family at no expense to you. You only have to say the word."

Grady hesitated for a moment, and then said, "I think we'll be alright for now, but I will definitely let you know if things take a turn for the worse. I think Jaimansen, or someone, believes I've found something that implicates him in some nasty business, but the truth is, I haven't found a thing. I'm hoping his two men will give up soon and realize that I have nothing."

"I wouldn't put much stock in that," the attorney general said. "I'm afraid they will stop at nothing to get what they want, or to intimidate you into staying quiet. Jaimansen is a very powerful man, as I'm sure you're aware. As I said, I can't tell you much right now, but I can say, you should be very careful. And please, consider the governor's offer of police protection. It can be provided round the clock for as long as it is needed."

"Thank you, but I don't want to frighten my family to death, not unless it becomes absolutely necessary. I also don't want to make it look like I do have something I'm hiding. It will only make the person seeking it more determined to get it from me. I don't even know exactly what Jaimansen has done, if anything. And really, you know as well as I do, there is no way that you can protect my family and me. If a man like Jaimansen wants to do us harm, there's no way you can stop him."

Two things were occurring simultaneously inside of Grady. He felt a certain sense of relief, because he was happy to know the attorney general was onto Jaimansen, but at the same time, it made him worry all the more about the serious nature of it all. He had the feeling that he was being drawn further and further into a story that was ratcheting up out of control.

"We may have to get the FBI involved soon," Attorney General Stevens said. "I'll let you know if we get to that stage. In any case, the main reason I called was to tell you that the governor has expressed an interest in meeting with you personally to give you his personal assurance that he will do everything in his power to protect you and your family. Tomorrow, if at all possible. He thought it might put your mind at ease. He's going to be in Creighton Beach honoring the "Teacher of the Year" at the Oceantides High School. Would you have time to meet with him at around 1:30 p.m.?"

Grady tightened further. A meeting with the governor? He certainly didn't want that. It only made the problem seem bigger. It already seemed big enough, and so unreal, with people dying, thugs following him, and with his house having been broken into. But he knew he couldn't very well refuse the governor's request."

"That would be fine," he said. "Thank you. Where will we be meeting?"

"I'll have my assistant get back to you with that information. Okay, well I've got to run, now. I have a meeting in five minutes, so you take care of yourself, and I'll be in touch soon."

"Thank you," Grady said.

At nine the next morning, Grady received a call from the attorney general's assistant telling Grady where and when he was to meet the governor. As he drove the thirty miles to the location, he was feeling very nervous about everything, and he couldn't see how it was going to help him with Jaimansen's strong-arm tactics. And though he did his best to make sure he lost the two henchmen before he went to 127 East Lynchester Street in Creighton Beach, there was no way he could ever be certain that Jaimansen didn't have more people on the hire to follow him everywhere he went. If the man found out he was meeting with the governor, he might feel compelled to take more drastic measures against Grady.

The address for the meeting was an office building owned by Joseph Kriel, a prominent Creighton Beach businessman and one of Governor Winde's strongest political supporters in Timpkin County. Grady had been there once, two years ago, when he was doing a story on the governor's election campaign. He remembered the building had served as Governor Winde's campaign headquarters for the county then. It was located one block from the Delancey River on a beautiful tree-lined street.

Upon entering, Grady announced himself at the receptionist's desk, and she told him that the governor was expecting him in room 301. Grady took the elevator to the third floor and found the room. The door was closed. He thought he should knock, and as soon as he did, the door was swung open by a grim-faced young man in a blue suit. After ushering Grady into a very spacious law office, the man immediately moved over by the adjacent wall and stood quietly by. Governor

Winde was seated at the end of a long, polished, mahogany table and was talking to an aide, a man in his mid-thirties, who was seated next to the governor. There was another young man standing on the other side of the room, directly opposite the man who had let Grady in. Both of these men now had their arms folded behind their backs and looked very much the way Grady expected security agents to look.

After a few seconds of further talk to his aide, the governor finally glanced up at Grady and smiled. He was an exceptionally tall, gangly man, only a few inches shy of seven feet, and only thirty-eight years of age, in fact the youngest Newmont governor in history, and he presented a striking, unusual figure, even when seated.

"Come in, please, Mr. Able," the governor said. "Please have a seat, if you don't mind." His voice was deep and resonating, and it had a calming effect on Grady. The man definitely had a winning charisma. Grady could see why he was a difficult man to beat in a political contest. He had that certain Lincolnesque look and confident demeanor of someone who just wasn't going to lose, and in this state, that kind of demeanor went a long way. "I'm so glad you could make it," he said. "Thanks for taking time out of your busy day to see me."

"You are highly welcome, Governor," Grady responded. "It's my pleasure. I'm sure your days are a whole lot busier than mine." Grady moved over to the side of the table and sat next to the governor's assistant. It was the easiest place to take a seat without making a fuss.

"Not at all," the governor said. "I've actually had quite a relaxing morning. It's always nice to get over to this part of the state, especially when all I have to do is heap praise on a woman teacher who deserves nothing less. That's the fun part of the job."

"Yes sir."

"I guess Attorney General Stevens filled you in on the difficult task we may have in front of us. I just wanted to let you know in person that I know the mess you have walked into and that I will use all the powers of my office to keep you and your family safe. We can't very much have journalists in our state being intimidated, now can we?"

"That's much appreciated."

"I don't want to take up much of your time. Have you had lunch?"

"Yes," Grady said. "I grabbed a sandwich before I left Tomlin Dunes."

And then the governor looked straight at Grady with such a look of concern on his face that Grady didn't know what to make of it. The Governor's look lingered for a moment, and it filled Grady with trepidation. There was something in those eyes that showed a hint of fear. "We've got to stop this before it gets out of hand, you know. This is very ugly business, indeed."

"Yes, sir, it sure seems to be, doesn't it?"

The governor then looked away and out the window of the office, and as he did, he said, "I'm counting on your support in this matter, Grady, and I hope you'll be circumspect as a journalist until we can get all our facts straight. If we tip off the bad guys too soon, we won't be able to root 'em all out." He looked at Grady.

"Well, Sir, as you know, I've got to get the story out, if and when I have one. But I can promise you this much: before I print anything further on the Linda Herrero story, I will give you a heads up, and if you tell me then that it might compromise your investigation, I'll put my best judgment to work on it. You can be sure that I won't print a story that I know will kill off any chance of reaching a conclusion to that story. That's also part of my job as a journalist."

"I'm not sure exactly if you just gave me the answer I was looking for, but I will take it that we have your cooperation, as much as is possible within your journalistic ethics."

"You have my cooperation, as far as I can give it."

"All right then, let's both do our jobs, and do them well, and maybe we can accomplish something good for the people of the state of Newmont."

"That would be great," Grady said.

"Well, Mr. Able, thank you for meeting with me on such short notice. My aide has informed me that you have a busy schedule and that you have a lot to attend to. Take care of yourself, and let me know if there is anything at all I can do for you."

"Thank you again, Governor. I will do that," Grady said, standing to leave.

The meeting had lasted less than five minutes. During that time, however, Grady began to feel a little better about what he was dealing with. It was good to have the governor of the state on your side. There was a part of that, however, that also brought more fear. He was being threatened and followed by men capable of who knows what, and he was still involved in something so big that the governor had become involved in a serious way, and it all added up to only one thing—danger.

Many thoughts ran through his head as he drove back to Tomlin Dunes, and some of them were very troubling. Once again, he began going through in his mind all that he had seen in Linda's things, and he remained at a loss as to where she might have hidden her dangerous documents, and once again he became determined to go through her things one more time when he got home. There had to be something he was missing. Or maybe there wasn't. Maybe there were no clues as to where she had hidden her evidence. Maybe those clues had forever gotten lost in the panic of that final, fatal week of her life.

Grady worried that Jaimansen would discover through the many tentacles he had strung out through Newmont government and elsewhere that the governor's office was now deeply involved in his activities. Grady hated to think of the possible consequences that could result from that. He suspected that a cornered Francis Jaimansen was not a good thing at all.

CHAPTER 19
«»

Coming up to see . . .

A month had passed since Grady's meeting with the governor, and a lot had changed. He began to feel that the physical danger from Jaimansen and his henchmen had passed. Grady hadn't seen the two thugs following him during that time, and he hadn't heard anything from Attorney General Stevens about any new developments in the investigation. On the discouraging side of things, however, Jaimansen had been good to his word. He had been applying a lot of pressure on Grady through the use of his media and legislative contacts and cronies. He had the money and the power to get his message out, and it was beginning to take its toll. He had pounded away at Grady during the past two weeks, asserting that he was a loose cannon of a newsman who would print any libelous story to sell his papers.

He was attempting to define Grady. Jaimansen called him "an arm of the left-wing media machine," which was absurd on its face. But these days, you could simply make an accusation, get the mainstream media (the same media, ironically, the right kept referring to as "liberal") to repeat it, even if it was in question form, and people would begin to believe it. Jaimansen's comments and opinions were showing up in papers all over the state, especially in those that had picked up Grady's original story about Marcy Appleton and Linda

Herrero, which had contained a mention of Jaimansen in reference to the contents of one of Linda's letters.

Everything in Grady's story had been journalistically measured, factual, and true. Nonetheless, Jaimansen could make hay with it. All he had to do was to ask most editors to print his rebuttal to the article, and they did so gladly. Newspapers, and news media in general, loved contention and controversy. It sold papers. It was also the right thing to do on their part, as far as Grady was concerned, because rebuttal was an essential element of news reporting and an essential element of a free press. But Jaimansen had power and money, and his efforts went far beyond mere rebuttal and an explanation of why his name had shown up in Grady's article. Jaimansen had his attack machinery marching in full force, and he even personally showed up on a local TV talk show in the Southeast Newmont area, decrying Grady's article as pure libel. Several newspapers had contacted Grady, as did a talk show host in Sienna, asking him to do an interview. He told them that when he had anything more to say on the Linda Herrero story, he would print it in his paper.

The effects of Jaimansen's negative campaign were beginning to be felt. Circulation had dropped off enough to make paying the bills more difficult each week. He had also lost several advertising accounts. On top of that, Grady hadn't found anything at all in Linda's things to give him the slightest lead as to where she might have hidden her troubling evidence for the last time.

It was a Tuesday when Grady woke up after a night of horrible nightmares, the last of which had him chasing after an elusive news story as a reporter. In the dream, there were hundreds of other reporters on the scene, pushing and leaning in with their camera crews and microphones to get a piece of the story for their newspapers and radio and television stations. In the dream, he couldn't see or hear what was going on, and he kept calling back to the city room at the Miami News Beacon assuring them he would get the story, that he just had to get in a little closer to report on it. One of the paper's senior news editors kept calling Grady every few minutes on his cell phone, asking him if he had made any progress. With this pressure hanging over him, in the dream, Grady had worked his way into the crowd to a point where he could see a television reporter giving a live interview with someone. His nightmare didn't reveal exactly who the person was, but Grady knew he was important. He could tell by the chill it put in him. He knew he had to get closer so he could see and hear what was being said, but he could only get occasional glimpses of the reporter, and he was not able to get a single look at the person being interviewed. When he had tried to shuffle further through the crowd to get closer to the action, he failed and completely lost sight of even the TV news woman reporter doing the interview. It was as if he had shrunk in size, and the massive bodies of the people in the crowd around him simply had the power to swallow him up. He awoke at that very point, and it left him feeling feeble and vulnerable and with an unrecognizable anxiety. As he sat straight up in bed upon waking, Grady couldn't remember what the event actually was, but it had been something very important.

With the nightmare still lingering in his mind, he drove the four miles to work, sipping coffee from his well-used travel mug and feeling groggy. He had one of those headaches he knew would last much of the day, and he was also feeling a tinge of nausea. It must have been that pizza he had bought on the way home last night from a new chain that had just opened up a franchise in town. He knew better than to buy from them, especially since there was a family-owned pizza parlor in town. He much preferred supporting local merchants whenever possible. He had been in a hurry last night, though, and for the sake of convenience he had tried the corporate chain pizza. He didn't want to believe it had been the nightmare from which he had awoken that was making him feel so awful, so he blamed the pizza.

The day quickly went further downhill from there. Much to Grady's shock, when he arrived at the Sands paper, there were picketers gathered around the front door of the newspaper building. Their signs said such things as "Liberal Propaganda Lies," and "Boater's Rights Now," and "The Tomlin Sands

Newspaper is Costing us Jobs," and "Do Not Buy This Paper."
He worked his way through the protestors, through shouts of
"traitor," "environmentalist terrorist," and all other manner of
ugly and abusive comment that rose up as he passed. He did
not make eye contact with any of the protestors. He just
wanted to get inside the Sands' offices and lock the door.

Grady sat at his desk and immediately got to work on the
upcoming newspaper issue and on the editorial, in particular,
that he planned on putting in. It lambasted the "barely legal"
crony capitalism in the state that, in his view, was responsible
for what was certain to be a horrible legislative session coming
up in a couple of weeks. He wrote that citizens should be
prepared for cutting and slashing from those programs that
helped those most in need, so that windfall tax breaks could be
given to special interests, businesses, and to those that didn't
need them. He was angry, and his headache only made him
more so, but he was also feeling exhausted and worn out. He
ended his editorial by saying, "I can only hope the governor has
his veto pen at the ready to reject any horrible pieces of
legislation that might reach his desk." He thought about the
consequences of mentioning the governor, especially in the
light of current circumstances, but he had a responsibility to
his readers, and to himself.

He thought about the protesters outside. Maybe Jaimansen
had been right when he had issued his threat to Grady over a
month ago. Maybe he could squash Grady like a bug without
much effort. He certainly had made progress in that direction,
and there was little Grady could do to stop him. The only real
weapon he had at his disposal to fight back was the printed
word on the pages of his own paper. He did have a lot of
staunch supporters in the area, and he had received many
wonderful letters praising him for his stand against powerful
interests in county, district, and state government, and for his
courage in taking them on from time to time. Many of these
letters urged Grady to continue on with the good fight. Some of
the citizens in the area saw Grady as something of a local hero,
a David, fighting Goliath, in many of the battles he threw
himself into.

And there were, of course, the death threats that came in. There were always those, probably from the same people who carried protest signs speaking of "rights and freedom" and calling him an "environmental terrorist." It was so utterly ridiculous, Grady thought. And the irony of it was how easily some people could be persuaded to take a strong opinion about something, and how easily they would go out in public and be willing to spout outright lies. Grady had never been an environmentalist, never in fact, had he belonged to a single environmental organization, though he respected those that chose to dedicate themselves in that way. He knew how fundamentally un-American it was to wrongly label persons who were in those organizations as terrorists. They were actually some of the most caring and responsible people you could ever meet. Even though he wouldn't call himself an environmentalist, the ugliness that continued to always show itself on the opposite side of every environmental issue was making him think seriously about becoming more involved. Someone had to stop the takers, grabbers, and destroyers. If it wasn't going to be the environmentalists, then who? They, after all, were on the front lines of caring about such issues, and that caring always carried with it a heavy price. Grady admired them, because they went on caring anyway. The ugliness had to be discouraging, but they continued on with their courageous convictions, believing as they did that it was possible to create a better world within the American system.

The whole Jaimansen mess was beginning to take its toll on Grady, mentally and physically. He had little energy these days, and he had frequent bouts with upset stomachs, headaches, and fiery heartburn that would sometimes stop him cold in his tracks with an explosion of pain. He didn't feel like much of a hero, and he was afraid that "Goliath" was going to easily crush him in the end, and the windmills at which he was titling would grind him into monster dust.

He was just finishing up the final paragraph of the editorial, when he heard a loud knock on the front door. Emily was not in the front office. He didn't see her in Charles' office, either, so she must have gone out back to check with Doug about something. Grady went to the front door and opened it. There, standing on the steps, was a thin, bespectacled man he didn't recognize. A few protestors were still gathered on the side-walk, yelling their fury toward the man and toward the Sands' building. The man's hair was slicked back, and he had on a plain, dark blue suit. Grady asked him what he wanted, in a somewhat irritated and less than polite tone. At that point, he wished only to be left alone, and he was annoyed, in a knowingly irrational way, that someone was at the door.

"Are you Grady M. Able?" the man asked.

"Yes I am. Who are you?"

The man reached quickly inside his suit jacket and pulled out a piece of paper that could only be one thing.

"I am here to serve you with an official summons to appear in Calhoun City Court. The details of the summons are contained within. Please sign this paper, signifying that you have been duly served." The wiry man then handed Grady the summons and the paper he was to sign. He had a pen ready for Grady to use.

Grady had received one other summons, and receiving this one now made his blood run cold. It was more than he thought he could handle, emotionally and financially. He took the summons, looked at it as if it contained some horrible disease, signed the man's paper and said a barely audible, "Here," and handed it back to the man. He continued looking down at the paper, even when it was back in the man's hand, not wanting to look directly at the man's face. The process server, having accomplished his assigned job, then quickly left.

The summons was the beginning salvo in a lawsuit brought by Francis Jaimansen. Grady looked at the summons and scanning down through the header information he imme-diately saw the words "libel" and "slander." Grady knew he could most probably beat him in court, because Jaimansen had no real grounds for bringing the suit. Jaimansen was doing so only to put more pressure on Grady and to make him expend more of his precious time and money fighting the suit. He was certain that it was all a part of his strategy to force Grady to give up pursuing the story surrounding Linda Herrero's death.

Grady had little money to fight the likes of a Jaimansen and the team of lawyers he was sure to put up against him. Jaimansen was likely going to use the case to get more of his propaganda into the media. It would be disastrous for Grady and the paper. He was suddenly feeling completely alone and desperate.

CHAPTER 20
《》

I now lie bleeding. I heard it coming but couldn't get out of the way. Every breath comes hard and with great pain . . .

The end of April:

Grady was worn out and feeling depleted of spirit, and more than this, there was something gnawing away at him just beneath all conscious thought. An important, but subdued, memory was trying to surface, but it could only make it to the edge of consciousness before floundering under the burden of a mountain of stress and confusion. Grady sensed the memory was there and sensed its importance, but it was an itch he couldn't quite scratch. He let it go. What kept it subdued was his worry about everything in his life, including his family, Mrs. Herrero, his business, and his ability to maintain himself as a strong, independent human being.

He was now into the second day of the civil suit that Jaimansen had brought against him. The trial was being held at the Calhoun City Courthouse, which required Grady to put up in a hotel and be away from his business each day. It was a seven hour drive from Tomlin to Calhoun. Emily stayed at home, so she could be with the kids and so she could also help with getting out the paper.

Grady sat next to his attorney in the hardwood chair provided for him as the defendant. His jaw was set, and a grim determination was hardening in him, a determination to not be defeated in the fundamental things in life, especially by the likes of a Jaimansen. Where was the governor and the attorney general, he wondered. Where were the arrests? The trial was not going well, and Grady needed some help.

Judge Harbinkle had not dismissed the defamation suit against him, as Grady's attorney had been confident should have happened. Grady thought cynically that the judge had probably refused to give a summary judgment against the suit because it had been brought by very powerful and well-connected lawyers, hired by Francis Jaimansen, lawyers that in legal circles weren't to be taken lightly. Political consequences could ensue. From what Grady's lawyer had told him, this judge they had drawn for the case always ruled in favor of business interests, whenever it was even remotely possible within his purview to do so. It had become clear to Grady, that with almost any other judge, this case would have never seen the light of day.

Grady's attorney, Jill Franklin, was a local Calhoun woman who was very bright, very good in the courtroom, could think well on her feet, but she had no experience going up against the level of attorneys that Jaimansen had hired to try the suit. They were giving her a legal chase around with their subtle pre-trial motions, by presenting esoteric case law, and by challenging her efforts at every turn, this all aided along by the help of the judge's one-sided rulings, of course. She had no doubt that in the end, she would win, even with the case being tried in front of Judge Harbinkle, even in the state of Newmont, such as it was.

"They simply don't have a libel case—not based on anything real, legally," she had told Grady. Despite this, she also knew that Jaimansen could bleed Grady dry, drag things out, and drag him through the mud with his public relations machine, and ultimately hurt or destroy his business. As I have said, most of the citizens in Tomlin Dunes had offered their support to him during this whole ordeal, and most of them kept up their subscriptions to his paper, but not all of them. If Jaimansen could propagandize enough, using the trial to make it look like Grady was an irresponsible journalist, running an irresponsible newspaper, the support could quickly dry up, and frankly, Grady couldn't afford to lose too many more customers or advertisers. Jill and Grady both knew this, though it was never mentioned.

Jill thought the trial would last no more than a day, maybe two at the most, because there just wasn't much to try, but Jaimansen and his lawyers had already forced it along well into the second day. The Plaintiff's attorneys were still presenting their case, with the defense to follow, so the trial would last three days at least.

Jaimansen sat smugly through it all, with a hint of an arrogant grin always apparent on his face. It wasn't going well, Grady kept thinking. There had been a lot extraneous testimony from a parade of people that Jaimansen's attorneys had dug up from Calhoun and surrounding towns and counties who testified that they had come to believe that Jaimansen might be involved in scurrilous or criminal activity, and all from reading Grady's innocuous article. Jill suspected that most of the witnesses had been bribed in some way. She had deposed each of them and had interviewed family members and friends surrounding them, and though in the case of each witness, there was somebody in their circle of friends or family who owned a Jaimansen boat, or had some other indirect form of business with Jaimansen, she couldn't find anything she could plausibly use in court to attack the validity of their testimony. In fact, she knew Jaimansen's lawyers had selected people to testify who had bought from Jaimansen's company in the past because later in the trial, they would use them also to prove the damages portion of the case. To prove libel in Newmont, you had to show both that defamatory statements had been made and that damages to the plaintiff's reputation had occurred as a result.

Jill saw it all as an absurd kind of legal theater, blackmail even, and Ms. Franklin quickly objected to each such question and statement, because it was preposterous on its face. But Judge Harbinkle had allowed Jaimansen's attorney full latitude, and so the trial dragged on.

The questioning of each witness had gone something like it had with the first witness Jaimansen's lead attorney, Robert Memphard, had called to the stand to testify. She was a Calhoun woman who had read Grady's article in her local newspaper, as the story had been picked up by many newspapers around the state.

"Mrs. Archer, I understand you read Mr. Able's news article in January of this year?" Attorney Memphard had asked the woman.

"Yes," the woman answered.

"The article was printed in your local paper?"

"Yes, I think it was picked up by one of the news wire services. They must have thought it was important."

"And did you form an opinion of Mr. Jaimansen after reading the article?"

"Objection," Jill said.

"Overruled," Judge Harbinkle said. "I think it's important to hear the reaction from a reader to the article. But I caution you Mr. Memphard, such testimony, in and of itself, does not prove libel. So be careful."

The judge said this to sound reasonable, Grady thought, but by allowing such testimony, the way it was being presented, he was prejudicing the jury.

"Yes, Your Honor," Attorney Memphard responded, also ever so reasonably.

The judge turned to the witness and said, "you can answer the question, Ma'am."

The Calhoun woman then said, "I felt like he was probably a pretty awful man, Mr. Jaimansen, that is, a dishonest man, who may have had something to do with some kind of government corruption, and he was hiding it. That was the opinion I formed from the article."

"Objection. There is no evidence, whatsoever, that the witness formed her opinion from any specific language in the article itself. She may have had an opinion, but an opinion is not evidence of anything libelous or defamatory. Your Honor, are you going to let this go on?"

"Overruled," said Judge Harbinkle. "How someone responds to words in an article, and how those words are used, can be a very complex matter. I want to hear what the witness has to say about her reaction. You'll have a chance to cross-examine the witness. My instructions to the jury will also be very clear about what they can, and cannot, consider when it comes time for them to begin their deliberations. There is a lot of case-law and precedent to guide us. But for now, I will allow the witnesses to answer this line of questioning."

Attorney Memphard continued, "Would you say that any reasonable person reading the same article would come to the same conclusion about Mr. Jaimansen's reputation?"

"Objection, Your Honor. Hearsay."

"Sustained. I told you to be careful, Mr. Memphard. That is out of bounds, and you know it."

"Yes, Your Honor," Mr. Memphard said and then turned back to his witness. "Then, let me ask it this way, Mrs. Archer. Without any evidence to the contrary, and only making your judgment based upon your own reasonable reading of Mr. Able's article, would you say that Mr. Jaimansen's reputation was harmed by what you read, at least in your eyes?"

"Yes. It made me suspicious of Mr. Jaimansen, and I think he might very well be a despicable person who may have been involved in some kind of illegal activities. That poor girl, Linda, ended up dead over it. When they tell you there is no evidence of wrong-doing, you can be assured that there probably is. They just haven't discovered it yet."

"YOUR Honor," Jill spoke up loudly. "There is NOTHING whatsoever in the article that claims that Linda Herrero's death was caused by anything related to the contents of Linda's letters. NOTHING. And there is also nothing in the article to suggest, even remotely, that Mr. Jaimansen was involved in anything illegal, or even 'despicable,' for that matter. And whether or not a person chooses to read that into the situation is purely subjective, and in this case, is little else but common speculation. There is not a single hint of accusation towards Mr. Jaimansen in Mr. Able's article, nor has the plaintiff's attorneys offered the slightest hint of any evidence that there is. And we all know why—because it just doesn't exist. On the contrary, Mr. Able cautions against any speculation about Mr. Jaimansen in the same article being discussed, which goes above and beyond the call of duty as a journalist. So, having no evidence whatsoever, lead counsel for the plaintiff is attempting to perpetrate this charade, a magic act, to create something from nothing."

"Your Honor, please," objected attorney Memphard. "The attorney for the defense is testifying now. Either that, or she is prematurely trying to give her summation, such as it is."

"Ms. Franklin, you know better," said judge Harbinkle. "You'll have time for all of that in your closing. I am, however, inclined to agree with your basic point. Nonetheless, I will allow the plaintiff to present his witnesses. I warn you again, though, Mr. Memphard, their testimony must move your case forward in some substantive way. The subjective opinions and speculations of the readers, alone, is not enough. It is a "reasonable reader" determination that must be met. On the libel part of this trial, the examination of these witnesses must provide evidence within the words of the article, itself, that they are both untruthful and damaging to the plaintiff's reputation, and done intentionally and with malice, at least in the court's eyes of what a reasonable reader would conclude. So move things along. Mr. Memphard."

"Yes, Your Honor, said attorney Memphard. "I have nothing further to ask this witness."

Jill then asked the judge for permission to approach the witness, and given that permission, she walked quickly forward. When she was standing right in front of Mrs. Archer, she tipped her glasses down on her nose so she could read the newspaper she held folded in her hands.

"I have the article here, and just so everyone is perfectly clear about what we are talking about, I will read you exactly, word for word, what it said in reference to Mr. Jaimansen and then ask you a question or two:

'A Mr. Francis Jaimansen was mentioned in a few of Linda Herrero's private communications to her friend Marcy

Appleton. Both young women are now dead, and so unfortunately, they cannot provide us with further details as to what connection, if any, existed between Mr. Jaimansen and the document they both referred to several times in a series of letters to one another. In a correspondence to her friend, Linda said, "Jaimansen is involved, and we are in danger." When I offered Mr. Jaimansen a chance to respond to this statement in the letter, he said, through his personal spokesperson, that he had no comment. This reporter tried several times to elicit a response from Mr. Jaimansen during the next few days, but none was forthcoming. That reveals nothing, however, because he has every right to not respond, and so at this point, this reporter has no way of knowing what Linda Hererro meant in her correspondence. And because of this, the reader should not jump to any conclusions from this reporting.'

"Not in any of the language Mr. Grady used in his article, is there a suggestion at all that Mr. Jaimansen has done anything wrong," Jill began, looking up at Mrs. Archer over the top of her glasses. "Only in a quote from one of Linda Herrero's letters is there a hint at a connection between Linda and Mr. Jaimansen. And that letter is a matter of fact and also a matter of possible public concern, in that Linda speaks frequently in those letters of corruption within the state government. In fact, Mr. Able ended the article with this warning, and I repeat: 'the reader should not jump to any conclusions from this reporting.' And so he made it very clear, didn't he? Mr. Able only reported the actual facts as they existed, including the quote, so I'm at a loss to see how you, Mrs. Archer, can possibly interpret that Mr. Able libeled Mr. Jaimansen, in any way. Can you please explain?"

"It's just how I read the article," said Mrs. Archer.

"Didn't you read the actual words in the article, as I just did? Or did you write your own words between the lines."

"Objection," attorney Memphard said. "Argumentative."

"Sustained," the judge said. "Restate the question, Ms. Franklin, and tone it down a bit."

"Do you think you might have been reading between the lines in your interpretation of the article?" Jill asked.

"I read the words, but I interpreted them the way I think they're meant."

"I see, so it isn't the actual words in the article, but your own way of interpreting them that gives you the impression that Mr. Jaimansen is a 'pretty awful man,' as you say.

"It's my own interpretation."

"Here's the article," Ms. Franklin said and handed a copy over to Mrs. Archer. Can you point to the particular language that made you come to your 'own interpretation?' Please take your time."

After looking at the copy for a few seconds, the witness said, "I think it's where it says the two women are dead, and Mr. Jaimansen was mentioned just before that. I think that's where I began to think the man may have had something to do with the women's deaths."

"But it doesn't say that in the article," Jill asserted. "It doesn't say that at all, does it, Mrs. Archer?"

"Not in so many words, but to me, it still says it."

"Then just how many more words would it take for it to ACTUALLY say that?" Ms. Franklin asked, her voice rising with emphasis and sarcasm.

"OBJECTION, your honor!" Mr. Memphard interjected.

"Withdrawn." Ms. Franklin said. "One last question, Mrs. Archer. Do you think Mr. Able wrote his article with malice toward Mr. Jaimansen, or was he just reporting what he had found out?"

"Objection. The witness can't possibly know whether Mr. Able wrote his article with malice or not."

"Sustained."

"Let me rephrase, then. Did you read anything in the article, or interpret anything in the article, that would make you think Mr. Able wrote his article with malice toward Mr. Jaimansen?

"Objection. Same reason."

"Not this time. I'll allow the question, since you opened the door to this by asking your witness to interpret the words of the article. You can answer, Mrs. Archer."

"No, I don't see any malice in the article."

"No further questions," Jill said. It was a definite victory and would support a big part of the defense she planned on mounting.

Counselor Memphard called nine more witnesses and pressed each to explain what it was about the language of Grady's article that made them believe that Jaimansen was a bad person and perhaps giving them the impression that he was even possibly engaged in some sort of illegal activities. Jill posed objection after objection, outraged at almost every single question Attorney Memphard asked, but Judge Harbinkle overruled her nearly every time. He did so despite what he had said about demanding that Mr. Memphard move the case forward, and he continued to allow the parade of witnesses to be brought forward. Jill cross-examined each of the nine witnesses much the same way she had with Mrs. Archer, getting each to admit there wasn't actually anything in the written words, themselves, in the article that made them feel the way they did about Mr. Jaimansen, but it was a mere reading between the lines. What she was not able to get them to admit, however, was that they didn't see malice in the words. All the rest of the witnesses answered that they did think perhaps there was some malice in the words written by Grady. There was no actual basis for these responses, but Jill suspected that the witnesses had been well-coached by the plaintiff's attorneys to hold to that line of reponse. Each was deliberately more careful after the debacle of Mrs. Archer's unhelpful answer to that question.

Grady could see the mounting discouragement on Jill's face, as he gave her an occasional glance. He sat there behind the defendant's oak table, feeling more and more helpless. He began to worry that Jill had been wrong, and that it was possible the jury would find against him because of all the seemingly damaging, though absurd, testimony of the many witnesses the judge had allowed to come forward on behalf of

Jaimansen's suit. It seemed ridiculous to him that such a lawsuit could be brought in the first place, and even more ridiculous that it could be allowed to get this far in court. He had written a clean article with every single word being true. He had always been told that the "truth was the best defense against any libel charge," but here he was, his whole livelihood and reputation as a competent journalist and newsman on the line.

Jill's tightened brow spoke volumes about what was transpiring, and what Grady thought he saw on the jurors faces during the witnesses' testimony wasn't encouraging. Because each of the witnesses were chosen because they knew someone close to them who had purchased boats from Jaimansen Crafts, they were also questioned by Mr. Memphard as to whether they would ever purchase another boat from the plaintiff. Each of them, of course, said, "No."

Grady wondered what kind of pressure, or what kind of bribery, Jaimansen had brought to bear on these people. He doubted very much that they actually felt the way they had testified about his article. It was such a farce, but a destructive one. When Jill cross-examined each one, he noticed that most of them did everything in their power to avoid looking her straight in the eye. She tried to make each of their statements seem as foolish and silly as she truly believed they were, but Grady could tell she wasn't sure she was getting through to the jury in any constructive way. People hated the press these days, and a natural sympathy resided beneath the surface for those who dared to take to task a member of that press.

Jaimansen had warned Grady that day at his mansion back in January that he would crush him if he pursued anything that might represent a threat to his "business" dealings, and Grady was finding out just what he meant. He hadn't known how powerful and devious the man could be. Even if Jill could get a guilty verdict overturned on appeal, which she continued to assure him they had plenty of grounds for doing, the damage that would accrue from such a verdict would be irrevocable, and Grady would probably find himself out of business. His newspaper was a small one, and he couldn't sustain the financial losses that would ensue to wait to get a guilty verdict overturned. It would take too long. Jill knew this, too, and that was some of the stress he saw on her face. It was ridiculous that Grady might lose this case, but here they were at risk of doing just that, mostly because of the attitude of the judge sitting on the case.

During the days leading up to the trial, Jill had asked Grady over and over if there was anything at all, any kind of hard evidence he could provide against Jaimansen, just in case they needed it. He said he had nothing, and that's precisely why he hadn't made any accusations in his article. "I've been doing this for a long time," he said to her. "And I know how not to libel or slander someone," he told her. And now the trial was winding down, and Jill was about to begin the defense, but as her only counter to all the witnesses who had testified, she was going to bring four journalism experts to testify, two professors of journalism, and two editors of major papers, each to say that the article fell well within what a journalist is expected to do, and not do—in keeping with the first Amendment. Her argument to the jury was that the words, as read by any reasonable reader did not constitute libel. However, with this judge and this jury, she wasn't sure that was enough.

There was no slander case, since Jaimansen's attorney's hadn't been able to come up with a single witness who actually heard Grady say something disparaging about Jaimansen. They attempted, through hearsay testimony from two witnesses, to insinuate that Grady had slandered the man, but even Judge Harbinkle wouldn't allow such testimony. That part of the trial had simply gone away.

Grady had been going over everything in his mind, trying to come up with something he could use from what he had seen in Linda's things, or in the facts of what had happened since that day he had seen Marcy floating dead in Warm Springs County Park, but his mind was blank. He sat there listening to witness after witness come forth, each making it sound as if he had libeled the unjustly accused Jaimansen. It was like trying to defend against an absurdity. What exactly could a reasonable reader of his article actually believe about Jaimansen? Only something in their imagination. He had nothing by which to prove the truth of that imagined guilt.

Grady's expression was sullen, and his thoughts were dry as a hot summer wind. He couldn't focus properly, and it all seemed surreal. It, in fact, seemed there was no useful outcome anywhere in sight, only searching, and agonizing, and failure.

He stared at a Mr. Armeson as he spoke of the terrible opinion he was left with after reading Grady's article. Mr. Armeson was a well dressed witness, entirely reasonable in appearance and demeanor, a perfectly good witness for the plaintiff. Grady watched, and as his confidence waned further, he began to wonder if in fact his article had been libelous, even though he knew that not a word of it had been. Mr. Armeson sure thought so, though, as did Mrs. Garlin, Mrs. Bransing, Mr. Towers . . . and on and on. Had the words he used changed meaning somehow? Did they now mean something different from what they meant when he wrote them? The trial was getting to him.

The judge finally recessed the court at about 4 p.m. that Tuesday. Grady had a brutal headache by then. He went straight to his hotel room. He didn't want to talk with anyone, not even Jill. He dropped onto the bed and rested there for the longest while. Darkness finally crept into the room. The only light now came from the large window which offered the glow of the parking lot lamps through the partially open drapes.

It was about 7:30 p.m. when a knock came on his hotel room door, and startled out of a troubled sleep, he switched on the bedside lamp. He dragged himself to the door and opened it. As if appearing straight out of Grady's nightmare, there he stood, in all his nasty glory, one Francis Jaimansen.

"Hello, Mr. Able," he said jovially. "I'm glad I caught you up." The man was alone, except for his driver, who was lurking in the darkness by Jaimansen's silver European luxury car out in the parking lot. Grady was on the first floor of the inexpensive hotel he was staying at on the outskirts of town.

Every muscle in Grady's body tightened. What could Jaimansen possibly want at this late hour? Grady was exhausted and out of the energy required to deal with any new wrinkles in his life, especially any coming directly from this evil man who had set out to destroy him. And here he was, appearing, as if called up by Grady's own torment of thought about what the man had done to him during the past couple of months.

"What do you want, Jaimansen? Coming by to gloat about putting me and my family through hell?"

"No, not at all. On the contrary, I came by only to offer you a proposition whereby we could both walk away from all of this nastiness. I really don't want any trouble. Can I come in?"

"No, I don't think so. You can say what you have to say out there."

"All right," he said and put that cold look on Grady that he had seen when he had interviewed him. He readjusted his small body slightly and the lean angle of his cane. "I'll get right to the point. I've just recently decided to acquire a newspaper or two, and it struck me that yours might be just perfect as a starter for my purposes. It's small, and it's on the east coast of Newmont. I'd like to have a voice over there."

"What in the world are you talking about, Jaimansen?" Grady said, his patience wearing thin.

"I've done a little research, and I want to make you a fair offer for your paper. I think $700,000 would be a healthy price to pay, and I'm willing to offer you that much. I'll even keep you on the editorial staff, if you want."

"You must be completely out of your mind."

"No, I'm not. You lease the space you run your paper out of. For $700,000 you could make all your troubles go away. That's a mighty nice chunk of change."

Grady blinked his eyes, tempted for the tiniest moment to consider Jaimansen's offer. The amount was, indeed, a lot of money, and the troubles that were swamping him were indeed heavy ones. He blinked his eyes once more, and then the rage came surging forward. It was a rage that had been building for many weeks. "You think you can buy anything, don't you?" Grady said. "I don't want anything to do with your money, Jaimansen. I'm afraid I couldn't stand the stench of it long enough to get it into the bank."

"That's too bad," Jaimansen said coolly. "I knew you were the stubborn, foolish type, but I thought I'd make you the offer. It's the gentlemanly thing to do, after all. I'm sorry you're too boneheaded to know a good thing when it's offered to you, so I'll bid you good night."

"You can go to hell, Jaimansen," Grady said as the man turned toward the parking lot and began limping away on his cane. "You can go straight to hell, and I'll see your lawyers in court tomorrow."

"It's a big mistake you're making," Jaimansen said as he turned his head to call back to Grady. "But yes, indeed, you WILL see my lawyers in court tomorrow." And just like that, Jaimansen was back in his luxury sedan and gone.

It was almost dreamlike to Grady, because he couldn't believe how odd and warped his life had become. He closed the door and stood there fuming, wondering in some small dark corner of his mind whether he had just made the biggest mistake of his life, just as Jaimansen had said. He quickly dismissed the thought, though, because he knew he hadn't made a mistake at all, not because everything would turn out okay, because it probably wouldn't, but because once you sold your soul to the likes of a Jaimansen, there was no coming back from the hell in which you would find yourself. There were times when you just had to do what was right, no matter the cost.

Grady returned to the edge of the bed, where he sat, and after a few seconds, he switched off the light. All his fears and worries had thickened in his mind. And then as he sat there, slipping deeper into depression, straight out of the blue it hit him like a ton of bricks. The barking dog. Jaimansen. He heard it in the back of his mind, remembered it clear as a bell. Just two sharp barks from a small dog. The sound of it, and recognition of it, rose gradually to the front of his mind and lingered there, and he fumbled for the light switch. He remembered his meeting with Jaimansen almost two months earlier. He remembered the subdued smile on the man's face, as he told Grady he would crush him like a bug if he got in his way.

He sat up and reached over to the bedside stand and retrieved his tape recorder, which he had brought along because he thought the tape of that conversation might have something important on it that Jill could use in his defense in the trial. However, there was nothing on it that could be used in a court of law because it had been taped without Jaimansen's permission. Jill had said it would be inadmissible. He clicked on the recorder, rewound the tape to the beginning of his interview, and played the entire conversation, twice through.

Jaimansen's voice, so certain, so cold in its threatening tones, once again put a chill into Grady. And there it was, distinct as could be—Jaimansen's dog barking at Grady with complete contempt for his presence. And Grady trying to sound calm and strong and trying to stay on an even keel, even though he had failed. And now Jaimansen's threat was proving to be everything Grady had feared it might be. The man was destroying Grady's life, little by little, day by grinding day. But now Grady thought he was finally onto something, and he immediately made a call to his attorney.

"Hi, Jill. I just remembered something important. Didn't you say you thought Memphard would be finishing up tomorrow and that we would be starting our defense?"

"Yes. He has one more witness, and then it's our turn."

"There's something I want to check out before you begin tomorrow. It's probably nothing. It's just a crazy thought, but I've got to make sure it isn't something important. I feel incredibly stupid to not have thought of it until now. How could I have missed it?"

"What is it?"

Grady's mind was now racing through a lot of different thoughts and possibilities. "It could be important," he said, not really hearing Jill's question. "I know a good sound analyst— used to be with a local rock band in Tomlin Dunes—works in the recording industry now. I'll give him a call immediately. I don't know if we can get this done tonight, but we've got to try."

"That's fine, Grady. We'll do whatever you want, but first don't you think you should tell me what you're talking about. Just what is going on?"

Grady looked through the window at the glow of the parking lot lights and realized how irrational his actions must have seemed to her, and he realized that he had been in another world for a moment, a world of concentrated thought, where new possibilities were rushing through his mind, but they were not coming without confusion.

"I'm sorry, Jill. Of course I'll tell you what's going on."

The rest of the night was spent tracking down Jack Miller, the sound analyst Grady knew, and making calls, having Jill get a subpoena, faxing it to the Temple Hills 911 Emergency Department, and convincing them to allow them to immediately procure a copy of the 911 tape of Linda's call on the night she was murdered.

When Jill heard Grady's speculative theory, she was tempted to ask for a delay in the trial, but didn't dare because she wasn't sure they were chasing anything more substantive than a mirage. She decided the best strategy would be to carry on with her defense the next day and present the new evidence then, if and when it indeed turned up.

When Grady finally got in touch with Mr. Miller and made his request to use his expertise, Mr. Miller expedited things by having the Temple Hills 911 people play the tape of Linda's call over the phone, so he could make a recording of it that way. He had told Grady it didn't matter that the quality wasn't perfect. He could determine the answer to the question at hand even from a degraded tape. The frequencies and modulation of sound would not lie. If it turned out the way Grady was hoping, which was a very long shot, at the very least, it would be sufficient to slow Jaimansen down in court and to perhaps give the jury something to think about.

Jill warned Grady that his tape of his conversation with Jaimansen would not, itself, likely be allowed as evidence in the trial. On the other hand, she said, "It's not a criminal trial, and there is no specific 'fruits of the poisonous tree' principle at work in a civil case, at least not in any concrete way that would prevent Judge Harbinkle from allowing testimony from an expert witness who had drawn his conclusions from the tape. She was confident that even if she was not allowed to have Mr. Miller testify, she could use his expert knowledge as leverage in other ways in the trial, if he discovered what Grady thought he might discover.

Grady had little confidence that his tape theory might actually produce anything useful. It was a stab in the dark. Right now there was a lot of dark to stab into, but there was one thing he knew for certain, he had to make that stab. His life and his reputation as a newsman depended on it.

CHAPTER 21

My beautiful young one wiggled her way up on my back in her playful way and slid immediately off into the water. She thought it such fun, she did it again, and this time she rode up there out of the water, precariously balancing on my slippery back for several seconds. I smiled inwardly . . .

3rd day of the trial:

The morning was dark and cloudy. The air was exceptionally warm and breezy as Grady walked with Jill up the courthouse steps. There had been quite a crowd of television and print media reporters drawn to the lawsuit as the politics of the Linda Herrero story and Francis Jaimansen's involvement in it became known. It truly had become a David and Goliath story that was irresistible to the press, and they frankly didn't care one iota who won. Either way it would sell papers and boost airtime ratings.

Spring was already beginning to give way to more summer-like weather. In Newmont, like much of the southeastern states, late March and early April usually ushered in the first hints of the hot humid weather that was to come. By mid-morning, the rain was beating heavily against the courtroom windows on the west side of the building.

Attorney Memphard had finished with the last of his witnesses. The testimony was just more of the same, with each question and answer indicating that Grady's article had persuaded people to believe that Jaimansen was engaged in nefarious and illegal activities, which he was, but which Grady and Jill knew were not referred to in his article, except a mention in Linda's quote from her letter. The absurdity of it all continued right to Memphard's last question to his last witness. It was amazing what money and pressure could produce.

"The Plaintiff rests," Memphard said at last.

"Ms. Franklin, are you ready for your defense?" Judge Harbinkle asked after Mr. Memphard sat down. "And as per our conversation and the subsequent subpoena you obtained late last night, I understand that you have some new evidence you wish to present at the beginning of your defense. I warn you, though, you are on a very short leash, since I have not yet had the opportunity to examine this evidence, and it is unusual procedure, at best, this late in a trial."

"Yes, your honor, but I think it might save this court and the jury a lot of time, if you will allow it."

"Objection," said Jaimansen's attorney. "I only heard about this this morning when I arrived here at court. Your honor, if council for the defense has new evidence, then we should have been properly notified, and not in this manner that could be prejudicial to my client's case. This is wholly out of line."

"Your point is noted, but I have decided that the evidence is important enough, at least as it was described to me, that I am going to allow it to be presented. I caution the jury, however, that you must carefully weigh the validity of the evidence, as it applies to this libel suit."

"May we approach, your honor?" Memphard asked.

The judge nodded for both attorneys to come forward, and when they were both standing before him, he said, "Let's hear it, Mr. Memphard."

"If you allow this evidence to be presented without knowing what it is exactly, and without knowing for sure that it isn't just a stunt by the defense council to prejudice the jury against my client, and to somehow put unwarranted doubt into their minds, it will go against all the rules of jurisprudence. I think, at the very least, you should examine the evidence, yourself, in chambers first."

The judge stared at Memphard for a moment in thought and then looked at Jill. "I think you make a reasonable request, and I'll allow it."

Jill had been hoping she would be able to persuade the judge to allow her to present her new evidence directly, but she knew that Robert Memphard was a very skilled attorney and would do everything in his power to keep that from happening, and would likely succeed.

Judge Harbinkle then gaveled for attention. "Court is recessed for twenty minutes," he said. He then led Jill and Mr. Memphard to his court chambers, which was a large office located just down the hall from the courtroom. As directed by the judge, a court clerk wheeled the tape recorder and stand into the judge's chambers, the same that Jill had brought to the courtroom to use in her demonstration. Judge Harbinkle took a seat behind his large mahogany desk, looked at Jill and said, "Alright, what exactly do you have Ms. Franklin?"

"In a nutshell, and as I told you last night, my client remembered something that triggered him to believe that Mr. Jaimansen was present the night Linda Herrero made the 911 call the same night she died. He was pretty certain that he was onto something, but there was no way he could be 100% certain without getting an expert to check into it further. As a result of the work of a Mr. Jack Miller, a professional, and highly qualified sound analyst, we now have evidence to back up Mr. Able's theory.

"And this new evidence revolves around the 911 tape of Linda Herrero's call to the Temple Hills Emergency Dispatch?" Judge Harbinkle asked.

"Yes, that we subpoenaed last night."

"Your Honor," Mr. Memphard spoke up. "What could a 911 tape of a call placed by Linda Herrero possibly have to do with this libel and slander case?"

"Everything," Jill answered before the judge could respond.

"You'll have to be a little more forthcoming, Ms. Franklin. I think I'm beginning to agree with Mr. Memphard that it might be highly prejudicial to proceed without a more solid foundation."

"Alright," Jill said. "There was the sound of a dog barking in the background on that 911 tape, and Mr. Able believed it was the same dog he had seen and heard barking during an interview at Mr. Jaimansen's residence several weeks back. We had the sound analyst, Mr. Miller, examine the recorded call to see if the sound matched a recording Mr. Able made of the interview with Mr. Jaimansen, during which, Mr. Jaimansen's dog barked in a distinct manner a couple of times. Sure enough, the dog barks matched on both tapes, and I have Mr. Miller here ready to testify to that expert opinion. Apparently, every dog has a distinctive bark, nearly like a fingerprint in its uniqueness. I have another witness ready to testify to that fact.

"And this suggests strongly that Mr. Jaimansen's dog was present during Linda Herrero's 911 call the night she died, and certainly it is not likely the dog was there without Mr. Jaimansen. At the very least, it goes to reasonably demonstrate that there was some definite connection between Ms. Herrero and Mr. Jaimansen, or else, why would his dog be present the night she died. The jury needs to know these facts, because as part of the defense, despite the fact that there is no evidence whatsoever in Mr. Able's article of libel, I am going to assert that even if one could believe that there were statements in it that could plausibly damage Mr. Jaimansen's reputation, we can back up the veracity of every single statement. We will demonstrate that any connection between Mr. Jaimansen and Linda Herrero certainly is evidence of that veracity, especially if Mr. Jaimansen was present the night of Linda Herrero's death."

Jill was bluffing in part with this, but she knew it was a bluff with some sharp teeth and a sharp smile, and it was a bluff she was willing to press forward. She was counting on Mr. Memphard's good judgment to take strong notice of what she intended to do in the courtroom, in front of the whole world. And Mr. Memphard did react immediately to what she said to Judge Harbinkle and proceeded on an expected tact of his own.

"Your honor," he said. "This is completely out of order. Any tape Mr. Able may, or may not, have made during a conversation with Mr. Jaimansen in his private residence, is certainly not admissible as evidence, since that tape was made expressly against the wishes of my client. I know this, because in preparation for this trial, we had discussed Mr. Able's interview, and my client assured me that he had not allowed him to record their conversation."

"Again, this is not a criminal trial, and there is no such hard and fast restriction here," Jill quickly responded. "It's all within your purview, to allow it or not, Your Honor. We are not intending to present the tape itself as evidence. We are going to put forth Mr. Miller's expert testimony about the comparison he made between the two tapes. That testimony will show that there is reason to believe that Mr. Jaimansen had a whole lot more to do with Linda Herrero than he is admitting. And the fact that there is every chance Mr. Jaimansen was indeed present the night Linda Herrero died, is one that will not escape the attention of the police, I'm sure. The court might even see fit to honor a request by the defense to have a tape made of the actual dog in question, in which case, the taped conversation Mr. Able made of his interview with Mr. Jaimansen will not be needed."

Jill knew this would have an effect on any bias the judge might have previously held, because if the tape indeed did reveal that Mr. Jaimansen was present in Linda's apartment the night she died, then Judge Harbinkle would want nothing further to do with aiding him. The implications were clear, and murder was nothing the judge would be willing to fool around with. It could cost him his career.

"This is preposterous," Attorney Memphard said. "Mr. Able's council is now resorting to threats. Your Honor, I beg you not to let her get away with such malfeasance."

"Oh, well Mr. Memphard, I would suggest that begging me is not the way to go at this juncture. It's sounds like the testimony Ms. Franklin wishes to present is evidence the court should have a chance to hear, and after hearing it, I will then decide where to go with it from there. However, as I said earlier, I will not allow any shenanigans by Ms. Franklin in presenting her witness. And if you wish to rebut the testimony with your own expert witness or witnesses, I will certainly make sure that you have every opportunity to do so. I may also allow the defense to get an official recording of the dog's actual bark. I haven't decided yet."

The look on Mr. Memphard's face suddenly hardened. The coolness in his eyes, however, did not waiver. His mind was clicking away as efficiently and reliably as an adding machine. "In that case," he said. "I would like a few minutes to consult with my client and then to possibly meet with the defendant's attorney, if she is willing." Attorney Memphard looked at the judge and then at Jill.

Both Judge Harbinkle and Jill knew what that look meant.

"Certainly," the judge said. "If you can bring closure to this whole thing, I think that might be a good thing for all concerned at this point, at least as far as this trial is concerned."

Upon leaving the judge's chambers, Mr. Memphard went quickly over to Francis Jaimansen, who was sitting with two of Mr. Memphard's assistant trial lawyers on a bench just outside the courtroom. Grady was in the hallway, and he watched Mr. Memphard as he spoke to his client. Jill was just coming over to where Grady was standing. Very few words were exchanged between Mr. Memphard and Jaimansen, and within only a few seconds, Mr. Memphard approached Grady and Jill.

"Okay. Let's see if we can work something out," he said.

"Let's do that," Jill said.

Attorney Memphard escorted Ms. Franklin to a vacant room adjacent to the judge's chambers, and once inside, and with the door securely closed, he said, "To avoid embarrassing my client with this absurd defense theory of yours, I'm offering to dismiss the suit and to pay all legal costs for the trial. You've won. The judge is obviously going to allow you to present that testimony, good or bad, solid or not, and it will be very prejudicial to the jury and damaging to my client, even if it is blatantly false in its implications. I have spoken with Mr. Jaimansen, and he has agreed to end this thing here and now. Do we have a deal?"

Jill looked unflinchingly at Mr. Memphard for a second, just to make him sweat a little. She thought she deserved at least that much. She then said, "Yes, I think so. I'll talk to my client and get back to you in fifteen minutes. I think it would be wise to ask the judge for a longer recess to attend to this business."

"I agree."

They were back in Judge Harbinkle's chambers within minutes, telling him what they had discussed. The judge agreed to recess the court until 2:30, so they could finalize their settlement.

Jill went to find Grady to tell him the good news, that the trial was likely over, that is, if he agreed to Mr. Memphard's offer. But to Jill's dismay and utter surprise, Grady exploded angrily, "You've got to be kidding, after what that man has put me and my family through. No way in hell I'll let that SOB off that easy. I want him exposed for the murdering bastard he is. People like Jaimansen are always getting away with every manner of crime without suffering any consequences—only because they've got so much goddamned money they can grease their way around anything. That's what they're good at, making money and bringing destruction to everyone and everything around them. I want that tape evidence presented."

"Well, you certainly could do that, and it is your right to do so," Jill said calmly. "But frankly I don't think it would be worth it. Think it through carefully. In my opinion, you need to settle this trial and be done with it. The police will investigate the tapes, and as far as getting the truth out to the people, well there's always the independent press for that, right?" She smiled at Grady. "Right?" she asked again. He smiled back wanly. "And this time," Jill added. "There's one thing you can be sure of, there won't be any further libel suits being brought by Mr. Jaimansen, not after the facts are out about that 911 tape."

"I guess you're right," Grady said sheepishly. "I guess I just wanted my pound of flesh for what Jaimansen has put me through, and for all the damage he has brought to others. Who knows how many other people he has ruined, or even had killed."

As her legal training compelled her to do, Jill wanted to caution Grady that there wasn't absolute evidence that Jaimansen had killed anyone, notwithstanding the 911 tape, and that it wouldn't be wise to go around saying such a thing prematurely. But she said nothing to him. She knew Grady needed to feel the way he did right then, and that all her legalistic advice could wait. She also knew he was a good journalist and wouldn't be saying anything in public without solid evidence to back it up. So she just looked at him and smiled warmly.

She rushed off to meet with Memphard, and they agreed that the trial should end. Shortly thereafter, at 2:30 that afternoon, the judge convened court and officially declared the suit had been settled. The press attending the trial went into a frenzy of questions for both attorneys outside on the front steps of the courthouse. Attorneys for both sides had no comment at this time other than to say that the libel and slander suit had been dropped by Jaimansen.

Grady couldn't believe it was over. It had ended so suddenly and had left him so unfulfilled, with no real judgment in his favor to remove all the false implications of guilt he had carried around with him for weeks, and as a result, it would still leave a cloud over his reputation, until the facts came out. But at least he could get back to work and begin putting the pieces of his life back together, maybe begin to slowly repair the damage that had been done.

One thing was certain, in the coming days, there would be a rising maelstrom over the tapes. Jaimansen was going to have his hands full for quite some time to come, but Grady worried that the man, with all his power and connections, would find some way to extract himself from trouble. Nobody had ever laid a glove on him before. The Linda Herrero and Marcy Appleton story wasn't over. He knew that much.

CHAPTER 22
《》

I saw them gathered. They were watching me, and I was watching them. They seemed friendly. I swam over to get a better look. There is something in me that tells me I should be cautious, but my curiosity sometimes gets the better of me...

By the time Grady got back to his hotel room, it was 4 p.m., and he was ready to pack up, get in his car, and make the long drive back home. He so wanted to see Emily and the children. He was in a hurry as he gathered all his things and packed up to leave. The feeling of anticipation of returning to Tomlin Dunes was building in him. He was very tired, and he was still on edge about the outcome of the trial, but all in all, he was in a pretty good mood. It was beginning to rain again as he hauled his sports bag, his laptop, and a briefcase full of papers he had brought for the trial to his car. He returned to his hotel room to make sure he hadn't left anything behind and to leave a tip on the dresser for the chambermaid. As he was taking one last look in the bathroom, his cell phone rang.

"Hello," he said in a light and cheery voice, half-expecting it to be Emily.

"May I speak with Mr. Grady Able, please?" a man said in a deep southern voice.

"Speaking," Grady said.

"Hi, this is Roland Grebes. I don't know if you remember me."

"Sure, I thought I recognized your voice," Grady said. "Of Anders, Grebes, and Williams law firm, right?"

"Yes, that's right."

"So what can I do for you, Mr. Grebes?"

"I really don't know how to begin. The more I thought about Linda Herrero and her death, after I talked with you last, the more I felt I had to set some things right. It might be too late, but if you are still interested, I have some information about Linda I thought you should have."

"It's never too late to do the right thing, Mr. Grebes," Grady said. "I'm glad you called." Grady was instantly suspicious of the man's sudden impulse to "set some things right." He suspected it was likely only motivated by the news of how Grady's libel trial ended. To be sure, plenty of rumors would have quickly circulated about the dog barks in the 911 call and the possible mysterious implicating connection it had to Francis Jaimansen.

"Yeah. Well, here it is. I understand that you have been trying to get hold of a certain document that Linda had claimed to have in her possession before she passed. Well . . ." Grebes paused for a moment, perhaps waiting for some response from Grady, and after not receiving one, he continued, "I think I know where she may have hidden it."

"How's that?" Grady asked, somewhat leery of anything the man had to say. He remembered his earlier visit to Mr. Grebes' law offices. He cautioned himself, though, not to let his indignation, suspicion, and cynicism get in the way of getting the answer to the one question he hadn't been able to flesh out from the beginning about this story. Any lead at all now would be welcome.

"Linda came to me about three weeks before she died and asked for my advice," Grebes said. "At first, I was shocked when she described the list she claimed she had in her possession. I promise you, though, she never told me specifically who was on it, and as a good and cautious attorney, I knew better than to ask. She just gave me the gist of it. I wasn't sure what to believe. It sounded quite off-the-wall to me. I advised her to hide the list and to tell no one for the time being. Then she told me she thought her life was in danger. Frankly, Mr. Able, I didn't believe her. But then when she turned up dead three weeks later, I didn't know what to believe, or what to do. I wouldn't allow myself to think the worst. I wasn't even sure there was a list. You can get yourself to believe anything when fear and panic takes a grip on you."

"So she told you where she hid the list?" Grady asked with growing impatience just beneath the surface and with a hint of it coming across in his voice. He didn't like Grebes one bit, and the more he talked with the man, the more he disliked him.

"No, not exactly. Linda came into my office a week later and told me she had hidden the list. She said she had hidden it and then moved it. She was in a very nervous state—sounded kind of crazy about it all—but she seemed to trust me, I guess because I'm in the same legal profession she was trying to get into."

Hearing this, Grady thought, *Yeah, she trusted a snake.*

"In any case," Grebes continued. "She talked quite freely about the adventure she and her friend Marcy had experienced in hiding the thing on some hiking trail in Maple Springs National Park."

Grebes went on to say, "I was very busy, and I let her chat on, but I really just wanted her to leave my office. Frankly, I didn't pay much attention to her, but I do remember something she said that morning. She made mention a couple of times of a 'Y-shaped' tree, the tree apparently she had hidden her list under. I don't think it's information that warrants going to the police with yet, because there is no official investigation surrounding it, and frankly, I don't know what is on the list, or if there is a list at all. I was hoping you might try to find it, and if indeed you think it contains any substance, you could let me know. We could then both report it to the police."

"Now that you've come clean about that bit of information, Mr. Grebes, maybe you can you tell me why you fired Linda?"

"Yes. Perhaps it is time for that, too," Grebes said without emotion. "A week before she died, I received a call from a friend of mine who has some serious connections with some very high officials in state government. He is a personal friend of Senator Sarcost. He told me if I cared anything about my career that I would have nothing further to do with Linda Herrero and that it would be wise on my part to let her go from the firm. He said that she was, and I quote, 'a no-good trouble-maker who could do a lot of damage to a lot of innocent people.' Please understand me, I didn't believe for a second, whoever those people were, that they were innocent, but I also didn't want to get mixed up in something that was none of my business. And Linda had been so paranoid, and just plain wild in her talk, full of anxiety about her list and all, that she frightened me, you know. So I decided it was best to just let her go. And then she died a week later. I know I told you that I had not received any pressure to fire her, and I'm sorry I lied to you about it when you were here, but frankly, the whole thing frightened me."

"I suppose you saw the latest news of my libel trial and how things might be unraveling for Mr. Jaimansen."

"Yes, I saw it mentioned on the local news today," Grebes said. "It's going to get real messy from here on out. That's why I thought it might be good to get a little ahead of the curve. And I guess my conscience was beginning to bother me."

"Well, Mr. Grebes, I'm glad to hear that you still have one. Thanks for the information. I'm headed home, and I promise you that I will do my best to find Linda's hidden document as soon as I can."

"All right. That's good. I'm afraid it's all going to explode into a big deal real soon."

"You can count on it," Grady said. "I'll be in touch."

Grady hung up the phone and immediately called Emily. "Hello, Sweetness," he said.

"Hello again, my successful newsman," Emily said. "Those windmills never had a chance."

Grady chuckled and then said, "Beyond the trial being over and what I told you in my previous call, I've got some exciting news, and a favor to ask. The news comes from Roland Grebes, of Anders, Grebes, and Williams, the law firm where Linda was employed before she was fired just before her death, the same law firm I visited awhile back. I just got off the phone with Mr.

Grebes. The Linda Herrero Story is starting to have all the earmarks of some serious corruption in the state government."

Grady told Emily all that Grebes had said. He then asked her if she would mind going through Linda's letters one last time. He asked her to look for one that mentions a hike she and Marcy went on in Maple Springs National Park down south. He remembered she had talked offhandedly about a Y-shaped tree in one of the letters somewhere near the middle of the stack. Emily was excited about the news and the prospect of perhaps finally being able to find Linda's document.

"I'll call you back as soon as I've gone through her letters," she said. "I'm glad the trial is over, Grady. It's had me worried, because I know you've been under terrible pressure. I can't even imagine what you've been through in that courtroom."

"It hasn't been much fun," Grady said solemnly. "Those attack-dog lawyers of Jaimansen were good, and plenty nasty."

"I know, Sweetheart. It's been awful. I can't believe this is all happening. But it doesn't matter. We have to put up a fight against people like Jaimansen. Somebody's got to. If we don't, what are we worth? You've said it many times, and I completely agree with you."

"We'll fight 'em, alright. I'm not sure where that might lead, but I am sure of one thing. I love you, and I love our children, and I love what we have together. Jaimansen can't take that away. No one can."

There was silence on Emily's end of the phone, and Grady knew she was silently crying. She finally said in a quiet, tear-filled voice, "I love you." She then hung up.

Grady had to choke back a few tears of his own. He felt he needed to be strong in situations of high stress and high demand, as men were usually taught, wrongfully or rightfully. So, his eyes became moist, and his chin tightened with emotion, but he stemmed the flow of tears after only a few brief seconds of perceived weakness. He thumbed off his cell-phone and sat on the edge of the unmade hotel bed, staring blankly into the red drapes covering the window.

Emily called back about twenty-five minutes later. Grady was already on the road by then. She excitedly told him that

she had found the letter, dated early February of last year. She
described the trail that Linda and Marcy had hiked on and how
they had joked about the Y-shaped tree. This was about nine
months before Linda had died. It became quite obvious to
Grady that for Grebes to mention that same tree in conjunction
with Linda talking about the hiding of her list, that it had to be
something. Grady was now filled with anticipation and wanted
to get home more than ever, so he could go see if there was
actually something to be found this time. If there was
something, anything substantive at all, he knew it would
change   everything,   and   he   wanted   to   move   the
Herrero/Appleton story along to some point of truth and
resolution, and he wanted to feel like the whole effort hadn't
been for naught. He wanted to just get home, too, so he could
see Emily, Krissy and Steven, and he also was worried about
how well Mrs. Herrero was holding up after all of this. He knew
she couldn't stay with them forever, nor would she want to. But
he also knew that she had to have some sense of safety and
some sense of family.

Grady arrived home around eleven that night and was
received at the door with warm hugs and smiles all around
from Emily, Krissy, Steven, and then finally from Mrs. Herrero.
The children had been allowed to stay up for this special
occasion. When Grady had received his full fill of this
outpouring of love, he returned to Emily and gave her an
especially long hug and kiss and then stood for a moment
gazing into her eyes, expressing clearly with that look all that
he felt for her. He had missed her terribly during the past week.
They hadn't been apart for that long a stretch since they were
married.

After the children had gone to bed, they sat on the living
room couch and talked quietly. Emily knew Grady was tired to
the bone, and when it got to be after midnight, she finally
suggested they both get some sleep. She knew if she didn't step
up and put a halt to the talk, Grady would stay up all night
chatting with her. He had a tendency toward the excessive
when it came to talking in the wee hours of the morning. He
had done it on several occasions in the past, usually over too

many Saturday night beers in the company of good friends who had the same tendency for never-ending laughter and conversation.

Emily and Grady slept soundly with the comfort and security of being together at last. Grady couldn't even remember having had a single dream during that night, and that was rare. He didn't get up once to relieve himself. He didn't roll over once in bed after his mind shut down and the wonderful depths of complete and restful sleep descended upon his thoroughly exhausted body and mind. He could only remember one time in his life when he felt more tired, and that was during his final tension-filled days in Chiapas, just before the Acteal Massacre there. Then, he had felt his life, and the life of those who had generously taken him in, were in constant danger. Then, sleep hadn't come for days at a time.

CHAPTER 23
《》

Have you ever seen me do a series of belly rolls? I am quite good, you know...

Grady slept like a stone until his alarm awoke him just after first light. He was facing one more busy day on his long Marcy/Linda story trek, one he was hoping would bear bountiful fruit at last. He met Nuck at 8 a.m. at his house on Edgewood Road. It was on the way, and they drove the hundred and seventy-five miles south to Maple Springs National Park located northeast of Lake Ponceover. They stopped for breakfast along the way and arrived at the park just before noon. Grady paid the fee at the park entrance, received a big warm smile from the woman at the gateway office, and drove in. After parking in the nearly full lot, they went immediately to the concessions building and rented a canoe for the day.

"I'm told there's a hiking trail going to the west off the spring run," Grady said to the attendant. "Could you tell us where that is?"

"Well, the park closed that trail a year and a half ago," the man said. "But I see no harm in telling you. Very few people know about it. It's strange you ask, though, because a couple of young women asked me a similar question about a year ago. Do you know them?"

"Yes, one of them is a friend of mine," Grady said, feeling he had no choice but to lie.

"I've walked it a couple times, and it's beautiful out there," the man offered. "You go about two miles down the spring creek, and when you see a huge oak tree that was blown over—its top has fallen into the water—you'll know you're really close. Go around the next bend and stay near the left bank. The old trailhead is all grown over now, and it's easy to miss. The Park has decided to let it grow in completely. There used to be a hike-in campsite out at the end of it, but when a young boy was lost out there and never found, the park commission decided to close the trail. It's a shame."

"Sounds like it. Thanks for your help," Grady said.

"You're not supposed to be walking that trail, or at least officially I'm not supposed to admit there are any trails. If you get caught, you didn't hear about it from me. Alright?"

"Hear what from you?" Grady said smiling. "Thanks."

It was a cool, bright, late morning by the time Grady and Nuck got under way. Beads of dew were still glimmering on many of the exposed leafs in the dense forest surrounding the spring. It took them about a half hour to get to the fallen oak tree mentioned by the park concession-man. They paddled slowly as they rounded the next bend and searched the left bank of the spring for any sign of a possible trail. They stopped at an area that looked somewhat open, but it led nowhere. They paddled another ten yards and found a heavy thicket of palmetto scrub with heavy growths of colorful lantana intruding here and there. Grady and Nuck peered in through the dense foliage and could see only more dense foliage.

"I don't believe there could be a trail in there," Grady said, and he began paddling the canoe along the bank. They searched carefully as they went along but found nothing that could possibly resemble a trailhead. Grady was beginning to think that perhaps the park concessions-man had given them bad instructions, so he continued to look along the bank all the way to the next bend.

Nuck noticed an animal trail of some sort along the way but was quickly convinced it was merely an otter run—too narrow to be a human trail, tunneling low as it did through a thicket of dense underbrush. The two men found nothing all the way past the next bend, and a look of discouragement began to take form on Grady's face. His patience with everything had worn thin. Every step he tried to make seemed to go nowhere.

Several canoes and kayaks passed them as they searched, and most of the people in them gave a canoeing-compatriot wave. Grady waved back and said a friendly "Good morning" to each. Nuck nodded his head and smiled reservedly but said nothing. Grady carefully watched each person as they moved along the spring, to make certain they went on their way without stopping somewhere to watch what he and Nuck were doing. Grady was becoming very nervous by now, perhaps even a little paranoid, worried that Jaimansen knew about Grebes' call to him and that he had set his two henchmen on Grady again. He didn't think it was likely, but he couldn't be sure. Jaimansen had to be very angry after his setback in the libel trial, and he had to be more dangerous than ever concerning Linda Herrero's hidden list, especially if it implicated him in further criminal activity and tied him more directly to Linda's death. Grady knew very well that until Jaimansen was behind bars, Grady and his family would never be safe. He looked around until the creek was clear of all people coming and going.

"Let's turn around and backtrack along the bank again," Grady said with determination.

Nuck immediately made several strong paddle strokes from the back of the canoe which turned the canoe 180 degrees in seconds. Grady helped in his clumsy fashion, but he could feel the power of Nuck's paddling was doing most of the work. A small alligator on the far side of the spring run stealthily ducked its two eyes beneath the water. An otter was swimming about in the spring waters, looking for freshwater mussels, seemingly unconcerned about the presence of any alligators, or canoeists.

Grady thought that he and Nuck must have missed the trailhead, somehow. He looked at every opening in the wild undergrowth and also looked deep into the forest all along the way, searching once again for anything that could possibly indicate that a trail might have existed at one time. They rounded the second bend in the waterway and were back at the straightaway where, according to the instructions given to them by the concessions-man, the trailhead was supposed to be located. They looked over every square inch of that section, but could find nothing.

Now thoroughly discouraged, Grady sat still, his paddle out of the water and dripping quietly. The canoe drifted under the influence of the gentle current in the spring. The water was crystalline, and at various places one could see the many boils that contributed to the waters of the stream. Grady and Nuck drifted back toward the fallen oak tree. And then suddenly Nuck noticed a pattern on the stream's bank that he hadn't seen coming the other way. It was the shade of green that caught his eye, maybe a lightness, probably revealed by the angle of the sun in that direction—he wasn't quite sure— slightly different from the rest of the surroundings. He began paddling the canoe up to that area of the bank, and Grady glanced back and saw the intent in his eyes. Nuck began searching for any recent footprints or any evidence that people had departed onto the land from their canoes, but he didn't see any. Grady began searching too. He knew Nuck was onto something. But if the trail hadn't been used in several months, the rains would have washed all such signs away.

As they came closer, Grady began to realize that the area that had caught Nuck's attention was the area of dense vegetation they had examined earlier and had dismissed because they hadn't found anything trail-like about it. He looked back at Nuck again. He knew not to say anything, because Nuck wasn't going to say a word until he was ready. Nuck began to see the pattern more clearly, and it looked to him like there was a new growth of ferns sweeping through the Palmetto shrubs, beneath their pervading dangling fronds, that showed promise.

Nuck maneuvered the canoe over against the bank, and Grady knew he intended they get out. Grady tied the canoe's rope to a branch and hoisted himself up and out onto the leaf covered ground. He held the canoe steady as Nuck swiftly made his way to the front and nimbly climbed out. Nuck immediately began walking around the heavy growth of Palmettos. He looked behind them and could now clearly see what had once been a well-defined trail. They returned to the canoe, checked for any signs of traffic in the spring, and pulled the canoe up out of the water and dragged it behind the dense foliage of the palmetto scrub. They then began following the trail. As they penetrated deeper into the woods, it showed itself more clearly.

They now walked swiftly along the trail, which in spots was overgrown quite heavily. Sometimes they had to make a detour into the woods to get around an especially dense area, or a fallen tree. Grady continued to search ahead of him, looking for the Y-tree Marcy had mentioned in her letter to Linda.

They had been walking for about a half hour when they did finally see a magnificent maple tree, standing all by itself at the top of a slight rise, and with the definite appearance of a Y formed from its two main trunks.

"That's it, Nuck," Grady said excitedly. "That's the tree Linda and Marcy had talked about."

They hurried forward toward it, and Grady's enthusiasm was beginning to build. He felt like a kid at that moment, on the verge of finding the pirate's treasure, but he cautioned himself that Linda may not have hidden her terrifying document anywhere, or if she did, there was still some likelihood that this was not the spot.

The sun was gleaming brightly through the tree branches, and the ground was light in appearance due to all the leaves that had fallen a few months ago and which reflected the sunlight. It was a golden spot and had a character that stood out from the rest of the beauty in the forest. It struck Grady as an absolutely spectacular spot.

He walked around the tree looking for a possible hiding place, but it didn't immediately reveal itself. He scraped away at the cover of leaves with a stick but found the ground to be quite hard directly under the tree, as there were large roots just beneath the soil.

At first Nuck stood a few feet back and simply observed as Grady went about his digging. Then he began walking about in wider semi-circles around the maple tree. Suddenly, he stopped when he saw an old rotten log lying on the ground behind three small maple trees. The middle of the log looked as if it had been disturbed, because the reddish brown pulpy remainder had shreds that appeared to have been placed back on the log in an unnatural way. Grady might not have noticed this immediately, but to Nuck it stood out like a sore thumb within the natural surroundings. He found a stick on the ground nearby and began digging into the soft pulpy area and deep within the hollow center of the log. To his amazement, because he was always amazed when he discovered something that was unlikely to be discovered, which he seemed to have an affinity toward doing, he found a seal-top plastic bag. He pulled it out and could see that it had been also sealed with duct tape. Inside the bag, clearly visible, were several neatly folded pieces of paper.

He looked over at Grady, who was still staring with a considerably discouraged look at the ground under the Y-tree where he had been searching. Grady then sensed Nuck was looking at him, and he turned to see his friend's eyes trained on him. When he saw the dirt-covered plastic bag dangling from Nuck's hand, Grady's heart skipped a beat and nearly stopped altogether, and then it began beating very rapidly. He rushed over to see what his friend had found. Nuck handed it to Grady, who carefully unwrapped the tape and unzipped the seal. He tried to hold it gingerly by its top corners. After wiping his dirty moist hands on his jeans, he carefully withdrew three sheets of paper contained within the bag. The first sheet was Linda's explanation of the significance of the second and third sheets and the context in which she happened to come by them. The second sheet was a list of names, with dates and money amounts, and investment instruments or deposits in banks. Grady had no idea how Sarcost's assistant, Richard Jacobs, at the urging of his brother, Perry, had come up with a list with such detail, but it was a devastating document if the precise deposits of these payments proved to be true, and Grady had no doubt they would.

It filled him with instant terror, as it seemed every new bit of added information did about this troubling story. He believed that Linda had been murdered because the list represented such an incriminating piece of verifiable evidence for every name on it. And now he held that key bit of evidence in his hands.

The money amounts were all quite large, and beside each was written a description of what the money had been paid to accomplish, or what was expected for the "contribution." Most of the people on the list were elected state officials, but at least two seemed to be people outside of government. One caught Grady's eye immediately. Next to Senator Sarcost's name was typed a date range covering much of the past year and the following:

5 deposits, totaling $75,000, Bank Merit account number 789456600, Cantover, Newmont — Kill SB 1387 (manaseal protection bill) in committee.

Grady could hardly believe his own eyes. Included in the list were the names of a few of the most influential people in the Newmont Legislature and quite large amounts of money next to each of their names. And there was one name that simply floored him and made his blood run cold. If these were political bribes, which they appeared to be, and if they could be tracked down and proven, even if only a few of them could be tracked successfully, then it would have the potential to bring down many serious heavy-weights in Newmont government, not to mention Jaimansen, himself. Now Grady began to understand why Jaimansen had been intimidating Mrs. Herrero and why he had hired thugs to follow Grady. He knew now, more than ever, that his life, and the lives of everyone closely connected to him, were in extreme danger, and that he had to act quickly. These people had to be stopped, and now.

After Nuck took several pictures of the freezer bag, the three sheets of paper, the Y-tree, and the log that had been the burial spot, the two men quickly retreated along the trail back to the canoe. As they paddled their way back to the park concessions area, Grady's thoughts were a muddle of panic and confusion. He could barely keep his mind on the canoeing, and he felt a numbness taking him over, as the enormity of their find began seeping into him in a way he knew would change his world forever—one way or another. There was no escaping it.

They returned the canoe to the rental area of the building.

"Did you find it?" the concessions-man asked Grady. The question caught him off guard with fright for a moment, as he thought he meant the list at first, but then instantly he realized how silly a thought it was.

"Oh . . . No," he lied. "No, we looked and looked but we couldn't find the trail."

"Yeah, it's pretty well grown over by now. It's not easy to spot. Like I told you, they don't want people using it anymore."

"Yeah," Grady said sheepishly. "Thanks anyway."

"No problem. I hope you had a good canoe trip, anyway."

"We did," Grady said.

On their way back to Tomlin Dunes, his mind churned, trying to come up with a reasonable course of action. For just an instant of overwhelming fear for his family, he thought maybe he should forget his "story of a lifetime" and simply hand the list over to Jaimansen. Maybe that was the safest thing to do, but his stomach tightened further as these thoughts chased about in him. And he instantly knew he would never hand the list over to a man like Jaimansen. Not in a million years. He knew he would likely just give the list to the FBI, the state police, and every other authority that might take action. Pursuing the story on his own, trying to confirm the accuracy and legitimacy of the list, would be nearly impossible under the circumstances. He couldn't take on the likes of a Jaimansen by himself. That was for sure. These other authorities, both state and federal, were equipped with the resources and manpower to investigate Jaimansen and his affairs properly, and all those on that list he had bribed down through the years. He knew very well that this was too big a scandal for a small town newspaperman to handle on his own.

By the time they arrived in Tomlin, Grady was mostly resolved to this plan of action. He knew he couldn't hold the list long in his possession. It was too dangerous, and there was no way Jaimansen's thugs would give up until they had their hands on it. He trusted no one, not even the attorney general, but saw no other way to go. A coordinated attack from all directions was necessary.

That poor young woman, Linda, he thought, having to face all that pressure of having possession of something so dangerous, and then having to die for it. It was horrible beyond belief. Grady hated the men who were pulling all the strings and manipulating the democratic system and even public opinion in Newmont solely to feed their own personal greed and ruthless ambitions. These were evil men, users of everyone who could be used, and Grady had long come to know that just about everyone was susceptible to being used. Unless a person was extremely careful as one lived one's life, he or she might fall victim to many a user. From advertising scams, to political lies, to get-rich-quick schemes, people were too easily marked for use. Those who didn't guard against it would be taken advantage of, over and over again. It was evil, and it produced even more evil—like the evil of the Jaimansen's of the world. He was a man created by people's willingness to be used, which required a willingness to throw away all of one's own personal principles, sense of morality, and reason. Every single name on that list had been used to create a greater evil in Jaimansen. Every time they accepted a bribe, or even when they took so-called legitimate campaign contributions that came with an expectation of performance from a person like Jaimansen, they were helping him grow stronger in his evil. And the stronger he became, the easier it was to bribe more people into doing his bidding. As long as people like Jaimansen could flourish within the political fabric of a state or nation, there was no democracy, at least not any worth mentioning.

Grady was not so naive as to think that this kind of thing didn't go on all the time, but he had never believed it to be so pervasive as the criminality of what Jaimansen represented in Newmont. The man had become so powerful and arrogant that he believed nothing could stop him. Grady remembered his conversation with him, and he remembered the in-your-face visit Jaimansen had made to Grady's hotel room during the trial. It sent chills down his spine again. Jaimansen would stop at nothing to get what he wanted, and Grady was convinced that the man would stop at nothing to avoid being brought down. The closer he came to that, the more dangerous he was. He had been operating pretty much out in the open, demonstrating complete confidence that there was no one who dared stop him. He worked carefully and methodically within the halls of government. He had a good instinct for sniffing out those he could make his offers of cash to—those he could use.

Grady knew that the power of money could be every bit as tyrannical as any tyrant sitting on a throne. He strongly believed the country was well on its way to being bought and sold by criminals who had been handed legal means to enact their power-grabbing schemes. And this led him to believe the country was well on its way to becoming a corporatized banana republic. In all his heart, he didn't want to believe it, but what he saw going on in Newmont made him believe it more and more.

In his own paper, he had tried to expose the lies and deceptions of politicians, so local voters might have some chance of knowing when they were being bamboozled and hoodwinked, which in Grady's experience was quite often. He had tried to chase down inequities in local business dealings, municipal contracts, hiring practices, zoning issues, and consumer dealings. He tried to cut through all the bloviating political talk and evasive nothing-speak. He had tried to dig into the guts of political and/or business policies and practices that would affect the citizens of the area in a potentially negative way. In recent months he had become more and more involved in trying to make sure people had information concerning issues that might have a deleterious long-term effect on the environment, because he saw more and more that there was very little environment left and that it was entirely vulnerable. The developers had done their best to plow it all under and pave it all over with concrete and commercial monstrosities. As long as there was money to be made, the uglification of Newmont, of the United States, and of the world, would continue, because there were always plenty of gutless, weasely, self-serving politicians to do the bidding for the powerful destroyers. There were always too many people who would allow themselves to be used—too many whores.

There was so little Grady could do about it. He felt helpless and frightened for what the future might hold in store for him, for his family, and for Mrs. Herrero. Most of the people on Jaimansen's list held powerful positions, and he didn't like the feeling of vulnerability it left in him—the feeling that a significant part of his state government was a destructive, secretive nest of ambitious and ruthlessly selfish people—an enemy within. With all the legitimate fears over terrorism, this was a fear that rose in Grady above everything else, because of what he had found in the Linda/Marcy story. With all the talk of patriotism, and with all the flag-waving that went on following the latest attack, he couldn't think of anything more unpatriotic than the corruption of the very government that was supposed to be loyal to those same principles of democracy which the flag represented. Big money was well on its way to destroying everything, and few people were doing a thing about it, because so far, that same big money had crushed most all other voices. It didn't matter how many lapel flag pins people wore, or how much they tried to wrap themselves in the flag—that proved nothing about their character—and it galled Grady that some of those same individuals had the nerve to actually accuse others—those brave enough to challenge the policies and practices of the powerful—of a lack of patriotism.

He knew it wasn't all people with power and money that were guilty of this most fundamental selfishness, but there were certainly enough of them around to destroy every last vestige of the environment, the democracy, and the constitutional principles and framework upon which the country was founded. He was angry and disillusioned, but he had it in his power to bring about some small change, and he fully intended to do just that. He just wasn't sure exactly how he was going to go about it, but an idea was piecing itself together in his mind.

CHAPTER 24
《》

Sometimes I feel like there isn't any place left to go where I might have some peace and quiet and some safety. Everywhere I go, I see those fast moving creatures disturbing the waters above, and they make a lot of noise. They also leave a nasty smell in the water after they pass . . .

It was close to six when they got back to Tomlin Dunes from their highly successful adventure in Maple Springs National Park. Grady took Nuck to his favorite seafood restaurant, The Surf, located on Hollow Bay Freeway in the northern end of town. They were both hungry, and Grady needed to keep up some pretense of normalcy, until he could figure out his next move.

When they were seated and looking at the menu, Grady looked across at Nuck's studious efforts at scanning the meals and prices, and said, "I will not be happy with you at all, if you order the least expensive item on the menu, especially after our success today. I know that's what you're looking to do. I've seen that look before," he added with a smile. "Celebrate a little, my friend."

The waiter came, and Grady ordered the Captain's platter, and Nuck ordered the "Fish of the day" dinner, which was the cheapest meal on the menu. Grady gave him a deep frown, but said nothing. He knew it was no use.

They ate and then sat at the table drinking coffee for awhile after, talking about the Boston Red Sox and their prospects for the upcoming season. Nuck enjoyed talking baseball, sparse though his discourse was. He had become a bit of a Red Sox follower because of Grady's constant, ebullient talk about the once always thwarted team. Nuck seemed to like the fact that most of the team's entire history until recently seemed to be one of struggle against a steady rain of defeat when close to the highest pinnacle of success in the sport. He liked the team's dogged determination every year, and the optimistic spirit of a fresh start they took into every new season, and he had grown to like the Boston and New England fans who put themselves on the line every year for their beloved teams.

When they had finished their dinner and left the Surf restaurant, it was already getting dark. Grady drove Nuck home, thanked him, and waited in his sand and grass driveway until his friend was in his house and his usual single, dim light was glowing in his small living room. It was only then that he drove off.

Nuck looked out the window and back up Edgewater road because he had noticed something he thought worth paying attention to. A pair of headlights appeared a couple hundred yards away as soon as Grady had gone a quarter mile down the road toward State Road 54, which was the back-way shortcut to where Grady lived in Tomlin Dunes. Nuck watched the car as it accelerated past his house. He was sure he recognized it from a description Grady had given him about it a couple of months earlier.

Grady turned left onto SR 54 and had gone about a mile when he saw the car lights in his rearview mirror. At first he thought nothing of it, until he saw how quickly they were coming up on him from behind. He was traveling 60 miles an hour, himself, and the vehicle behind must have been going well over 80. He watched it carefully as it came up right behind him. He slowed to let it pass. "Go on by, you reckless idiot," he said under his breath. He hated tail-gaiters. The car stayed close to his bumper, though. Above the harsh glare of the car's headlights, Grady could see there were two figures sitting in the front seat. Then suddenly, the car swerved out to pass and the engine roared with a surge of power. The car pulled up directly beside Grady, and the man in the passenger seat motioned him over to the side of the road with what looked like a gun. Grady knew that car well. It belonged to Jaimansen's two thugs. He wondered if they had been following Nuck and Grady all day.

"Pull the fuck over, you asshole," Tom yelled out from behind the wheel as he swerved his sedan sharply toward the side of Grady's car. Grady, of course, couldn't hear him, and even if he had heard him, he had no intention of pulling over. Joe waved the gun out the window in a menacing gesture. Tom then jerked hard on the steering wheel to his right and slammed into Grady's car. Grady tried his best to steer against the ramming force from the sedan, but despite his best efforts, he was pushed over onto the shoulder. When the front right wheel went off the road onto the damp gravel and dirt, it dug in and pulled the entire car further to the right, and he found himself without any ability to steer the car at all. He went careening completely off the road and crashed into some dense brush at the bottom of a bank.

His air bag had inflated, and he wasn't badly injured, but by the time he could get out of his seat belt and attempt to work his way out through the thicket his car was lodged in, Tom had brought the Caddy to a screeching halt just up the road, and the two men were upon Grady with their guns drawn.

Seconds after Nuck saw Jaimansen's thugs drive by in their large maroon sedan, he went quickly into the small wood frame garage attached to his house, climbed into his old rattletrap of a station wagon, and went racing noisily down the road after them. The muffler had rusted through two weeks ago, and it was thundering away in the night. He had been meaning to get it fixed but hadn't found the time.

He was hard pressed to keep up with the sedan, since his car could only manage seventy-seven miles an hour before it entered that zone where every stitch and rivet of the car was on the verge of flying off in every direction. He stayed close enough, though, to see the car turn onto SR 54, and he followed.

After going two or three miles down that mostly straight highway, two sets of taillights came into view up ahead, one just off the edge of the road and the other further down the bank, off the side of the road. He switched off his headlights, slowed the car, put it in neutral, turned the engine off to keep the noise down, and coasted cautiously forward. When he was close enough to see that two figures were standing near the brush behind Grady's car, he pulled over a couple hundred yards up the road, shut off the engine, and quickly, but quietly, got out of his car. He left the door open. He could do so, because the inner dome light didn't work. He kept close to the edge of the brush and weeds at the bottom of the slope, so as to not be easily seen.

The two men didn't seem to notice him, and so he moved stealthily closer.

"Get out of there," one of the men yelled at Grady.

Grady emerged through the brush slowly, and the man nearest him rushed forward and gave him a stout whack on the back of the head with his gun barrel.

"You're gonna tell us where that list is, NOW—and that's all there is to it."

Holding the bloody bruise on his head, Grady turned to face the man. "I don't have the list yet. But I think I'm close to finding it."

"What do you take us for? I know you have it. We've been following you for weeks, and we followed you all day today."

"I'm telling you, I don't have the thing," Grady said. "I'd have to be pretty stupid to try to lie to you way out here in the middle of nowhere." He made a quick glance over the top of his car up the road, hoping to see someone driving up, but he saw no car headlights for the entire stretch of visible highway and not even a hint of glow in the darkness from a vehicle around the bend a mile back. It was a very dark night. Clouds had moved in to further blacken an already moonless sky.

Tom gave Grady another whack with his gun, this time on the side of his head, to show him he meant business, to show him he had no intention of leaving Grady alive unless he turned over the list to him. "Joe here is going to look through your car, and you had better hope he finds it. 'Cause if he doesn't, I see no reason for you to be alive. No one will ever find your body. I can promise you that. If you try to make a fool of me, you'll pay for it. I want that list, and I want it now."

The first place Joe looked was in the glove box, and there it was in all its glory. The plastic bag containing the list that had caused so much damage to so many people's lives—just sitting there on top of the other contents of the glove box. "It's here, boss. He's been lyin'."

Tom gave Grady two quick whacks with the barrel of his pistol and then kneed him in the privates. At that moment of staggering pain, Grady was sure that his time on Earth had come to an end. He suddenly realized that this was how he was going to die. The pain had neared that threshold just above sustainable consciousness. His head felt like it was swelled to three times its size, and he had a fleeting image of it all swelled and bloody, which, indeed, it was becoming. He blacked out for a moment and fell to the ground. Both his hands were clutching his privates.

And just as Tom was giving Grady a second kick to the stomach, Nuck launched himself on top of Tom from the darkness, seemingly from out of nowhere. Nuck brought the large man swiftly to the ground, and using his many years of self-styled martial arts training, mostly his own version of various more formal disciplines, cobbled together from his own perspective of them, he battered Tom senseless in a matter of seconds. Joe yelled out in the darkness from the other side of the car. "What's happening? Tom?" Tom did not answer.

Joe came around the back of the car to see what was going on. His gun was drawn and ready for action. Nuck jumped at him from a stooped position where he was waiting next to the left rear bumper of Grady's car. Tom remained on the ground, moaning, and he tried to get up. With a flash of swift, silent movement in the dark, Nuck dislodged the gun from Joe's hand, kicked the man's left leg out from under him, caught his right arm in a quick and powerful grip, and then vaulted his entire body over Nuck's shoulder and onto the ground. As Grady watched from his fetal position, he saw this Herculean figure that was Nuck, a rescuer from the bowels of darkness, moving as a cloud moves before the moon, swift and sure.

Tom tried to get up, to join the fight to help his partner, and as he did, Grady reached out and grabbed his foot. Tom kicked hard until he had freed himself, and then he got up onto shaky legs.

"Watch out Nuck," Grady yelled out.

Nuck wheeled around and with a single spinning kick made with the elegant motion of a ballet dancer, he caught Tom squarely on the side of his head, and it sent him sprawling limp to the ground once again.

Nuck and Grady drove up to The Donut & Coffee Shoppe at 5:30 a.m. in Nuck's ever so loud station wagon. Neither man had gotten much sleep after a very long night, first spent in the emergency room, where Grady's wounds were treated and bandaged and he was released with warnings about not engaging in too much activity—he had a concussion. Next, they spent another two hours at the Timpkin County Sheriff's Office in Creighton Beach, answering questions and filling out forms. Jaimansen's thugs had been arrested, after having been initially delivered at gun point by Grady and Nuck, and they were booked on assault charges, with further charges pending.

And after that, and after getting their coffee, it took Grady and Nuck just over four hours to get to Hasselford. Grady was now in pursuit of a plan to bring this whole Jaimansen business to an end.

CHAPTER 25
《》

I have no natural enemies, at least that's what my experience tells me . . . except . . . I keep getting the feeling that my human friends aren't as friendly as I once thought. I keep seeing bodies turning up, and I've seen the causes for it with my own eyes, and I've seen it more than once. No one can tell me that I haven't seen humans in the grip of those horrible speeding creatures above . . .

President Balder was scheduled to meet with Governor Winde at 10 a.m. that Saturday morning and then appear at a press conference on the steps of the statehouse, mostly a puff and fluff event. He had attended a $200 a plate fundraising dinner the previous night at Harmons, a restaurant known for its wealthy and powerful clientele and for its extremely high prices. The food was said to be good. It was one of those image restaurants that survived more on its reputation for who came to it than for its cuisine. If you didn't go to Harmons, then you couldn't call yourself a somebody in the town, or in the political machinery of the state.

It was already eleven o'clock, and the red carpet leading up the steps to the lavishly adorned podium was not yet peopled with the main political dignitaries of the event. The Presidential Seal was on display on the front of the podium, and several large American flags and a single Newmont flag were posted behind for all to see. There were two smaller American flags popping out of holders on each corner of the podium.

The president was pushing hard for the new anti-terrorist bill that many civil libertarians had already declared as unconstitutional on its face—it was even more invasive than the Patriot Act passed several years earlier. These were scary times, and the legislature had passed far-reaching measures with implications that went a long way toward seriously eroding constitutional protections for individuals and their personal privacy. Newmont had one of the strongest personal privacy laws built into its constitution of any state in the country, including Florida, and President Balder knew that it was going to be a bit of a hard sell there. He needed the governor, and the governor needed him. So far, the public was buying it all, because they were frightened. His job approval rating had slipped, though, in recent months down from a high of 64% to only 48% now. He needed Governor Winde to win his re-election bid, because Newmont was a crucial electoral vote swing state.

Grady waited. He was used to this type of thing. The press was everywhere, as they always were with any visit from the President. It was primarily a photo-op, and any quasi-official event such as this was usually one of those vacuous press conferences where the president praised the governor for all his good work in Newmont, and the governor praised the president for all his good work for the nation. No serious questions would be asked, because there weren't any seriously hot issues on the news radar screen right at the moment, other than the anti-terrorist act, which the majority of the press had fully demonstrated they were too spineless to challenge. Even worms had more backbone, Grady thought. He saw them as lemmings these days, marching off in lockstep toward the cliff's edge, because they were mostly paid by large corporations who had an interest in reelecting a pro-business president, and because they had gotten so lazy and incompetent in their jobs as "journalists" that the long history of good, hard work that had once given a glow to that title had all but lost its luster.

Perfunctory, conciliatory, soft-ball questioning was usually the order of business at such events. They were rigorously staged, with the president's team writing almost the entire script, and offering no surprises. So bland, they were in fact, that most reporters called them "fillers," because all they would do was fill space in papers and in TV news shows. Stories about a president's visit always had wide public appeal, but the articles usually would say absolutely nothing, other than what the president had programmed the media to say. Most people liked it when the president came to town, regardless of the politics of the situation. They only became upset when the president's motorcade and the secret service activities swirling about it demanded the closing off of certain roads, thereby delaying their commutes to work by two hours or irritating them because their favorite avenues for local travel had been shut down.

Presidential visits, on the whole, however, provided the press an opportunity to pander to a feel-good atmosphere, which most of the public readily lapped up. Today was going to be different, though. Grady was confident of that much.

He then received word from his wife, who was already inside the capitol building, that President Balder and Governor Winde had left their meeting together and were headed along the main lobby to the front door and would be at the speaker's podium very shortly. Moments later, they walked out together, along with many of the highest elected officials in the Newmont Legislature and key members of the governor's appointed cabinet, including the Secretary of State, the Secretary of Education, the State's Attorney General, and the State Treasurer.

The Newmont Secretary of State went to the podium first and spoke briefly about all the good things that were being accomplished in the state as a result of Governor Winde's great leadership. She then introduced the governor. He stepped up to the podium and gave a brief speech about how everything was on the improve in the new state, even though the economy had been stagnant now for more than two years, education ranked among the lowest in the country, social programs had been slashed to the bone, children under the state's care continued to turn up abused or missing on a weekly basis, there was no end in sight to the accumulating debt that had already reached record numbers. Moody's had just lowered the state's bond rating to B minus, which didn't bode well for future borrowing, and the irresponsibility of the governor and the legislature on fiscal matters insured that massive amounts of such borrowing would be necessary into the foreseeable future—very expensive borrowing.

"We're looking good in education," the governor said. "Our 'Better Schools', program is working well. We have allowed private companies more flexibility in becoming involved in profitable enterprises in our public schools. Their profit is everyone's gain. Our economic outlook is looking good. If we stay the course, we'll soon be leading the nation in economic growth. Businesses are coming to the state in record numbers, and tourism is on the rise again . . ." Blah, blah, blah. Grady had heard it all before. Politicians and their speeches tended to sound very similar, no matter which party they were from these days.

The governor finished up with his most predictable, and entirely insubstantial speech, and then he said, "And now, the man you have all been waiting for, my good friend, President James Balder." He smiled over at the president and began clapping his hands. Many stalwart supporters in the crowd applauded enthusiastically and waved their little flags furiously. President Balder smiled back at the governor, and then at the crowd, as he moved to the podium. He shook the governor's hand heartily and then stepped up to the mike. He lowered it a little to match his height, which surprisingly was only a couple of inches less than the unusual tallness of the governor.

He gave a brief speech, mostly filled with throwaway, cheerleading lines that preached to the choir of the over-raucously cheering strong supporters that had been mustered to show up this morning. You always had to have a friendly crowd around you. And for this event, if you didn't have an official event name tag, in fact, you weren't even allowed anywhere near the podium. They would have sold tickets to control who came and who didn't, but to do that might have gotten the press calling it a fund-raiser, and the president wanted this photo-op with the governor to have a much more official look than that.

He spoke for about ten minutes, and then he opened up the proceedings to questions from the official press. This was done to placate the media and to lend officiousness to the entire affair. They wanted it to be very "presidential."

Grady looked on with great interest. This was the moment he had been waiting for. The first question was a silly one from a reporter of one of the local newspapers. "How do you like the friendliness of Hasselford, compared to that of Washington?"

"Oh, it's great! You have some very friendly people here in your beautiful town, and they are very patriotic, which you don't see enough of in Washington these days." The president was offhandedly referring to the cold reception he had been receiving lately from many people in congress over his anti-terrorist bill, including a few from his own party.

"Do you expect passage of the American Freedom Act bill?" asked another reporter.

"Yes, I do. I think it's a good bill, and it has a lot of support." The president then pointed to another reporter, to Nuck Flanders, in fact. Grady hadn't expected such good luck, and in fact it hadn't been in his plan at all. He had positioned Nuck far away from himself and had given him an official press badge, which for the first time since Grady had known Nuck, he hadn't fought. This time, Nuck hadn't insisted, as he always had in the past, that he was only a photographer, and that he wanted nothing to do with being a reporter. Grady looked across the sea of reporters, microphone booms, and cameras and saw that Nuck was stunned into silence. He pointed to himself in a questioning manner, and when the president nodded that indeed he had selected him, a man came over and handed Nuck a mike.

And Grady said to himself, *At last, we can make up for some of the hell we have been through. At last, maybe we can do something for Marcy and Linda, and for Mrs. Herrero.*

"Tomlin Sands Newspaper, here. Are you aware . . ." Nuck began with an uncertain quaking voice, one that was barely audible.

"Please speak into the mike," said the president "Not everyone can hear you."

"Oh, okay," Nuck said looking nervously down at the microphone he held in his hand which was connected wirelessly through the PA system. He hoisted it up a little, so it was nearer his mouth, but was disinclined to getting it too close. Grady knew that he really didn't want to be heard. There was a look of terror on his face. "Do you know that Governor Winde has been involved in bribery and corruption, and that there is evidence to implicate him fully in it, evidence that is surely now in the hands of local authorities and the FBI?"

"Implicate?" Grady thought. He had never heard Nuck use a word such as that. It made him smile.

The president looked at the governor with surprise and a questioning look. He covered the mike and leaned over and asked him in a whisper, "What's this?"

"I have no idea," the governor responded.

Nuck, the reporter, then continued, "I have a copy of a list of payoffs that were made during the past three years, including a detailed description of where the funds went after each individual received them." Nuck held up three sheets of paper. "There are a lot of important names on this list within the state of Newmont, including Governor Winde's name. Do you, or the governor, have any comment."

"I don't know anything about this," President Balder said and then covered the mike again and spoke to a man behind him, likely a presidential advisor.

He then looked forward again and said, "I'm afraid I have no idea what you are talking about, and unfortunately without having seen your so-called evidence, I cannot possibly venture a response. I'm sure it's all some kind of mistake."

"This list has a few names on it that reach all the way up to people near your own white house, influence-peddling and the like," Nuck continued. "I'm sure you will have a chance to look at it in the very near future. And I'm also sure the authorities will be looking into the criminal activities of a Mr. Francis Jaimansen, for whom the list was made. I understand that a warrant for his arrest was just issued within the last few minutes. Two of his associates, one Thomas Jackson and a Joseph Moebe are currently spending some time in the Tomlin County jail in connection with some of Mr. Jaimansen's activities. I have word that they have given a statement to the FBI and state police."

"I'm sorry, but I've just been told that we have to leave," the president said to the crowd, ignoring Nuck entirely now. He looked around nervously and with great agitation showing on his face. "Unfortunately, I have to be in South Carolina in two hours, and if I don't hurry, Air Force One is going to leave without me." President Balder then beamed out his campaign smile momentarily, and said, "Thank you all for coming." He waved as he hurried from the podium and became quickly swallowed up by the political dignitaries and a swarm of secret service agents that surrounded him. He then vanished into the capitol building. Governor Winde vanished with him, but not before putting a very nasty, threatening, retreating look upon Grady, who was in the front row of reporters. It was over for the governor, though, and he knew it. Nuck's devastating questions would take the lead in the media coverage of the investigations, resignations, convictions, and the large amounts of serious prison time that was surely to follow. Grady smiled inwardly, and at long last, he felt a sense of freedom glowing within. He felt cleansed in some deep and satisfying way.

Before coming to the state capitol, he had made sure to give a call to Lieutenant James of the state police, and he faxed him a copy of Linda's three sheets of damning evidence. He also called the FBI and Newmont's Attorney General, who couldn't necessarily be trusted because he was so close to the governor. The Timpkin County Sheriff's Department was already involved, because they had under their arrest Jaimansen's two thugs. As a final stroke of fairness, and to make sure the story got out in a big way, immediately following the debacle of the president's news conference, Grady also placed a call to Larry Holliston, the reporter he had been referred to by his friend at the Miami News Beacon, the man he had spoken with the day after Marcy had turned up dead, the newsman who had been working on a story about the rampant influence peddling that was going on in Newmont government. He also faxed him a copy of the evidence and a copy of the story that Grady had written, with Emily's help, and which had already been printed in a special edition of The Tomlin Sands. It was being delivered throughout the Tomlin Dunes area at that very moment. Grady felt the man deserved a heads-up, so he could put together a breaking story of his own. After all, he had worked on the corruption story even before Grady had gotten involved, and he received a mention in his own news article, which would surely be picked up immediately by the news wire services.

CHAPTER 26

I think I hear another one coming. It's making that terrifying noise they always make. I have a little one nearby, and I also see friends nearby, and some of them also have young ones. It's coming, and I keep seeing more and more of them coming. Where do we go from here? I only wish I knew . . .

Grady and Nuck returned home to Tomlin Dunes from Hasselford and were unexpectedly met by a crowd of townspeople in front of the Sands, each holding a copy of the special edition sheet. As the two men passed through the warm gathering, they stopped to stand amongst them for a few moments. Many cheered and came up to shake their hands and to congratulate them on their good work. The rest of the crew from the Sands came out of the building, including Emily, who beat Grady and Nuck home, and they received spontaneous cheers all around, too. Newmont had its good side. The Bermuda triangle could work in strange ways, some people continued to insist.

The small crowd treated them as heroes, and so did I. I was there that day, and I felt a sense of pride beaming from within me, not something that is common for me, because I am usually the cynic's cynic, probably even more so than Grady. But on that day, I couldn't subdue the pride I felt in a friend, and in a community, and in a way of life that still struggled on to stay truly free. My eyes moistened, and I think I saw tears on

Grady's cheek, and even on Nuck's face. It was something to behold.

A man came up to Grady and said, "I'm sorry to say that I was one of those who dropped my subscription to your paper, because I thought you were defaming a businessman just for some liberal agenda. I was wrong, and you showed me something today." Grady knew that it was the nature of the news business, though, when your business is trying to print the truth.

On the following morning, when Grady drove to the Paper, the sun was shining brightly, just as it should have done on a day such as this, and the air was warm with the fresh breath from the heart of spring, and there was the smell of orange blossoms and Jasmine in the air. It was a Newmont morning. It was why so many millions of people wanted to move to the state. The politics of the subtropical paradise had gotten ugly, but at least some of the ugliness was on its way to being fixed, and that made this morning all the brighter for Grady. Nuck accompanied him as they entered the Tomlin Sands, and even Nuck seemed to carry himself with a posture that was a little more erect. Ned Lower waved a strong "Hi" to both of them and said, "Boy, when you print a story, you sure print a story!"

Grady grinned broadly at Mr. Lower and replied, "Sometimes it's just what you have to do." He waved, and Mr. Lower gave a quick wave back and then disappeared into his antique shop, three doors down from the newspaper.

As soon as Grady entered the small lobby of the newspaper, he asked everyone to join him in his office. They all found a seat in the three available chairs, on a couch next to the wall, and on a table against the adjacent wall, with Nuck preferring to stand as usual. After the excited morning chatter had died down, he said, "Things have now changed for The Tomlin Sands Newspaper, as you probably all realize. We have acquired a degree of respect that we didn't have before, and with that respect comes a lot more responsibility for all of us. Everyone worked tirelessly through this entire ordeal, and I can never thank you enough for the great job you all did. You kept the paper going. I can assure you that we would have never had this outcome if you hadn't been here working as hard as you did. So, thank you, from the bottom of my heart. Grady looked around his cluttered office and looked into the eyes of every person in that room. They were people who had always remained faithful and full of dogged energy and optimism about the newspaper. It was a family, ragged around the edges at times, as were all families, but nonetheless a family.

"Now, onto more pressing business. I have decided that we all have earned a day off, and so next Thursday we are closing the paper down for a day, and we're going out to Lincoln Park and spend a day together, just relaxing and maybe even having some fun for a change." This news received a resounding cheer.

And good to his word, Grady, Emily, Krissy, Steven, Mrs. Herrero, Nuck, and all the employees at The Tomlin Sands went to Lincoln Park the following Thursday for a day of well-deserved rest, relaxation, good eating, and fun. For the first time in his adult life, Grady really began to feel some sense of confidence that he could live up to a dead father's dreams for him as a newspaperman, and as a worthy son.

It was a good feeling, with family and good friends all around, and he sat on the lush, spring grass, his back against a 100 year old live oak, his legs crossed casually, and he watched his wife and Nuck and Mrs. Herrero playing a loose form of soccer with the children. Mrs. Herrero seemed to be enjoying herself just a little for the first time since Grady had met her. It had helped that the cause of her daughter's death had been officially removed from the ranks of suicide.

Grady had been playing soccer with his family a few minutes earlier, but now he just wanted to sit back for awhile and take it all in. He was no longer the lost Grady he had always felt himself to be. His marriage to Emily had certainly eased much of that, but always present in him had been a tenacious fear that he would never measure up to the demands of his chosen profession, that he would be a failure and a complete disappointment in the end. Starting up the newspaper had helped him assuage some of those dark worries, but now that he had proven himself, at least once, as a solid journalist and newspaperman, and against all odds, as a man who could stolidly get at the truth of a big and dangerous story, who could demonstrate enough courage to print it for the public to read, no matter the consequences, he started to feel like he had built a place for himself within his own expectations. His inner stuff felt more reliable.

The rest and relaxation felt good, too. The camaraderie felt better. A nice warm breeze blew across the open field where they had set up to have their picnic. There were few people in the park on a Thursday, and so they had the place pretty much to themselves.

As Grady sat there against that beautiful old tree, basking in the glory of the day, he wondered if he would ever feel quite this same glow again as he went through life. Certainly the birth of his children had brought a special kind of feeling and glow and excitement, but the feeling he had now encapsulated some of that, encapsulated all that was good in his life, and was better in a sense than any feeling he had ever had about himself before. He knew that probably when tomorrow rolled around, and the next serious problem was dropped on his desktop, he would begin to feel again some of the old worries and self-doubt, but for now, that kind of weakness was far removed and seemed impossible. It was a truly good feeling.

Several days later, Jaimansen was charged with conspiracy to commit first degree murder, and after a lengthy trial that lasted more than nine months, he was sentenced to death by lethal injection. The governor was forced to resign and was prosecuted, too. He received fifteen years for his part in the bribery and kick-back scheme. A lot of other people had to resign as well. And everyone on the list served at least one year of prison time. Some of those connected to President Balder's administration in the corruption scheme had also been convicted, and a Senate investigation was under way into how far up the line those connections went and whether or not the president himself was involved in any way. The U.S. Attorney General was going to be forced to become involved or resign.

And so that is that.

The telling of this tale is now done, and it must be said that all the facts and fabric of it, and even some of the reading between the lines that were necessary to fill in the details, came from information either retrieved from court records in Newmont or from interviews with the principles involved. But above and beyond anyone else, I am forever grateful to Grady, Nuck, and Emily for their tireless efforts to help me successfully complete this project. And I still don't know Nuck's real first name, if indeed he has one. He insists that it is simply Nuck, and one doesn't ask him such things too many times, because he will give you that calm, steady, questioning look that will raise the guilt inside you, as if you knew all along that it is absolutely rude for you to be probing into his privacy. Nuck always had the ability to shame a person with a look.

I hope this story will leave you with a mind full of caution about how citizens must attend to their own democracy, if they want to keep it intact. There is no place like Newmont to deliver such a caution, because only in a place such as this, wild and wooly as it is, can such a story unwind.

I can only hope that Newmont's haziness and dislocation in time and space can become more fixed, that one can easily identify how, and precisely where, its landmass, and spirit, attaches to the country. As of the telling of this story, that was entirely impossible to ascertain. Grady was also hopeful that Newmont would rise above the wild skin that covered it, a skin which kept it from being productive as a fully functioning, principled, and democratic state, to operate with some maturity. Survival was at stake, but there were hopeful signs that the state could overcome its harsh and corrupt beginnings. Good people live in the state, as a whole, and I am a little more confident that they will prevail in their goodness.

And Grady, what can I say about him? I see quite a bit of my longtime friend in his son, and it is inspiring to see in him the good side of human strength. It has made me believe that the world can be made a better place, even if it what it takes is a hard swim upstream in very restless waters.